Ultimate Goals!

Ultimate Goals!

Martin Dobson

SPORTS
BOOKS

Published by SportsBooks Ltd

Copyright: Martin Dobson ©
October 2007

SportsBooks Limited
PO Box 422
Cheltenham
GL50 2YN
United Kingdom
Tel: 01242 256755
Fax: 01242 254694
email   randall@sportsbooks.ltd.uk
Website   www.sportsbooks.ltd.uk

Cover designed by Alan Hunns

A CIP catalogue record for this book is available from the British
Library.

ISBN 9781899807 59 8

Printed in the UK by CPI Bookmarque, Croydon CRO 4TD.

The book is dedicated to my wife Carole – a very special person. Thanks for all the love and support. And to four fantastic children and five special grandkids.

Each and everyone of you has put a big smile on my face – and for that I will always be grateful.

Acknowledgements

Firstly to my publisher Randall and everyone at Sportsbooks Ltd for their professionalism and encouragement. Anne and Jeff for the witty anecdote, Shutty's recollections, Ruth's linguistic skills and Debbie's insight.

Thanks also to Pat and Lindsay for their super contributions. Walshy, Mooro – and Steve's expertise. Thanks fellas. Helen's colourful tales – brilliant. And finally, Sheila and John for their honest advice. Many thanks to you all.

1

It was an innocent mistake after bringing home the shopping from the local supermarket. A weekly chore she grudgingly accepted. No big deal. The heavy bags split, but no help was around. She struggled up two flights of stairs and entered the pokey flat. After heaving the groceries onto the kitchen table, she closed the door.

A bag ripped open and a large can of tomato soup fell onto the floor, flipped on its side, and effortlessly, almost mechanically, as if triggered by remote control, rolled towards the front door. As it came to a halt the door was pushed open and in marched a figure she knew well, fuelled by alcohol. The figure nonchalantly picked up the offending item. Looking serene and in total control, he proceeded to smash the tin into the side of her face.

She awoke, cut and bruised. She picked herself up and staggered to the tiny bathroom. Alone. She bathed herself. She stemmed the flow of blood and placed a plaster over the deepest wound. She looked at the ring on her finger; a single diamond stone that she treasured; her one true possession. Other belongings had been sold or pawned to get the essentials: food on the table, the bills paid.

A day or two hidden in the flat, away from prying eyes, would do the trick. The lesions would be gone. She sat on the toilet seat and cried.

The following day she reflected on the violence and wondered why she hadn't foreseen it, when she'd been through it so many times before. What a fool! It wasn't as though he hadn't already warned her. The factory was dishing out redundancies, reducing labour and stopping overtime.

A three-day week was all he could hope for, so he had good reason to be angry. She should have been more careful. It was her fault. He was under pressure. It was up to her to make sure everything was fine.

As long as Ricky was all right, she'd take the punishment. If he laid one finger on the boy, she'd kill him.

Ruth Grant had often thought about leaving. But where would she go?

Denial kept her from taking action. But one thing was for sure; the violence was becoming more frequent. Before, it was easily handled. Now she had doubts. The bruises were deeper and taking longer to heal; the hospital visited regularly. The slip-ups, the falls, the occasional trips, the cuts from chopping vegetables; how many other excuses could she make?

It was up to her to sort it out. It wasn't the responsibility of the authorities, the police, social services or psychologists. They wouldn't believe her story anyway, and it would only further aggravate her partner. It was little consolation to know that thousands were experiencing the very same at that precise moment.

Ruth, Ronnie and Ricky lived on a depressing Midlands housing estate in Crixton, where assaults and criminal damage were an everyday occurrence. Yob culture had terrorised the local population, driving away the law-abiding families. Half of the residents had fled from boarded up, torched-out properties.

It was a living hell for the rest, who were subjected to vindictive acts of abuse. Cars were vandalised and no sooner had obnoxious graffiti been removed, then more offending material would appear. Long gone were the days when residents took pride in their homes, adorned with colourful plants and hanging baskets. That pride had been snatched away, with the few possessions they once had.

Windows would be randomly smashed and threatening 'phone calls bombarded the locals in the early hours; but complaints to the council fell on stony ground.

Ronnie Baxter had gained a tough-guy reputation but even his flat hadn't completely escaped. Dog excrement, pushed through the letterbox, was a gentle reminder that no one was off limits and many a time Ricky had been awakened by screeching tyres in the early hours. Burnt-out cars littered the waste areas. Shouts and screams shattered the night's silence.

Ricky grew up in this world of violence. He had been familiar with it for so long it no longer caused concern. There was no order to his home life; no boundaries to what was expected. Predicting behaviour was difficult. Ricky had so far kept away from the thugs but the day would surely come to either unite or confront.

Ruth felt trapped. She'd been on the council's relocation waiting list for ages. The chances of moving were bleak.

2

The Watkins family lived in a three bedroom Victorian semi in the town of Burding in the north west of England between the cities of Liverpool and Manchester. With a growing family and limited space, Steve spent every spare minute bringing it back to its former glory. Steve was married to Linda and they had two kids, 12-year-old Jake and younger sister Chloe, in her last year at junior school.

Steve had set up his own building business specialising in extensions and home improvements. It was tough early on but he got a break. He made an appointment at the doctor's surgery to sort out an eye infection, diagnosed as conjunctivitis, and drops were prescribed. Medics had little time for small talk but on this occasion Doctor Graham confided in him that his kitchen needed a complete overhaul. Steve offered his services. It was the biggest job he'd quoted for but after presenting the final estimates, he was given the go-ahead. Profit margins had been cut to the bone.

On completion the Grahams were delighted and the reaction was immediate. The work flooded in.

Jake loved football – whether it was playing with his mates at school, watching the big matches on TV or getting out the Playstation at home. His bedroom was bedecked with blue and white. Pictures of his heroes from Burding Town FC covered the walls and his duvet was straight from the club shop.

The magical game enthralled the young man. Jake was in his first year at secondary school, Burding Comprehensive, situated only half a mile from his home. He had settled in well and the school had a great reputation for discipline, values and academic results. Maths and Chemistry were the subjects he enjoyed most, whereas Geography and French, even at this early stage, were something to be tolerated.

But what he looked forward to most were the sports lessons: two in the gym and an outdoor session on a Wednesday afternoon. Jake was scrawny, thin but tallish for his age. He was competitive, loved winning and was always around a ball of some description, working on his touch and control.

Jake had a dream. He wanted to be a professional footballer. Not only that, he wanted to play for England. It was all pretty clear. How he'd get there, he didn't have a clue.

He rushed in from school hot and flustered. School had gone okay. Miss Chatham's history lesson covered the D-Day landings in Normandy June 6 1944 and her drawings and plans on the overhead projector had made the magnitude of the event a lot clearer. What an undertaking. The allies were in unison in their attempt to overthrow Nazi Germany. Thousands of soldiers, many as young as nineteen years old, had lost their lives on that day.

He scampered up the stairs two at a time. His room was a tip. Everything stayed where it fell. He put on a CD and blasted the place out. He changed into his favourite tracksuit bottoms and got out his schoolbooks.

Jake was last at the table as Linda served up the potato hash.

'Good day, son?" asked his dad.

'Not bad.'

'Pass the onions.'

'Where's the brown sauce?' asked Chloe.

'Sorry I've forgotten it love, can you get it?'

Steve told them about a problem he was having converting a farm building. The owners kept changing their minds about what they wanted in one particular room.

'The old fella wants to put in a games room. You know the kind of thing-a snooker table and a bar – whereas his missus wants to use it as a study. Her hobby is painting and we're stuck in the middle. Can't put in things like the electrics until they decide. We've just got to plough on with other things. It's a toss up as to who gets the nod.'

The front doorbell rang. 'I'll get it.' said Jake.

'Hello, you must be Jake?' said a man in a dark suit and carrying a folder.

'Yes.'

'Well, I'm Mike James. Is your dad in?'

'I'll just get him.'

'Dad, it's someone for you.'

Jake left the man standing outside while Steve made his way from the kitchen table.

'Hello Mr Watkins. I'm Mike James. I'm a scout at Burding Town FC. I'd like to talk to you about Jake. If it's not convenient I'll come back another day.'

'No, no, come in. And it's Steve.'

He showed him into the front room and offered him a drink.

'Coffee please. I'd like Jake to sit in if that's all right,' said James.

'Yeah, sure. I'll get him.'

'No way!' shouted Jake when he was told.

'Come on he wants to talk to you.'

'Sorry for barging in on you but I didn't have your 'phone number, and I always feel that it's important with these things to meet face to face. I'll tell you why I'm here. You played against St Jude's on Saturday, didn't you Jake?'

'Yes.'

'Well I was there. I'd gone along to look at a player from their team but came away very impressed by your performance. So much so that we'd like you to join our Under 13 squad.'

Jake was gobsmacked.

'What do you think?'

'It's always been Jake's ambition to play for the Town,' said Steve. 'But we never thought it'd be so soon.'

All Jake could mutter was, 'I don't believe it.'

'The Academy is run very thoroughly,' said James. 'We have experienced coaches to look after each age group and ex-players Tim Ashton and Nobby Clarke are in charge of this squad. Both have UEFA coaching awards and know the game inside out. The group trains twice a week and plays its games on Sunday. D'you think it's something you'd be interested in?'

'That's wicked,' replied Jake.

'I take it that's a yes then. I'll get back to you in a couple of days to arrange a meeting with our Director of Youth, Alex Cummings. After that everything will become a little clearer.'

Jake didn't believe what was coming out of this guy's mouth – the chance to pull on that famous blue and white shirt.

' If I can just take your home telephone number and perhaps your mobile Steve and I'll make contact again soon.'

'Thanks for coming. Goodbye.'

As James walked down the path Steve closed the front door. The whole family reacted like jumping beans.

'What about that? Have we got another Michael Owen in the house?' asked Steve.

They made their way to the kitchen to find the rice pudding was stone cold.

'A minute in the microwave will do it,' said Linda.

'Who do you think should wait on us tonight then?' giggled Chloe.

'What about the young superstar?'

With a beaming smile, Jake picked up the first two dishes. He inadvertently put the timer on to ten minutes. In their excitement no one noticed. The sticky contents were finally cleaned up after half an hour.

Two days later, Jake, Linda and Steve made their way to the Sterling Stadium and were met by Mike James and Alex Cummings.

'Good to see you,' said Cummings. 'Let's take a look around.'

Ten years before the club had moved to the brand-new stadium but during that time they had been relegated twice. On each occasion they had successfully regained their Premier League status. The facilities were as good as anything around, providing banqueting suites, corporate hospitality and excellent viewing from all parts of the ground.

'It's important that we're back in the big league after the heavy investment in the stadium,' said Cummings. 'It's meant that financially we've been able to compete and the club's now in a healthy position. With an average crowd of over 25,000, we reckon we can push on, in what's now the second tier of the Prem. Take away the likes of Chelsea, United, Liverpool and Arsenal and we'd give anybody a game.'

'A bit hairy last season,' said Steve.

'We flirted with the bottom end of the table but had a good run in. But it was worrying at one time.'

What really thrilled Jake was being shown the home dressing room. Walking through the light blue doors he could feel the atmosphere. A tactics board was placed on the wall.

Jake could almost hear the instruction from the manager. 'Jake I want you to play it simple for the first few minutes. Get hold of the ball and put your opposite number out of the game.'

There were several motivational messages on the walls.

Attitude is only a small word but it's a big thing.
We do not quit.
Keep trying, keep persevering, something will happen.
The only place success comes, in front of work, is in the
dictionary.

Cummings took them out of the changing room, through the tunnel and onto the pitch.

'Well Jake what do you think?' asked Cummings, pointing to the new stand.

'Fantastic, Mr Cummings.'

In the office were photographs of local boys who had come through the ranks to play in the first team.

'I like Tommy,' Jake said.

'Oh yes Tommy Holt. Took him a bit of time to get established but now the gaffer feels he's indispensable. Super attitude and can play several positions. Probably the first name on the team sheet.'

They sat down.

'Thanks for coming down tonight,' said Cummings. 'As Mike explained the other day, we'd like to bring Jake onto the Youth Programme. Playing for us does mean that Jake won't be able to play for anyone else.

'There'll be growth spurts at certain times and everything must be monitored correctly both physically and mentally. We have a first-

16

class physiotherapy department and the Academy also has its own doctor. So every boy receives the best medical attention.'

Alex's secretary brought in a pot of tea. Linda poured, Cummings continued.

'At the football club we are also very aware of Health and Safety and Child Protection issues. The staff have been on courses and fully understand their responsibilities.

'If there are any problems, with schoolwork for instance, then we have an Education Officer and he is the first port of call. All right so far?'

'Seems clear enough,' said Steve.

'Good. Well, all this information is in a booklet, which every registered player receives. If you're happy to get involved, then the documents can be drawn up and signed at a later date. That takes care of the formal side, now let's talk football. What do you consider to be your best assets, Jake?'

Jake was reluctant to say anything in case Cummings thought he was bigheaded. But in the end said, 'My touch and passing are okay.'

'That's what I've been told. You have a bit of pace as well, don't you?'

'I've always been the quickest in my year group. I find that part easy.'

'Pace in the modern game is vital... and fitness, of course. Being able to get up and down the pitch. It's a tough programme but we'll be looking for signs of improvement. There'll be some laughs for sure. It's not regimented but you are here to learn. The standards are very high.'

'I understand.'

'And then there's injuries. Worst thing for any footballer because not being able to play is so frustrating. And worrying. So make sure that when you're fit, you don't waste a single moment. There's a lot to consider. Any questions from you, Mr and Mrs Watkins?'

'No. When we get back home we'll have a chat to see what Jake wants to do. But I've got a feeling I already know,' said Steve.

'Anything from you, Jake?'

'Will we get our own kit?'

'Of course,' said Cummings. 'If you've got a minute, I'll show you what we play in this season.'

Cummings left the room and Steve said to Mike, 'He knows his stuff.'

'No messing with Alex. He's straight as an arrow.'

Cummings returned with two shirts, a pair of shorts and socks. And a pair of boots. 'Try these on for size, Jake,' said Cummings placing a shoebox in his hands.

They shook hands, said their goodbyes and walked over to the car park.

It was too good an opportunity to turn down and Steve rang the club the following day.

'He's made a decision?' asked Cummings.

'Yes. He's really excited and would like to come on board.'

'That's great news. I'll have my secretary sort out the forms and I'll get back to you when they're ready to sign.'

3

Ruth had arranged to see her sister, Anne, the next day. Their lives had gone in different directions. As a 17-year-old Ruth was a happy kid but then it all changed.

The Christmas holiday in Riccione, Italy, was her first abroad and what a wonderful break she'd had, chilling out and enjoying the nightlife. The attention she received from the local boys really boosted her confidence. One in particular, Antonio, with his dark hair, handsome face and muscular body sent her heart skipping whenever they met and towards the end of the holiday, laughter filled their every moment. Antonio's broken English was irresistible.

On the last day of the holiday, he invited Ruth for lunch at the family villa saying his mamma was a 'superba cookie'. Two brothers and two sisters, all younger than Antonio, parents, grandparents and neighbours greeted Ruth with loving gestures. 'Ruthie we 'ave 'eard sooooo mucha abouta you.' The spread was delightful. Italian specialities: bruschetti, mozzarella cheeses, tomatoes, pasta dishes, lasagne and tortellini, salads, chicken and fish dishes. There was wine and beer.

Antonio's parents were a hoot. Throughout the meal they kept everyone amused with stories they'd told a thousand times. Luckily for Ruth they could all speak English, although some were easier to understand than others.

'Hey Mamma, you remember Gina, the lady in the village who was a supa swimma but when she died, she wanted to be buried in her swimmin costume? Come the heavy rains and floods, her coffin was lifted and floated out along the main street. It's as if she couldna resist one last fifty metre backstroke!'

Antonio showed Ruth around the villa. They found a quiet corner, where they would not be disturbed. Their kisses were passionate – their touches tender and exciting.

A few weeks after arriving home Ruth discovered she was pregnant. Her first relationship and this had happened. Her family gave her love and support, but she still felt alone and frightened. Her friends' advice was more direct. 'Get rid of it. You'll have no life. What can you do with a kid on your back? Get real'.

With weeks of torment and doubts, she pondered, 'How could a happy time turn into such a nightmare?'

After much soul searching, her ambitions to go into the nursing profession would take a back seat. She had decided to see it through. She would have the baby.

What about Antonio? Should she tell him? When Ricardo arrived he was a beautiful baby, with his father's distinctive dark hair, brown eyes and olive complexion. Ruth's pride and joy.

A few relationships developed over the years but they came to nothing. Ruth took a part time job at a distribution centre but her relationship with Ricardo or Ricky, as he preferred to be called, would never be compromised. Ricky was a decent kid. He didn't have the good things in life but he did have a special relationship with his mother. More like brother and sister. They looked out for each other. It had been tough for both of them. Their bond was special.

At a company social event Ruth met up with Ronnie Baxter from the transport department. She'd seen him a few times in the general office and shared a table in the canteen. Although he was a little worse for wear on the night, he was good company and Ruth enjoyed herself. 'Have you seen that gin fig? More like a bleeding rug on his head. He's got a real sweat on and the edges have curled up. It's swivelled round 180 degrees.'

Ronnie was single, had never been married and lived in a rented flat nearby. They became close and after several months he moved in with Ruth. Ricky was fifteen years old.

Ronnie was financially embarrassed and his drinking was the problem. It was out of control. He would stop off for a couple after work but the amount drunk and time spent increased and his mood swings were becoming unbearable. His language became crude and Ruth worried for her child's safety. But she was resilient. She'd been through a lot and she was strong. But things were starting to deteriorate.

She looked in the mirror in the dingy bathroom. The ice-pack hadn't done its job and signs of discolouration on her forehead were already appearing.

Opening the tiny bathroom cabinet she rummaged through its contents: headache tablets, plasters, razor blades, toothpaste. She went to her bedroom to see if she could find the concealor lotion. Nothing.

She would have to call in at the chemists. She put on her drab overcoat, picked up her bag and closed the door.

A shopworker came over, offering assistance. 'Can I be of any help, madam?'

'Yes. I was walking our dog and I caught my head on a tree branch. I was wondering if there was anything to cover the bruise?'

'Certainly madam.'

The assistant applied liberal amounts of a creamy pink lotion and the result was acceptable. Ruth fiddled in her purse for the coins, made the purchase and stepped through the door, confident that her secret had been well hidden.

Ruth needed help in picking a birthday present for Anne's little girl. Choosing for an 11-year-old, going on twenty-three, wasn't easy.

'Ruth come in.' Anne welcomed her sister. 'Great to see you. I'll put the kettle on. Everybody's out and it's heaven. Sit down. How are you keeping?'

'Fine. I'm glad you rang. You don't mind looking around for Heather's birthday present with me, do you?'

'Not at all. A bit of retail therapy is just what I need. Heather is hyper at the moment. She's got this thing about wanting to be an actress. I know all kids are the same aren't they, heads in the sky, want to be on TV or stage?

'These programmes are to blame – they make out anybody can do it. I've been to a few auditions and you queue around the theatre for hours and hours and afterwards, there's no guarantee there will be anything at the end. It gets their hopes up and it isn't fair. Here's the coffee. How's Ron and Ricky?'

'Ronnie's fed up at work. They're talking about laying people off and we need the money. He's a bit stressed and Ricky is a little down too. I don't know what it is but he's been quiet for the last few days. He says everything's okay – you know the kind of thing – "don't hassle me". But there's something bothering him.'

They drove into the town centre and made for the 'Kids' Delight – Clothes for today's teenagers' store.

'Where do we start? What about a top? Skimpy, colourful. What about this?'

'Not her colour, she hates yellow. Thinks it looks like custard and she hates custard. I'm beginning to wonder what she does like to eat these days.'

They chose a skirt and top but when it started to rain they made their way over to the covered shopping area.

With no umbrellas they scampered across the town centre and through the automatic glass doors.

They shook themselves and raindrops fell from Ruth's mangled hair.

Anne shrieked. 'How did you do that?'

'What?'

'That bruise on your face.'

'I had a fall.'

'That's no fall. You've been hit, haven't you? Is it Ronnie? I knew he was a wrong 'un. I'll bloody swing for him, I will that. Come on, I want you to tell me what's going on. And I want the truth.'

Anne ordered coffees and blueberry muffins and they sat on the table furthest away from the till. The rest of the place was empty.

'Now lady, I want you to come clean. How did this happen?' said Anne, concerned.

'It was my fault,' said Ruth quietly. 'Ronnie's been under pressure at work and it was down to me to make sure things were all right at home. I dropped something.'

'And he hit you?'

'Yes.'

'What with?'

'A tin.'

22

'The bastard,' said Anne. 'When was this?'

'Last night.'

'And I'll bet it wasn't the first time, was it? Look Ruthie, this can't carry on. You have to do something about it.'

'I should have seen it coming.'

'It's not your fault; stop making excuses for him. Have you been down to the social or got in touch with anybody for help?'

'No.'

'If you want I'll come with you,' said Anne taking her hand. 'Look, love, I'm worried about you and I'll help you anyway I can. But it's up to you.'

4

As with most teenagers, Jake took a lot for granted – like the taxi service his parents provided to ferry him about all over the place. Steve and Linda would arrange their busy schedules around the coaching programmes and junior matches.

The sessions were held in the indoor facility, which had an excellent artificial playing area. Gone were the days of the rock hard ankle breakers. New technology meant that moulded rubber boots could now be worn and skin burns were definitely a thing of the past.

Jake welcomed the Youth Department's policy of rotating coaches for different age groups. When he was a member of the U15's, former players and UEFA 'A' licence coaches, Jonathan Breckin and Sid Suggett, introduced the squad to a more tactical appreciation of the game. The boys were asked to play in different positions and formations, enhancing their football education.

Everything was going to plan, although Jake did have to get through one awkward stage – and it had nothing to do with football. The spotty, teenage kid syndrome seemed to descend on him from a great height. One minute he was a happy, laughing kid, joking with his mates and then, without warning, he underwent a social metamorphosis – self-conscious, embarrassed, even introverted.

It was like having a personality bypass. Previously, in girls' company, there was no hassle. They were friends, good to hang out with. But now he felt uncomfortable. He became reserved, almost moody. Sex had reared its ugly head. He adopted an awkward gait and a shuffling movement. He avoided people, spending more time on his own. But the worst part of the mind-blowing experience was the spots – followed by the involuntary blushing.

'What's all that about?' he asked when he stood before the mirror. He was a good-looking lad but now resembled a pepperoni pizza. He tried squeezing 'em. Was there ever a good way of removing zits? Did they ever spurt in the right place? His mum picked up a tube of clear liquid from the chemists, which helped. He could treat the craters but the blushing was something else. A completely innocent remark would send him into flushville. He wouldn't have wished it on his worst enemy. He felt like a right dork!

But through his worst moments he had something to cling onto. He could play football. He could run about and kick the ball. He could forget about those irritations and worries. And he was good. He was one of the better ones and he was aware of the respect he had from the other players. He loved playing – the other stuff didn't matter. If he could spend all his time on the field, then he'd be okay. It lifted his confidence.

In the summer he got involved with the athletics team to specialise in the one hundred and two hundred metre sprints. He was champion in both events at school and was picked for the county side against a very strong Durham squad, which included an England international in their ranks. Jake took him all the way before being edged out on the tape.

Swimming galas, tennis tournaments – he had a go at most things. Freestyle swimming developed his all-round stamina and breathing, whereas the tennis and gym work built up his upper body strength and growth. He was lucky not to suffer any medical problems; one such was the Osgood Schlatter's disease, which affected the knee area, and halted some of the guys' progress.

Jake made himself useful by helping his dad during the summer holidays. Steve had expanded his business. He'd gone into partnership with a financial backer and had received planning permission to build thirty exclusive apartments in a secured, landscaped development, targeting the professional end of the residential market.

Jake took on the role of the 'gofer' – the carrying of cement bags, the filling of skips, the burning of pallets: fetching, carrying and delivering. He was also the chief 'brewer-up' for the painters, joiners, electricians and plumbers. They all got to know him. And they had a laugh. They knew about his footballing skills.

'Show us a piece of Bestie skill, Jake. Now there was a player.'

They told him to, 'Get stuck in mate. Don't take any crap. Put yourself about'.

They also wanted to know if the footie groupies were following him about. 'I'll be your agent, Jake. Nice job if you can get it. Ten per cent for doing bugger all. Piece of piss.'

'When you get your first bung, Jake, let me know,' said Fred the Sparkie. 'I've got just the place to stash it. Biscuit tin in me garden shed. Just under hob nobs. Next to me girlie mag. The missus hasn't a clue. My bit of heaven after I've planted me daffies.'

Jake laughed at the banter, added the sugar and passed round the mugs. Life was good. The spots were disappearing – as were most of the embarrassing moments.

For his fifteenth birthday he'd been given gift vouchers and bought himself a brand new, size five football, the best in the shop. He kept it in his bedroom. He practiced 'keepy uppies', spent hours heading it against the bedroom wall, and occasionally knocked over the bedside lamp and smashed the bulb. In his mind's eye, he visualised places on the wall, which represented different parts of the goal. He'd head into the far corner, volley to the right of the 'keeper, back-heel over the line, dummy the 'keeper before slotting into an empty net.

Once, Chloe came in unannounced, and wondered what he was doing. 'Are you talking to yourself? You'll get locked away for that.' 'Out!' shouted Jake, 'and don't ever come into my room again, without knocking!' It could have been embarrassing – for both of them.

But that ball, that top class, state of the art, finest example of manufacturing excellence even occupied his bed. He didn't snuggle up to it. It was at the other end, being caressed by eager toes and compliant soles. The two of them had to have a special relationship. They had to be friends. They needed to bond. For Jake, he just felt comfortable around that ball. It was his best pal. Nothing was going to come between them. Treat it the right way, look after it, and things will be fine. Take it from him then there'd be trouble.

He was born on Bonfire Night, 5 November. He didn't look into it with any significance, wasn't into astrology at all, but Chloe, who was, showed him a chart of a typical Scorpio. Passing it over she said, 'I'll have to watch you lover boy. I'm not bringing any of my mates over here. No way!'

'What you on about?' he replied.

Some people would have us believe that Scorpios are less than delightful folk. They stand accused of being secretive and suspicious with a tendency to nurse grudges. Scorpios are also supposedly full of anti-social habits including a tendency to be rude and to speak explicitly about taboo topics. Plus traditionally they are sex mad!

'Chance'd be a fine thing.' said Jake.
He read on.

The truth is, it's no wonder Scorpios are secretive. Who would want to own up to belonging to a sign with such a reputation? It is my pleasure to quash those stupid misconceptions and set the record straight. Scorpios don't nurse grudges. They are actually, very forgiving. They just don't forget anything. They are not rude, just honest, direct and unpretentious. They don't set out to shock people; they are just shocked themselves by the prissy attitudes that some people have towards basic human functions. And as for being sex mad… Oh gosh! I appear to have run out of space.

He smiled. Then he read the 'Key to Success'.

If you were born under Scorpio you might fear that you have drawn the short celestial straw… Actually, though, you have hit the heavenly jackpot. Your intense sensitivity may be a trial at times, but it's your greatest asset. If you trust it and nurture your sincere desire to do the best in every situation…everything in your life will yet prove perfect.

At least it hadn't said anything about the state of a Scorpio's bedroom. Not like his mum. Yeah, a couple of cups had grown mould on them, but so what?

Jake bought himself a guitar – a secondhand Spanish type, but he had an experience that put him off for life. He was getting to a decent standard – the rest of the family had stopped looking for the protective cotton earplugs – when it all changed. Chloe had got a kitten and called it Oscar. It was her pride and joy. She looked after it and always made sure it had access to the cat flap that dad had fitted to the back door. But like all good intentions...

One day, the moggy sneaked into Jake's room. How long can a cat wait before something has to give? Oscar did show some initiative. Looking around for a litter tray it found a perfect alternative – the guitar was laid out, invitingly, on Jake's bed. Oscar's aim was sure and exact. On Jake's return, he sensed that all wasn't as it should be – but he didn't catch on immediately. There was certainly a strange smell that greeted him but his trainers often smelt like rotting vegetables.

Slipping the guitar strap over his shoulder he was ready to strike the first chord when he hurled down the instrument, breaking it in two, while the unwelcome deposits scattered to the four corners of the room. If it hadn't been for that pesky numpty, maybe Jake's career would have taken a different turn.

In Jake's last year at school he was selected for the England schoolboy U16 squad. The game was against France at Leicester City's Walker Stadium and he came on for the whole of the second half. The team drew 2-2 and Jake set up the equaliser, fifteen minutes from time. All the family were there, proud to see him don the national shirt.

Steve, Linda and Chloe stood up after the final whistle and clapped and cheered as the players made their way to the changing rooms.

'You never know, love,' said Steve. 'Perhaps your son is destined to perform on the bigger stage.'

'As long as he's happy, doing what he's doing. That'll do for me.' Linda said.

'And bringing home loads of cash!' shouted Chloe. 'Then he'll be able to take me on a shopping spree.'

5

The minute Ronnie had come into his life, Ricky knew things would never be the same. They had an instant dislike for each other and Ricky sensed a real danger. Initially, they skirted around each other, in order to keep the peace. Ricky always thought his mum had chosen crappy boyfriends and inevitably those relationships fizzled out.

That's how things were: nothing permanent, nothing concrete, nothing on which to build a sound future. Why should this one be any different? Surely mum would see through this obnoxious prat. Even though Ronnie engaged in a charm offensive, tried to press the right buttons and said all the right things, Ricky's instinct told him something different – this guy was a waster.

Before Ronnie moved into the flat, Ricky's problems had only been on the other side of the front door.

Ricky made excuses whenever Ronnie was around – hanging out with mates – anything, just to be away from the repugnant creature. That was fine with Ronnie. He didn't want any snotty-nosed kid causing hassle, getting between him and Ruth. Ricky summed him up in two words, 'a plonker' or to be more exact, 'an out and out plonker.' What was mum doing? Was she feeling sorry for the guy? She's a good-looking woman. Why would she ever dream of being with this waste of space? Was there something Ricky was missing? But for his mum's sake, he had to give it a go.

It was Ruth who suggested that Ricky should spend a day with Ronnie helping with his deliveries, in order they should get to know each other a little better. It was arranged during the half-term holiday and, in the lunch break, Ricky was even allowed to drive the van on some disused land under the motorway arches. It all looked promising until Ricky missed a gear and caused a piercing racket, as he pushed down hard on the accelerator pedal. Ronnie whacked him on the arm and snapped,

'Don't do that again, son, or I'll have fun putting you back together. You've had it easy, so far, well let me tell you, this is where it all stops. You're going to get out there and graft like the rest of us. No more sitting around on your arse. Understand?'

Ricky didn't answer. 'Are you listening to me, boy?'

Ronnie's face was inches away from Ricky's right ear and his eyes were bulging like organ stops. Ronnie pushed him aggressively against the door, opened the glove compartment and dug out a half bottle of brandy, stashed away under a pile of empty fag and crisp packets. He took a large swig and ran his dirty arm across his mouth.

'Like I said, you little prat, from now on, you do as I say. Is that clear? And if I ever get mouthed back at in front of your mother, so help me, I'll do you serious damage.'

Ricky sat there shaking. Ronnie pushed him out and told him to make his own way home. 'Don't forget kiddo. One mention of this to your mum, and your life won't be worth living.'

Ronnie laughed, as he slid over to the driver's seat, slipped into first gear, and sped away.

Ricky let himself into the flat. All was quiet. He assumed the place was empty. He made himself a drink and a piece of toast and sat down at the kitchen table, when he heard the bedroom door bang shut. Ronnie stumbled into the room wearing a T-shirt and boxer shorts, looking dishevelled, unkempt, and obviously the worse for drink. He took a swing at the boy. Ricky ducked and shot behind the table.

'You've been nicking my ale, haven't you, you little toe-rag? Nobody takes me for a mug. Nobody.'

Ronnie took off his belt, wrapped it around his wrist and caught Ricky on the back. It hurt like hell but with Ronnie's senses dulled, Ricky skipped past the drunken oaf, to escape through the front door.

Down the steps, across the forecourt, onto the high street. He picked up pace and he ran and ran – he had to get as far away as possible – until he could run no more.

He sat on the wall by the town library and buried his hands in his face. Tears flowed down his cheeks. He felt abandoned, and alone. He felt angry. He had no one to turn to and he was desperately unhappy: almost suicidal. If he'd had a gun, he wouldn't have hesitated to use it.

Eventually, he wiped away the tears, stood up and walked across town. He waited outside the supermarket. He didn't know what time his mum finished her shift at her new job but he would wait as long as it took. Ruth was surprised to see him.

'Ricky, what are you doing here?'

'Thought I'd surprise you, mum.'

'Everything okay?'

'Yeah, no probs,' said her son, kicking an empty drinks can, twenty yards, with tremendous force.

The following day all three sat down at the breakfast table and Ronnie didn't say a thing, until Ruth went to the bathroom. He leaned over and whispered, 'I hope you never had a word with your mum, lad, because if you did, and I get the earache, you know what will happen, don't you? Don't you, son?'

Ricky nodded. He pressed his finger into the underside of the table and rotated it fiercely. He imagined Ronnie's eyeball being gouged from its socket.

Ricky continued to make excuses for never being around the flat. He hung around street corners with other likely kids, got involved with petty crime, stealing from the big retailers. They'd all take turns. Down the pants, in the heels of shoes. They knew exactly where the cameras were. Just bits of thrills. A buzz. It was warm in there, the security guys kept moving 'em on, but they became experts at ducking and diving.

Ricky did anything to get through the next day. He smoked. He sank a few beers. He smoked some grass. The first time he lit up, he spewed his guts out. But from there on, it became easier. The aggro, for a short time, disappeared.

It affected his schoolwork, but he kept his head down and didn't draw attention to himself. He sat there, quietly. The teachers were rabbiting on about all kinds of shit.

'History, geography, science – bloody hell, give me a break! How's that going to get me a job?' How's that going to get Ronnie off my back?'

The days floated past. 'Keep your nose clean, Ricky, baby. Sound. Just let it all drift...'

He started laughing and couldn't stop. Only when the tears reappeared, did he fall asleep.

6

Jake's progress was excellent, and the staff were delighted with the way he'd committed himself to the club. He made tremendous strides through the junior ranks and even though representatives from other clubs had made subtle approaches about his availability, the temptation to play elsewhere never became an issue.

At the end of his secondary education, aged sixteen, he was delighted to sign a two-year scholarship with Burding Town.

He was just under six-foot tall, slim, broad shoulders and had finely-carved features with clear blue eyes and a close-cropped hairstyle. He wore a black and white, anti-racism wristband with a 'Stand up, Speak up!' message.

He had matured into a fine athlete but was still at the development stage and he knew he had much to learn to be anywhere near the finished article.

On 1st July, the first day of pre-season training, it finally dawned on him that he was a professional footballer. He was paid £75 a week. Football was now his main priority but education was still important. Jake had passed five GCSEs and the curricula on offer were many and varied.

A building skills course included joinery, plumbing, and brick laying and would mean he could help his dad in the summer but in the end he plumped for a Sports Science course, reasoning that if things didn't pan out as planned he could still be involved in a sports environment.

The Government was telling everybody to get off their backsides and do some exercise so perhaps it was the best option.

The manager at Burding Town was a wily old bird, Ged Marsh, nicknamed the 'Silver Fox' because of his full head of white hair. Marsh liked to indulge in a glass of malt whisky as a 'relaxation' and had plenty of amusing stories about his time in the game. He was 'old school' but was finding it a lot more difficult with all the media attention. Everybody wanted a piece of the action.

Gentleman Ged had a benevolent manner. He would get the best out of his players by a softly, softly approach; a quiet word in the ear or an arm round the shoulder when dealing with a problem. Through experience he knew what each player needed to get him performing. Only occasionally would he lose it and the players would quickly see the other side of his personality. But now he was tired. He'd done it for fifteen years with four different clubs and his wife was pressurising him to finally put down the deposit on the Spanish villa. For Ged, though, it was still in the blood. The game. How could he walk away? What would he do? He was only 59.

Jake liked the boss even though he hardly saw him, but not every member of the staff had similar endearing qualities when dealing with players. The youth team coach was a guy called Matt Downie and he quickly gained a reputation as a 'smart arse'. Downie had never played the game at any level but had all the UEFA coaching badges and brown-nosed his way up the pecking order, right into the manager's good books. He took on a completely new persona whenever the gaffer was around. What the lads saw every day was a cynical, critical bastard.

It came to a head when the under-18s played against Manchester United. It was a game they desperately wanted to win but any kind of result would have boosted their self-belief. They went one down early in the game but then equalised, against the run of play, just before the break.

The team had worked hard and put in plenty of effort but United had some really gifted players and always held the initiative. In the dressing room at halftime, Downie screamed, 'That's *******
rubbish. You're all shit-scared and playing like puffs. I've never seen such garbage in all my life.' As soon as he spoke his credibility went through the window. They knew he was taking crap.

They sat in silence. They were an honest bunch of players and he'd questioned their commitment. They went out for the second half petrified of making mistakes and United swarmed all over them, scoring another three without reply. With confidence shattered, the Burding youngsters shuffled into the dressing room and sat down, fearful of saying a word.

Downie smashed his way through the door and with one almighty flourish scattered all the teacups and water bottles off the table. For the next fifteen minutes he subjected the players to another tirade of abuse. The expletives wafted over their heads. The damage had already been done.

Six months of demanding physical work was starting to take its toll and Jake went through a period of inconsistency; a man of the match performance was followed by a listless display, lacking in spark and enthusiasm. Jake confided in physio, Jimmy Franks.

'Everybody goes through it Jake. Your body is taking a hell of a lot of punishment but listen; it will level out. Don't put yourself under pressure. Just remember to rest when you can, take the odd vitamin tablet, eat the right food, drink plenty of water and you'll get stronger and fitter. Don't forget, you're still developing and I reckon you've got another couple of inches of growth yet. So be patient, it'll come good.'

The few words reassured the young man.

His life had certainly turned upside down, having to cope with the tough training sessions plus the educational modules. College day was Thursday and on Friday afternoons he attended lectures on subjects like media training, laws of the game and disciplinary matters. It was all-consuming and tiring. The words of Alex Cummings hit the spot. 'Physically and mentally it will be demanding, but just hang in there.'

The Christmas break came as a welcome relief with no games being scheduled for the youth team over the holiday period. The big day was always spent at his grandparents. But grandma had started to show the first signs of dementia and it was suggested the routine be changed. Grandma was having none of it.

On Christmas Day, Jake showered, looked in the mirror and smiled. What could be better than getting paid to keep fit?

Whilst towelling down, he clicked on his mobile. He'd received a text message from his cousin Julie. 'I'm sending you an email. Love Julie. Merry Xmas.'

He put on his dressing gown, sat on the bed and read. He started laughing.

How to shower like a woman. Take off all clothing and place in a sectioned laundry hamper according to lights, darks, whites, man-made or natural. Walk to bathroom wearing long dressing gown. If husband seen along the way, cover up any exposed flesh and rush to bathroom. Look at womanly physique in mirror and stick out belly. Complain and whine about getting fat. Get in shower. Look for face cloth, arm cloth, loin cloth, long loofah, wide loofah and pumice stone. Wash hair once with cucumber and pineapple shampoo with 83 added vitamins – 'cos you're the one!

Condition hair with cucumber and pineapple conditioner with enhanced natural crocus oil. Leave on hair for 15 minutes. Wash face with crushed apricot facial scrub for 10 minutes, until red raw. Wash rest of body entirely in ginger nut and jaffa cake body wash. Rinse conditioner off, taking at least 15 minutes. Shave armpits and legs. Consider shaving bikini area but decide to get it waxed instead. Scream loudly when husband flushes toilet, causing loss of water pressure and turning it red hot. Turn off shower. Squeegee all wet surfaces in shower. Spray mould spots with suitable mould remover.

Get out of shower and dry with towel the size of small African country. Wrap hair in super-absorbent second towel. Check entire body for remotest sign of spots.

Attack with nail clippers or tweezers (if you can find them). Return to bedroom wearing long dressing gown and towel on head. If husband seen, cover up any exposed areas and then rush to bedroom to spend an hour and a half getting ready.

How to shower like a man. Take off clothes while sitting on bed and leave them on the floor in a pile. Walk naked to the bathroom. If wife seen, shake 'old man' at her and shout 'Wey Hey!' Look in mirror and suck in gut and admire manly physique. Get in shower. Don't bother to look for washcloth, 'cos you don't need one. Wash face and armpits. Laugh at how loud farts sound in shower. Remember to leave some fetching hair on the soap. Shampoo hair but don't condition. Make Mohican hairstyle with shampoo.

Pull back the curtain to see self in mirror. Rinse off and get out of shower. Fail to notice water on floor because curtain has been outside of shower for whole time. Partially dry off. Look at self in mirror, flex muscles. Leave shower curtain open and wet bath mat on floor. Leave bathroom light and fan on. Return to bedroom with towel around waist. If you pass wife pull off towel and go 'Yeah Baby!' while thrusting pelvis towards her. Put on yesterday's clothes.

Jake laughed out loud. He rang her.

'Hey, Julie, out of order.'

'What you mean?'

'This thing about us fellas!'

'Well, I have some experience you know.'

'Sounds like it,' said Jake laughing.

'It was going round the office. Thought you'd like it.'

'Brilliant. What you doing today?'

'Family do as usual, then we're going to the pub. What about yourself?'

'Grandma's. And to be honest I think we're ready to leave. Mum's shouting, so I'd better get my skates on. Have a good day and all the best to everyone.'

'Same to you. See ya.'

He put on his black trousers and the new shirt Chloe had bought him. He sprayed on his favourite aftershave.

The family clambered into the car and Linda said, 'Now listen, when we get there, grandma will want help, so I'll be in the kitchen most of the time. I said we'd get there early so you two could make yourself useful.'

'Who's going to be there?' said Chloe.

'I'm not sure. I know mum's invited some of her neighbours and Auntie Marje and family are definitely coming.'

'They can't have asked that Pete and his missus again, can they? Last year he was sick all over the dog.'

'Stop it.'

They were the first to arrive and grandma met them at the door.

Linda donned an apron and made her way to the kitchen.

'Merry Christmas mum. Give us a kiss. Now what needs doing?'

'Can you sort the prawns out first, love? I'll be with you in a moment.'

Grandma hugged Chloe and then spoke to Jake. 'Merry Christmas sweetheart. How are you?'

'Great thanks grandma. Fit as a butcher's,' said Jake towering over her.

'Well you should be at your age.'

'You're looking well grandma. Can I help with anything?'

'Yes love. Grandpa's sorting out the beer barrel. I don't want him spilling it everywhere. You know what he's like.'

'No problem.'

Jake made his way through to the garage.

'Hello son. Good to see you.'

'Happy Christmas grandpa.'

'Thanks for the hedge trimmers,' said his grandpa, placing the icebox on the table. 'I'll be careful not to cut off any limbs – silly old bugger!'

'I'll come over and do it for you, if you want.'

'Thanks. I'll let you know. Let's get this barrel sorted. We've got to fix the nozzle.'

'How's it going anyway?' asked Jake. 'Grandma okay?'

'She's been better. Getting forgetful. Mind wandering, that sort of thing.'

'It's getting worse?'

'You could say that. She went to the shops on Monday for last minute presents. Wanted some gift tokens and a sweater. You know what she came back with? A tin of bloody sardines and a monkey wrench.'

'No way.'

'But I'm as bad. When you get as old as me your whole body aches. Cod liver oil used to lubricate the joints but even they've given up the ghost.'

'Things were a bit different in the old days.'

'Just a little,' said grandpa, looking around for a hammer. 'When I was your age, eh heck what year would it be?

'You'll have to help me out son.'

'Well you're 80 now, so it'd be around 1941.'

'That's right, two years in't war.'

His grandpa had never talked about the war before and Jake, remembering the class on the D-Day landings, was curious.

'Were you called up?'

'No. I was already on the railways. Started at fifteen, cleaning out the boilers ready for inspection. Called me a bar boy then before I went on't foot plate.'

'Where did you go?'

'Fairly local, although we did go over to Yorkshire quite a bit. I remember a bomb hitting the track, day after we were there.'

'Dirty job?'

'Used to come home filthy. Mother told me to strip off outside. She'd got tin bath ready.'

'No shampoo or conditioners in them days?'

'Carbolic soap lad. Took first layer off. Can you sort those glasses out?'

'Sure. I suppose your mum would cook you something special after all that?'

'Tripe and trotters.'

'Sorry?'

'Cows' inners and pigs' feet lad.'

'Sounds tasty.'

'Bit a vinegar, went down a treat. Looking back it was pretty basic but it's all we could afford.'

Grandma popped her head around the door. 'Everything all right, you two?'

'Grandpa's been reminiscing,' said Jake laying out the glasses. 'Telling me all about the good old days.'

'Good old days?' said grandma. 'Don't get me going.'

'How did you two meet?'

Jake knew the story but he loved hearing it and he knew his grandmother liked telling it.

'First met the silly old fool when I took my dad his sandwiches. I only had an hour for lunch and it was a twenty-minute walk from Booker Street to the goods yard. That's when I met your grandpa.'

'No Ethel,' butted in grandpa. 'First time we met was when I came in't shop.'

'Was that the confectioners?' asked Jake, setting up a table.

'Eh, tell Jake about rationing.'

'I had to sort out the coupons. Two ounces of butter, two ounces marg, two ounces of lard and half a pound of sugar. That was to last a family for a week.'

'That was for each person,' said grandpa, irritably.

'Ah. That's right.'

'Highlight for me was Friday night when grandma used to paint her legs.'

'Pink with yellow spots?' said Jake laughing.

'There were no tights or stockings in them days so we used a bit of false tan and painted a seam down the back.'

'What false tan?'

'Gravy browning.'

'Boiler inspector would have got a bit excited, eh grandpa?'

'I'd have knocked his block off.'

'Enough now boys. Jake, I'll have to take him to see the guests. Can you manage?'

'No problem grandma. I'll sort out the music.'

As his grandparents disappeared into the lounge, Jake sifted through the CDs. Grandad had fitted up the garage with a sound system but the collection of music wasn't that inspiring. Not even a Christmas 'singalong' album. Jake went to the car to find something more suitable. Motown, Christmas best of... He tested the volume.

Grandma rounded everybody up for lunch and the little ones were seated together, alongside the main dining table. Lots of fancy hats, balloons and crackers. The adults took their places and curiously, many seemed reluctant to sit next to Uncle Joe.

The recently divorced 30-year-old weighed around seventeen stone and had a tendency to break wind. The trouble was; Joe was the only one oblivious to this. He worked for the local bank and spent most of his time at the computer keyboard. Understandably, he had his own office.

What a fabulous table grandma had prepared. The turkey was passed around – the veg and potatoes followed. Sausages, gravy, stuffing, apple sauce.

'Brilliant grandma,' said Jake. 'Did grandpa help in the kitchen?'

'He did peel the spuds, love,' she said putting her hand on Jake's shoulder. 'But he gets in the way.'

Grandad opened the wine, muttering, 'At least I can do this right.'

Jake was sitting next to Marie, the daughter of his grandparents next door neighbours – dark hair, great looking and a figure to die for. He introduced himself and asked her. 'Left school, or are you working?'

'I'm doing a course in secretarial skills. Eventually, I want to be a PA. What do you do?'

'I'm a footballer.'

'Hey, cool! Who do you play for?'

'The Town.'

'What, the local club?' said Marie pouring herself a glass of wine. 'So you're a professional?'

'I'm on a scholarship. A bit like an apprentice scheme. It's my first year.'

'Are you in the first team?'

'Steady. I'm not at that level,' explained Jake. 'I play in the youth team.'

'When's your next game? I'd like to come and see you.'

'The reserves have got a game next week and I might be in the squad.'

'Can I come?' asked Marie. 'I've always wanted to see a real game. My dad only watches it on TV.'

'Yeah sure,' said Jake, intoxicated by the smell of her perfume. 'If you fancy it, we'll meet up afterwards.'

'Sounds good.'

'Jake, pass the spuds,' said Joe, whose plate was already straining from overload. 'What about those players who got accused of assault? What do you think?'

'Who's to say? But I think it's been blown up out of all proportion. Sounds like they could have been set up. A lot of girls see it as a way of making a fast buck. They know which nightclubs the players go to and afterwards go to the press. Some papers even hire girls. It's ridiculous.'

'Yeah, but they're not dummies, are they?' said Joe. 'With all that brass about, they know they're easy targets.'

'The first team lads at our place like to go out for a few beers after the game but they know when enough is enough. But, I suppose, you'll always get some looking for a bit more.'

Marie joined in. 'But they've got minds of their own and a tremendous lot to lose, haven't they? Most are married with families and it's a powder keg ready to explode. Do you get any help or advice from the club?'

'They're always on to us about how we should behave both on and off the field. And it's not only about the dodgy things. A 17-year-old might score a hat-trick in a televised game and suddenly he's in big demand,' said Jake, adding more gravy.

'If he doesn't watch what he says he might look stupid and sound like a right bigheaded sod. So the club prepare you for that kind of thing.'

Generous measures of port were served along with the cheese and coffee and while the older members of the family indulged, the kids were happy to play with their motorised remote control cars and video games. Jake volunteered to wash up, and Marie joined him in the kitchen.

'I'll wash and you dry. Or do you want to get the marigolds on?'

'No that's fine,' replied Marie.

'What do you think of the family?' asked Jake.

'Great. They're special.'

'Have your parents enjoyed it?'

'Well they can't stop smiling so I think that's a yes. What have I to do with all these left-overs?'

'Put them to one side. The dog will have them later.'

'A dog? I haven't seen it. Where is it?'

'In the garage,' informed Jake. 'If you fancy it, we'll take him for a walk later on.'

'Love to.'

'We'll have to get back for the party games before everybody falls asleep. It's tradition,' pointed out Jake. 'Grandpa is usually zonked by ten.'

'Pass me another tea towel. This one's soaking.'

They cleared the decks ready for the next round.

'When I've got a few bob I'm going to buy grandma a dishwasher. If there's one more greasy tray I'll go crazy. Come on, let's get out of here.'

Max was an English setter with a great temperament but had an irritating habit of leaping up. They strolled through the woods and time passed very quickly.

On their return, Uncle Bert had taken centre stage. 'Now listen up everybody – the younger kids would like to entertain you. First Louise will sing. Nice round of applause please.'

After a Sugar Babes favourite, Liz was next on, impersonating a comedian.

The kids did well and Bert gave them a chocolate selection box. They took their bows but were reluctant to move. Fame had gone to their heads. By the time the karaoke had been set up in the corner of the room Jake had cuddled up on the couch next to Marie.

'Mamma Mia here we go again, my my.... '

Grandma and grandpa duetted Sinatra's classic 'Something Stupid': 'I can see it in your eyes that you despise... '

Jake whispered in Marie's ear, 'what about that? They're still in love after all these years?'

'Absolutely,' replied Marie. 'No way they're faking.'

'Grandpa was telling me that it's getting more and more difficult for grandma. They went to an Italian restaurant last week and she ordered a basic chicken and chips. She thought it had some sauce on and refused to eat it. Had a right strop on. Called the waiter over and told him to take it away. Said she hated Italian muck.'

'Sad, isn't it? And it's not going to get any better.'

Jake slipped his arm around the back of the settee to nestle on Marie's left shoulder.

Finally, when everybody had downed their drinks and told their stories, beds awaited. Some staggered, some crawled, some were already fast sleep. Those staying at grandma's crept upstairs.

Jake walked Marie to her front door.

'I've had a great time,' said Jake. 'I'm glad you came. Any chance of seeing you again?'

'Of course,' smiled Marie. 'I'm coming to your game, or have you forgotten?'

He leaned over to kiss her on the cheek but Marie took control. Their lips met for a passionate embrace.

He sat next to Chloe for the journey home.

'Hey, lover boy, I saw you snogging,' said Chloe giggling. 'I suppose you'll be visiting grandma a lot more from now on in.'

'Come here you!'

7

First day back after the holiday break, Ronnie bundled his huge frame into the white Mercedes diesel van. For the overweight bald driver, this was sweet isolation, a beam of sunlight on a dark, depressing day. He watched the people outside, shuffling under windswept brollies, thankful he was surrounded by the comforts of the 2.4 litre German thoroughbred.

A few gear crunches later; he was on the open road. His first delivery was to a residential place owned by the social services. There must be a better system to this loading. The prats back at the depot had mixed all the items together. Now each one would have to be checked.

The fitter was already on site but someone or something had rattled his cage.

'What's up?' enquired Ronnie.

'What's up? I'll bloody tell you what's up mate. Waterworks that's what,' came the sharp reply.

'Sounds bad,' said Ronnie, not interested. 'Never away from the bog then?'

'What you on about? No, you silly bugger. This radiator. They want it shifting to the other side of the room but they haven't switched off the bleeding boiler. All the pipes are red hot. Got my fingers burnt.'

With the floorboards removed, the myriad of copper pipes resembled an underground rail link.

'Couldn't find a container, so when I disconnected the valve, steaming hot water shot out.' His hand was glowing like the tip of a red-hot poker.

'There's always problems at whatever job you're on. Last one, they wanted flush lights on the ceiling. Did anybody find out if the ceiling was solid or not?

'Did they bollocks. I tell them it can't be done and they start shouting at me.

'Not to them surveyors or designers, oh, no! It's me. And I usually get it from some old biddy who's going through the change.'

'Listen fella,' said Ronnie irritably. 'I'm only the delivery man. Can you give us a hand?'

First drop of the day and he was already getting flak. 'Where do you want the units?'

Ronnie's blood pressure was going into overdrive.

A woman appeared in a white outfit and took charge. She told him to put everything in the spare room until the plumber had finished his work.

The landing was narrow and several pieces were large and awkward. Manoeuvring around the staircases proved almost impossible. The floral wallpaper took a hammering but the damage to the collection of potted plants was hidden discreetly.

The day had started off badly for Ronnie. It wouldn't get any better. In fact, it was to get considerably worse.

8

Jake was included in the first reserve game in the new year, coming off the subs' bench for the last twenty minutes of a game that ended all square. Burding's second string had to defend for long periods and although Jake would have much preferred to be introduced earlier, he still made a telling contribution. At least Marie thought so.

'I thought you did very well,' she assured him.

'I wasn't on long enough,' Jake said, obviously disappointed.

'But the team looked very young.'

'That's the problem,' he pointed out. 'Some clubs look on it as a development league, you know, to bring on the younger players, but others who have massive squads play their senior players. Did you know they had six internationals in their side? Anyway, what kind of day have you had?'

'Good. I'm temping at the moment. Started on Monday with this solicitor's practice, just handling the 'phone calls, doing some paper work and general dogs body things.

'It's a family firm and they've made me feel really welcome. Fits in well with the course I'm doing.'

'How long you there for?'

'About a month. I'm filling in for somebody who's sick,' Marie explained. 'So it could be longer.'

'How about a drink?'

They found a small wine bar in town. At seventeen he was still uneasy about being seen in such an establishment.

'What you having?' Jake asked her.

'Glass of white wine please, medium.'

The bar was busy but they found an empty table.

'So you enjoyed the game?'

'It was good to see a live match.'

'Not much atmosphere was there?' said Jake, moving his chair closer. 'Not like a first team game.'

'No, but sitting right next to the action, you can see how hard you guys work. What did the coach say to you when you were coming on?'

'Just told me to relax and enjoy it.'

'You know when you took that throw-in?' asked Marie. Jake nodded. 'Well one of your teammates shouted "Peggy!"'

'Yeah.'

'What was all that about?'

Jake laughed. 'Most of the lads have nicknames and that's mine.'

'What? Peggy?'

'Jake the Peg. It's a song from way back,' explained Jake. 'I'm Jake the Peg, with my extra leg...'

'Ha Ha. It could come in useful.'

'Might get complicated if I did step-overs. I'd tie myself in knots.'

'What about the other lads?' asked Marie, feeling totally relaxed.

'Nicknames, you mean? Well there's Clive Jackson, he's called Wacko. You know, Wacko Jacko. Then there's Jonah Sonsissko. He's a Senegalese international and he's called Kiddo.'

'Where do they get that from?'

'The Cisco Kid. Cowboy programme on TV ages ago. It's the Skip that remembers it. Dan Jones, he's the captain, and he's always known as Skip. Welsh international Ivor Smeeten is Taffy, not very original I know and then there's Alan Simpson, the 'keeper. He's got a few – Bart, Hommie or just Simmo.'

'It's like being back at school.'

'Never grown up. The Spanish guy Juan Torres comes in for some terrible stick as well.'

'Why's that?'

'On good days he gets called Bully but when he's had a stinker he gets Kerr.'

'Kerr?' said Marie confused.

'Work it out yourself.'

The bar staff were shouting last orders. 'Come on. I think it's time to get Peg Leg back home.'

They made their way over to the taxi rank.

'Norfolk Road, thanks.'

They snuggled up in the back of the taxi. 'You're gorgeous,' said Jake.

'Give us a kiss, then,' Marie said, hugging him close.

'Thought you'd never ask,' said Jake looking directly into her eyes. 'How many boyfriends have you had?'

'A few.'

'Only a few? I'll bet.'

'You're such a looney,' she laughed. 'I'm only eighteen you know.'

'Yeah well you're great looking. All the guys must have tried to pull you.'

'Kiss me.'

'I'd never have believed,' said Jake touching her face, 'I'm kissing such a beautiful girl.'

'I'd never have believed,' said Marie stroking his hair, 'I'm kissing such a handsome footballer bound for the top.'

'If only.'

'You never know. You've got to have dreams.'

'Like a million others.'

'Yeah, but for some they come true. So why not you?'

'Come here. I wouldn't mind if I didn't make it as long as we were together.'

'Steady.'

'You're the best thing that's happened to me,' said Jake.

'Not a lot happened in your life then?'

'I did win a goldfish once at the Easter fair.'

'You're joking,' said Marie rolling her eyes.

'Got to believe it,' smiled Jake. 'You know how?'

'Haven't a clue.'

'Throwing a ping pong ball into a glass bowl.'

'Never.'

'Yeah. It was the last one. I really tried with the first few. You know, concentrated like mad but they went nowhere. With the last one I closed my eyes and just threw it anywhere. It bounced around all over the place and then dropped in.'

'What did you call it?'

'Guess.'

'I don't know. Jaws?'

'Cyril.'

She laughed. 'How long did you have it?'

'Two weeks.'

'Cat got it, did it?'

'Mum changed its water,' Jake explained. 'It was freezing cold. It tasted great with a chip butty.'

'Don't be awful.'

'Give us another kiss.'

'There's a limit you know.'

'On what? Kisses?'

'Yes.'

'And what's the limit?'

'One hundred.'

'One hundred? That's not many.'

'No you didn't let me finish. I was going to say one hundred million.'

'Right, better get cracking. There's lots to get through. Hands are a bit cold though. Any suggestions?'

'Cheeky. I've only known you for two minutes.'

'Long enough then.'

'Kiss me again and I'll let you know.'

Training in soggy gear on freezing cold days was a hard slog during the long winter months and the sunshine and pristine pitches were now a distant memory. Jake's inclusion, though, in the reserve side had given the 17-year-old a boost, just at the right time. Most of the stuff he was trying was coming off.

He got a surprise on Tuesday morning when he was told to report for training with the first team. Several regulars were either injured or on international duty and, to be fair, Jake knew he was only making up the numbers.

But he put that to one side. He played without fear and at the end of the session some of the guys had an encouraging word. They seemed to accept him.

On the Thursday before the Easter games he was in for another shock. The manager called him into the office.

'You'll be travelling down to the Villa game with us. You're in the squad. I've been watching your progress Jake and I've got good reports from the staff. It's just a start but well done.'

'Thanks Boss.' He couldn't think of anything else to say.

Long journeys to away games were the bane of every professional footballer but they all had their own individual MP3 players, mobile phones and video games to wile away the hours. And this long journey was made even longer when the manager had to take a 'phone call.

The card school was the favourite long before all the modern technology.

'How about a game of hearts, young 'un?' shouted the skipper over to Jake. Joe Smith called to his room mate Willie Short. 'Hey Shortie get your arse up here now. Card school.'

Willie was studying form. He liked to bet, nothing heavy, but he browsed through the papers each day, to see which stables were hot and where the top jocks were riding.

'Be with you in a minute.'

'What's the rules?' said Joe.

'Pass to the left, hundred out,' said Skip, shuffling the pack. 'Got a winner Willie?'

'Rubbish meetings today,' pointed out Willie. 'Bits and bobs but there's one racing at Newmarket in the 3.40. Got a chance. Been second in last two starts, could go one better. Weights good and it's a decent price.'

'What's it called?' said Skip, arranging his suits.

'Berks Jerk.'

'What kind of name's that?'

'Comes from a long line of Jerks.'

'You're not involved with it are you Willie?' said Skip laughing.

'Leave it out, Jonesy. Get your money on it but if it's a loser, don't come looking for me.'

'Who dealt this load of crap?' piped up Joe.

'Always moaning, that's our Smidgy.'

'Yeah but I've got nothing less than a bleeding eight.'

'Stop whinging and pass 'em on.'

51

Jake had a great hand, full of diamonds including the two, three and four. He was in with a good shout.

After several hands the coach stopped. Motorway hold up. Sitting in the middle lane they spotted a clapped-out saloon whose occupants were having a domestic.

'See them?' said Joe. 'Mother's face is a picture. Looks like a bag of spanners. She's giving the old fella a right bollocking. Eh, hold on a minute: bit of crumpet in the back.'

Teenagers. Impish. Smiled. They looked up flattered by the attention they received from a coachload of athletes.

'Hey lads we've got a couple here,' said Willie playing a spade. 'What you gonna do when you pack in the game, Skip?'

'Good question. At 33 I've not much time left.'

'Haven't you got a business of some sort?'

'My mate runs it,' said Dan. 'I look after the financial side. It's doing okay. We're onto something different now. A security system for vans. We're doing some tests but it could be a winner.'

Joe picked up the round. 'Looking back, would you have done anything different?'

'Not really, there wasn't the money about in the early days. But you guys have it made.'

'How about Jake who's just starting off?' said Willie, about to deal.

'Dig in there and get a pro contract,' advised the skipper. 'First thing, get the games under the belt.'

'And choose your mates right,' cut in Smidgy. 'Watch out for hangers on. Listen to people who've been in the game and done it. And be honest with yourself. It's the only way to succeed.'

'It's not easy.'

'Of course it's not,' said Skip, 'or everybody would do it, wouldn't they? It's a short career, you might think you've got loads of time, well let me tell you, it's over so quick you wouldn't believe. When I was eighteen, I thought thirty was ancient.'

Willie played a heart.

'Where's that come from?'

'Hey, I've got plenty.'

They counted the scores and it was Jake's turn to deal. They hadn't moved for half an hour and the guy in the saloon was still pointing at his wife, arguing the toss. The girls were craftily swigging something from a blue bottle. From their reactions it wasn't designer water.

When driver Dave eventually inched the luxury coach along the carriageway at a snail's pace, the players rose to applaud.

'Hey, not too quick Dave! Easy with the right foot!'

'He'll be stopping at the next services,' pointed out Willie. 'His bleeding tachograph will be jumping off the scale.'

As they got going, the reason for their slow progress was obvious. They witnessed a scene of absolute devastation. It was difficult to know exactly what had happened amid a tangled mass of twisted metal, broken glass and burnt rubber but a small red saloon was on its roof and an articulated lorry slewed over on its side.

Stationary cars were lined up on the hard shoulder, crumpled and battered, alongside the flashing lights of the emergency services vehicles. The injured were being carried on stretchers to the waiting ambulances.

Somebody's loved ones wouldn't be returning home that night. If the gaffer hadn't taken that last call, delaying their departure, who's to say what might have happened?

Dan Jones put away the cards. The players returned to their seats. They got our their mobiles. They phoned home. Afterwards they adjusted their headsets and closed their eyes.

9

Ronnie hated his job and people were really getting on his tits. From that very first delivery he'd had to deal with faulty goods, wrong directions, misinformation and a flat tyre. The administration department was making his life a misery.

The road works were a disgrace. He'd driven all over Europe – Spain, Italy, France, and their systems worked okay. So why not here? He was always jammed in the middle lane, making him late for each appointment, which meant plenty of flak from dissatisfied customers.

Ronnie decided it wasn't going to be one of those 'customers are always right' days. He used to take the aggro dished out and apologise for any delays or mistakes.

But not today. And if that greasy toad of a depot manager got onto him, with a 'Why didn't you do that filter drop first?' or 'Where've you been?' he'd decided he would nail him. It'd be nice to see his face cave in with a right uppercut.

Knocking off time couldn't come quickly enough.

The weather was still foul, miserable heavy rain, dark clouds and a cold wind. He promised he'd be home early as Ricky had somewhere to go – parents' evening or something. But he needed that one drink. He couldn't face the domestic situation without a booster.

His 10-year-old Ford saloon rattled to a halt in the 'Pig and Whistle' car park. Must get that exhaust fixed and that whining fan belt. He'd sort it tomorrow. He slammed the door shut, not bothering to lock it. It had never been knicked. Who would want it? The insurance would come in handy though.

He entered the pub through the back door.

He eased up to the bar and ordered a pint. He saw a few regulars but opted to be on his own. He preferred his own company. He'd drunk regularly ever since his Grandad sent him out to the local 'offy' where he'd slip an extra bottle for himself. Finished it by the time he got home. He never suspected a thing. Silly old bugger.

Drinking gave him confidence but also got him into some tight spots. Fights were normal.

He'd always liked a drink. So what? His drinking was under control. Some said he had a dependence on the stuff.

'Crap', thought Ronnie. 'I can handle it. No danger.' He'd been feeling edgy and suffering sweats but anyone with half a brain would know, it's not the booze – it's the stress at work that's the problem.

That night he got smashed. The shorts followed the pints. The other punters gave him a wide berth – he became nasty and vindictive. His language was vile.

The pub manager came over. He had seen him in similar drunken stupors and always managed to ease him through the doors. He told him to walk home, leave the car keys and sleep it off. To Ronnie it sounded like condescending bullshit. He knew what he was doing. He didn't need a toffee-nosed 'J Arthur' who'd cleaned him out of his wages to tell him what to do. With a swift headbutt he caught him on the bridge of the nose. The crack echoed around the deadened night. Hospital job for sure.

Ronnie shuffled off into the night – a pissed up, violent and broke, van driver.

10

Dave broke every speed limit to get the team to the hotel in time for their pre-match meal but they still arrived an hour late. Their preparations had been knocked off track.

After the meal, the gaffer gathered the boys together in the meeting room to announce the team. Jake would be one of the five subs. A tingle went up and down his spine when his name was called but he tried to stay calm and show no emotion. Everything inside was shaking.

The manager stressed the importance of a 'disciplined professional performance' and spent the majority of his talk going through the defensive strategies they'd been working on all week. The team had been leaking goals and it was time to get back to basics and build on a solid foundation.

All the players had a responsibility to get behind the ball and make it difficult for the opposition and it started, as in all good sides, with the strikers. If they were prepared to graft, then it would trigger a chain reaction throughout the side.

Ged Marsh finished with 'Concentrate for ninety minutes. If you do that, we'll get something today. Don't switch off.'

Jake's involvement at Villa Park was restricted to loosening up stretches along the touchline. The game ended 0-0. They would have settled for the point before kick-off. Burding was at the wrong end of the table and facing a relegation battle and an upturn in form and results was essential if they were to survive. It wasn't an ideal time to blood promising youngsters and Jake got the feeling he would have to be patient to get his chance.

Jake collected all the strips while the players showered. Kit man Dougy France barked out the orders. 'Shirts in one bag youngster, shorts in another.'

When it came to the jock straps and slips, Dougy called out, 'Best put them in a bin liner first son. Laundry woman will do her head in when she sees that lot. Dirty bastards. Can't clean their own arses these days. They get everything else done for them, probably want that doing as well!'

Jake showered and helped Doug and Dave to get the skips back on the coach. The manager said they'd leave at six o'clock sharp. Anyone not on, would be left. Skip had a word with Jake. 'Round 'em up Jake, will you, when it's time? Cheers mate.'

Jake signed a few autographs outside the ground but he was gutted when one young kid shouted, 'Who's that? Never heard of him.' Dave closed the door and the coach headed home.

'We've got a microwave on board Jake,' said Doug, standing up, checking to see if everyone was on board. 'I'll give you a shout when it's time to feed 'em.'

Jake went over to Welsh international Ivor Smeeten, now 32, who was enjoying some of the best form of his career. An introverted man, he did not like the attention off the field but to Jake he was a role model.

If Jake produced half of what Ivor had achieved in his career he'd be well pleased. Ivor was reading the programme.

'Fancy a coffee, Ivor?'

'Thanks Jake. White, one sugar.'

Jake went to the back of the coach and returned with the coffee.

'Enjoyed your first trip?'

'Brilliant,' said Jake easing himself across from Ivor and placing the plastic coffee cup on the table. 'I was nervous when the gaffer said I was on the bench. Funny really, whenever anybody went down I thought I'd get on. So I suppose it was a bit of an anti-climax in the end.'

'I know how you feel.'

'When did you make your debut?' asked Jake.

'I was eighteen, playing centre mid at the time and the manager only told me an hour before the game. We played at home and won 1-0. I was shattered after the game but kept my place for most of that season.'

'You've had a great career, playing in Italy and winning all those caps.'

'It's been hard work, but enjoyable.'

'Dan was telling me about some of the things to look out for. You know, to be aware of.'

'One thing you must expect and that's criticism,' said Ivor, glancing out of the window. 'Try not to take it personally. Get mentally tough and block it out.'

'Good shout.'

'And be yourself,' he added. 'Don't try to be like anyone else.'

'Is that what you did?'

'I don't show my emotions. I try to keep everything under wraps. That's the way I am. I think it's the only way I'm going to play my best football. But you come up against all kinds. You know that Pete Glass? Yeah? Well he's confrontational, always shouting his mouth off, upsetting officials, winding up opponents. Fans love him, don't they? They say he's giving everything for the club, every ounce of passion and sweat.'

Jake was aware of his reputation. 'Last week he was sent off for abusing the lino.'

'Right. But they say he wears his heart on his sleeve and they make allowances for him. But I get accused of not showing that same fight and aggression. I'll tell you what I did the last time we played against each other. The papers were saying Glass would "Tear a strip off me" or "Ivor for chop".

'One was "Cut Smeet to Ribbons" you know the kind of headlines the red tops do? Well, it got my blood boiling. I've always felt he's a very limited player; he reacts that way to disguise his weaknesses. One thing's for sure; I wasn't going to be bullied by him. I prepared for that game even more than usual.

'When we got out on the pitch I was in just the right emotional state – fired up but in control. You'll know what I mean when you've been in the game a little longer.'

'Was the game at home?'

'No, and the atmosphere at their place was electric. It was a full house and we were the underdogs. A draw would have been a good result but from the first whistle we were at their throats, winning possession early and pinging it about all over the field. Glass was niggling me early doors but I felt in good nick and whenever he dived in I skipped past him. The challenges started to come in later and higher.

'He'd been booked but the prospect of him being sent off didn't seem to bother him. When your game's in the zone it's like heaven: nothing will get the better of you. Glass was still ranting and raving, tapping ankles, elbowing and giving it plenty of verbals but he was always second best. He did everything to upset me.

'At one stage I even went against my instincts and said, "Hey Glassy, you can have a kick if you want."

'He was livid. His face was a picture. I thought he was going to explode. We went on to win 4-0 and his contribution was zilch. I felt I had won the battle and I got good reports. I knew I was top dog on the day. I had kept my emotions under control, didn't shout them to the press or the fans. No arm waving, no slagging off. Just controlled aggression.

'I tell you this because journalists will try to find some flaw in every player. If you are aggressive they'll murder you – "shouldn't be on the pitch, indisciplined". If you're quick, "he hasn't got the touch or he falls over too easily".

'Listen, you know as well as I do that when a player is flying past an opponent and gets a nudge, no matter how slight, they'll go down in a heap, won't they? They can't help it; their balance has gone. But the experts say he dived. That shows they've never played the game at any level. I know there's one or two who'll make a meal of it but they'll get found out – generally the players are honest.

'"Keepers who make great reflex saves will be slaughtered for being poor in the air or for kicking badly. Knock, knock, knock, and if you are not mentally strong it can make you into a nervous wreck. So don't read papers. Get them when you've won, played well, scored a hat-trick, scored the winning goal, top of the league. Whatever. They can't have a pop at you then. Does it make sense?'

'Everything you've said,' said Jake.

'Fancy helping me with this quiz in the paper? Yeah? Right then. Who had a top ten hit in 1961 with "Let's Twist Again"?'

'Now you are joking.'

'You must know that.'

'I hadn't been born,' said Jake with a short laugh.

'But it's a monster.'

'Come on then, who was it?'

'Your actual Chubby Checker.'

'Chubby who?'

'Checker mate, top man. What about this one. "Which celestial body is also know as the Dog Star?"'

'Britney Spiers.'

'Ha! Ha! You'll never win a million. What about crosswords?' said Ivor turning over the page.

'Never done one.'

'I'm hopeless as well. Let's see if there's something we both have a chance with. Tom... something actor, whose film roles included Richard Sherman in *The Seven Year Itch*. Five letters.'

'The only Tom I know is Hanks,' said Jake. 'But I don't know if he was in that film.'

'It's not Cruise. That's six letters. What's the capital of South Australia?'

'How many letters?'

'Eight,' said Ivor.

'Let's go through them. Canberra, Sidney, Perth, Melbourne. It's got to be one of them, hasn't it? I don't know any others.'

'Me neither.'

'Must be Canberra then.'

'See – together we've cracked it,' said Ivor. 'Last one. Postman's drop.'

'How many letters?'

'Thousands.'

'Bastard.'

'Nice one. How do you feel?'

'Like a plonker.'

'Get your own back next week.'

'If selected.'

'You will be son,' said Ivor, boosting his confidence. 'If not you could always open a café. That coffee was excellent!'

Jake found an empty seat and got out his mobile. He rang Marie.

'Fancy going out later on?'

'Yeah, course I do.' Marie said. 'You were on the bench?'

'Didn't get on. The boss was happy with the way things were going. Finished in a stalemate.'

'I heard a bit on the radio. Sounded a dull game.'

'But we got a point. That'll help us as the other results went our way. And after all the problems we had on the motorway...'

'What happened?'

'Big pile-up. Stuck in traffic for ages. It was all a mad rush after that.'

'You were caught up in that? It's been on the news. Three people are dead.'

'Should have seen the mayhem. Nightmare.'

'No problems coming back?'

'None at all. Sat with Taffy.'

'The Welsh guy?'

'He's sound.'

'You're not bad yourself.'

'With not getting on I've got energy to burn,' said Jake, grinning to himself.

'Well, we'll have to find a way of getting rid of it, won't we?'

'Any suggestions?'

'I'll tell you when you get back.'

'Hey Jake. Get your arse back here,' shouted Doug. 'Grub's up.'

11

'Tony, can I have a word?'

'Sure.'

'I'd like to talk to you about Ricky Grant.'

'Let's go into my office.'

Arthur Lampton was the class teacher at the Freedley Comprehensive School. Tony Hutchinson was responsible for the discipline and child protection issues.

'He's fifteen now, isn't he?' said Hutchinson easing into his chair behind a big mahogany desk.

'Year group eleven.'

'How can I help?'

'I've seen a change in his personality,' said Lampton. 'And I saw some bruising on his body when he was changing for gym.'

'Have you asked him about it?'

'He told me he'd fallen over the bins in the school yard.'

'What do we know about the parents?' asked Hutchinson scribbling some notes on a thick pad.

'Not a great deal, I'm afraid. We've no details of any previous problems.'

'Any of the other teachers seen a change in Ricky?'

'Yes, Margaret tells me he's switched off completely.'

'He could have a problem and has just withdrawn into his shell,' said Hutchinson.

'That's right,' agreed Lampton. 'He doesn't get involved in discussions anymore and will never volunteer an answer. Just closes up when asked a direct question and doesn't want to integrate with the other kids.'

'Any hint of drugs or other substance abuse?'

'Couldn't say,' said Lampton shaking his head. 'At this age he could be experimenting with all kinds of things but it's difficult to know.'

'Have you considered bullying?' Hutchinson suggested.

'I've thought of that, but he's a pretty strong lad who seems like he can look after himself and I'm pretty certain he wouldn't dish it out himself. But you never know.'

'Can you remember when we used to take those loose cannons – the Rat Pack – on a week's camp? What a motley crew they were. Remember the cave episode?'

'Which one was that?' said Lampton.

'We had them crawling on their stomachs through an eighteen-inch gap under the rock face. It was freezing cold and pitch black.'

'That was before my time.'

'We asked for volunteers and all the bullies were at the back, crapping themselves. We had another test involving a stretch of water. It was very cold, and we told them there was a walkway only a few inches wide and a hundred foot drop on either side, so they had to be careful and feel for the ledge. You could see the concentration on their faces. Of course there was no drop, was there? They could have walked across at any point. But it was a good exercise in character building.'

'And the bullies wanted to bottle out again?'

'But after Tom Kenyon sailed through, a fat lad with the jam jar glasses, they couldn't back out, could they?' smiled Hutchinson. 'It wouldn't have looked good for their street cred.'

'What's the best result you've ever had from a student?' asked Lampton.

'For me,' reflected Hutchinson, 'it would have to be Mark Evans. We've all had the easy ones, haven't we, those that float through their GCSE's, A levels and then breeze into university? But I tell you what, Evans will take some beating.'

'Wasn't he the lad who failed in every subject?'

'Sneaked through in RE. He had nothing going for him. Didn't seem to have one redeeming feature. He looked a real sight for one thing; very slow on the uptake, struggled in everything. His parents didn't want to know and he ate like a bleeding pig. His size ballooned but during those years when I was a raw teacher straight out of college, he struck a chord with me.

'I got to know him and, you know what, Arthur, we helped each other through. I saw him only last week. It was around eleven o'clock at night and I bumped into him down Osmond Street. I asked him where he was going and he said "chippy" and afterwards to the "Fascination Club. It's strippers' night". Did I want to come?'

'Different class.'

'When I retire and have a leaving do, he's one ex-pupil I'd definitely invite because in many ways that lad changed my life and how I perceived people. He taught me so much. Although he was the butt of the jokes he laughed when they were taking the mickey and took it the right way. In the end they became good mates. As time went on I saw a hell of an improvement in his confidence and self-esteem.'

'I know exactly what you mean,' said Lampton. 'Mine was a lad called Letworth from my old school. A real difficult kid. Effing and jeffing all day and his behaviour was terrible. Always getting into scrapes. I suspected his dad was the cause.

'He was a right pain in the butt, but then he got a job in Scotland I thought, great, that's the problem out of the way. The lad was intelligent he'd pass all his exams if he knuckled down, but he wouldn't do it with his dad around.

'So I got him in and suggested work experience, to try and get him back on track. He wasn't very happy with that but he was interested in electrical engineering and my brother-in-law, Chris, runs an installations company.

'He took him on for a week. Well Letworth never missed a day, did everything that was asked of him and when I spoke to Chris afterwards he told me he had been a model worker. Fitted in brilliantly and his behaviour was spot on. In fact, when he left school he took him on full-time.'

'What was he like when he returned to school?'

'He'd changed completely,' said Lampton. 'We had no problems with him at all. Even though we didn't find out exactly what the problem was, his attitude had changed. But do you know what was the most pleasing aspect?'

'Go on.'

'First day back he knocked on my door and said, "I've come to say sorry. I'm sorry I caused you and the other staff all those problems.

What you've done for me in those five days has changed my life. Thank you.'"

'That says it all.'

'Get one like that every ten years and it makes it all worthwhile. Keeps you going. These kids are coming from behind and if they're prepared to meet us halfway they've a chance.'

'You know it's not just these kids,' said Hutchinson. 'Everybody needs someone they can go to and say 'I have a problem'.'

'Correct.'

'Anyway, coming back to Ricky,' said Hutchinson. 'It sounds like I need to get him in for a chat.'

'What about involving the parents?'

'It could aggravate the situation. Leave it with me Arthur. I'll keep you informed.'

'Ruth Grant please.'

'Speaking.'

'Oh hello, this is Tony Hutchinson, Ricky's year group teacher.'

'Hello.'

'Could you pop in to see me to have a chat about Ricky?'

'Nothing wrong is there?' said Ruth a little concerned. 'He's not been bunking off, has he?'

'We can't really discuss it over the 'phone.'

When Hutchinson got a knock on his door later that afternoon he was as calm as he could be.

'Come in.'

Ricky entered the room and was told to take a seat.

Hutchinson was hugely experienced in these situations. He continued to work on his computer. 'I won't be a minute,' he said. He occasionally glanced over to see the youngster fidgeting. Three minutes elapsed. To Ricky it seemed like an eternity.

In almost a whisper, Hutchinson broke the silence. 'Why do you think I've called you in, Ricky?'

'Dunno know sir.'

'Anything wrong?'

'Well maths wasn't right good yesterday. Mr Brooks had a go.'

'Why's that?'

'Didn't do all the homework.'

'Where's your bag?'

'In the classroom.'

Hutchinson walked across his room, opened the door and stopped the first boy he saw.

'Go to Ricky Grant's class, Room 5, pick up his bag and bring it straight back to me.'

The boy returned with the bag.

Hutchinson faced Ricky. He looked directly into his eyes. He started to unzip the bag.

'Is there something in this bag that you shouldn't have?'

'No sir.'

'Is there anything in the bag you want to talk about?'

'No sir.'

'So it's just your course work, books and things?'

'Yes sir.'

'I've asked your mum to pop in. Why do you think I've done that?'

'Don't know sir.'

'Did anything go wrong at home this morning?'

'No sir.'

Ricky was feeling distinctly uncomfortable.

'Did your mum shout at you today?'

'No sir.'

'Is it all right if I take a look through your bag?' said Hutchinson calmly.

Ricky became tense.

'Perhaps you would like to empty the bag and show me what's inside?'

There was a knock on the door. It was Ruth.

'Please come in and take a seat.'

Ruth sat next to her son with Hutchinson behind his desk.

'I've asked you to come in because we have seen a definite change in Ricky's behaviour. He's become very withdrawn almost to the point of not wanting to be around anybody else.

'He doesn't interact with his classmates and completely disassociates himself from school life. This has gone on for a few weeks and we've become concerned. Have there been any problems at home?'

'Not that I am aware of,' said Ruth looking at Ricky. 'That's right isn't it, love?'

'We'd like to get to the bottom of it and nip it in the bud as soon as possible. Is there anything that you would like to tell me that could shed some light on the matter?'

'Well, sometimes I argue with Ronnie. He swears a bit when he's angry but every relationship has its bad times.'

'I'm not here to delve into your personal relationships Ms Grant.'

'Call me Ruth.'

'Ruth, my only concern is that we give Ricky the support and help he needs. Before you came in, I asked him to empty his bag.'

'And did he?'

'No.'

'Why not? You've got nothing to hide, have you Ricky?'

'Would you like to see what's inside?' said Hutchinson.

'Of course. Give it to me.'

She strewed the contents on the desk. Books, ruler, pens, calculator – all came tumbling out. Right at the bottom was a small tin box.

Ruth opened it.

Inside were three cigarettes. Hutchinson confirmed that they were cannabis joints.

Hutchinson had come across this scenario many times. Once rumbled, boys would often open up and seek help. For others, a young offender's institution could be round the corner.

'Thank you for coming in Ruth. I would like to have a word with Ricky on his own, so if you wouldn't mind waiting in reception.'

Hutchinson opened the door for Ruth and then brought a chair alongside the boy.

'Ricky, how did you get the drugs?'

'A mate of mine,' said Ricky staring at the floor.

'Was the lad from this school?'

'No.'

'How long have you been taking drugs?'

'A few weeks.'

'Where do you smoke them?'

'Around. Sometimes in my bedroom. It helps me get through.'

'Get through what?'

'Things.'

'Like what?'

'Ronnie.'

'Your stepdad?'

'He's not my stepdad.'

'Mum's partner?'

'Yeah.'

'What's he like?'

'A drunk.'

'Does he threaten you in any way?'

'I can handle it.'

'Does he threaten your mum?'

'Yes.'

'Have you seen it?'

'Yeah.'

'What happened?'

'He came home one night drunk, shouting and swearing. It woke me up. I went down stairs. He'd smashed the TV. Mum was crying. He told me to go back to bed. Told me it was nothing to do with me.'

'Did you?'

'I went to see if mum was okay; she was holding her arm as if she'd been thumped but she told me she was all right. There was some more shouting and that night mum slept in my room. She was shaking.'

'Has this kind of thing happened before?'

'Once or twice.'

'What are your feelings towards him?'

'He's a drunk and a bully and I just wish mum would get him out of her life. We'd be okay together.'

'Ricky, we've something in common. My father had a drink problem. My mother did everything she could to get him off it, but it affected me. I was only a kid. I started getting nervous twitches and acting stupidly. Once, I ran out of the house early one morning and called the police.

'They picked me up and took me to the police station. I felt safe. I would never have thought about running away before because they were my parents. They were adults and that was my home.'

'That's right.'

'The next day it was all quiet as though nothing had happened.'

'Yeah,' said Ricky. 'Everything goes back to normal but you know it won't last.'

'Ricky, just remember my door is always open whenever you want to talk. Is that clear?'

'Yes sir.'

'A lot of kids make mistakes at some time. Who hasn't? Everybody experiments. There's lots going on in your life but going down the drugs route isn't going to help. You do know that, don't you?'

'It gets me away from the mess.'

'I know and it takes a strong character to face up to all the aggravation.'

'How did you cope, with the dad thing?' asked Ricky.

'Somebody took me on board. A counsellor. She was brilliant. Helped me through. But my brother wasn't so lucky. He's also got a serious drink problem.

'Last time I saw him he said, "Why did I grow up to be a drunk?" And I said, "Because dad was a drunk". "In that case, why didn't you grow up to be a drunk?" I told him. "Because dad was a drunk".

12

Jake was putting in some solid reserve performances and was rewarded with a place on the bench for the first team fixture against Chelsea. He got on for the last ten minutes but with the team losing 4-1, Houdini would have found it difficult to turn the match around.

Things were getting serious. The 'R' word was rearing its ugly head and everybody was aware that unless results improved, it would be inevitable. Every morning before training, all the fixtures affecting clubs at the foot of the table, were scrutinised and discussed.

Burding Town v Middlesbrough Home. 7.45pm kick-off.

Boss Ged Marsh strode in purposefully. He made a couple of surprise omissions from the squad. Clive Jackson and Gerry Ingram, regulars all season, had been left out.

The team was announced. Jake would make his debut.

The boss went though the tactics. They were to play a basic 4-4-2 formation with Jake occupying a holding midfield role. Middlesbrough were currently in a European position but their recent form was poor. They'd won just once in their previous five league games.

Ged Marsh was in no mood for small talk.

'Middlesbrough are physically strong. They don't take any prisoners so we must be ready to match them in that department. We must also stay disciplined. They'll have a good following and the atmosphere will be electric. Remember to sort out the set plays early. You've each got a man to mark at corners so keep it tight. We can't afford to give away any soft goals.

'The danger men are Downing and Mido. You know all about these two. Mido is strong, plays as a lone striker, is always on the shoulder of the last defender and goes down both channels. His goal record is excellent. He's the main threat. We need to put him out of the game and Jonesy, that's your responsibility. Talk to the other lads if you've got a problem.

'In fact, I want plenty of verbals from everybody on the pitch. It's not just down to the skipper. I want eleven captains out there. Last game, it was far too quiet.

'Downing has silky skills as we all know. He'll line up in a left of five in midfield. He could even be pushed further forward into a more advanced position, so we need to work it out quickly if there are changes.

'He's got a great step-over and whips in dangerous crosses, so defending the near six-yard box will be vital; that's if we can't stop the initial cross.

'Important to watch the ball when he's in possession, otherwise he'll cause problems. Jonah, that's where we need you to double up on that side to give cover.

'Keep these two quiet and we've got a great chance. Any questions?'

The room fell silent. They knew the importance of the game.

Marsh clapped his hands. 'Right, Alex will take you out. Get warmed up and we'll go through our set plays.'

After an hour they were back in the changing rooms.

'Report at six fifteen,' said Pinder, 'and get some rest.'

Jake returned to an empty house and texted Marie. He then rang his mum. She had a part-time job at a shoe shop and was thrilled to hear Jake's news.

'Of course I can make it. Have you spoken to dad?'

'Just about to.'

'I'll see you later,' said his mum.

Steve took the call while sorting out some electrical work in an apartment block. 'Fantastic son, absolutely brilliant. I'll definitely be there. I might not see you before the game, so good luck and try to enjoy it.'

'I will, dad. See you afterwards.'

Jake got his head down after a plate of pasta and a glass of fruit juice. He dozed flittingly. Was it anxiety or excitement? Maybe both. Winning was the single most important thing. Burding were desperate for the three points.

Willie Short picked him up in his three-litre Mercedes people carrier. 'Nervous, Jake?'

'Not too bad.'

'Get a good touch early on,' said Short planting a playful punch on Jake's arm. 'You'll be all right.'

Eddie, the car park attendant, wished them both luck.

'Thanks mate, let's hope we do it,' replied Willie.

They exchanged banter with the home supporters on their way to the dressing room. All the lads had on their best suits. They looked cool apart from Tommy's, which got a bit of stick.

'Eh Holty, wife done another shopping trip at Oxfam?' shouted Simmo.

'It's called style mate,' he said, looking at himself in the mirror. 'Something you know nowt about.'

Among the thumping rap music, Jake picked up a programme and read the manager's notes.

Results have been poor because of injuries and suspensions. But there's been no lack of effort or commitment from the players. We're in it together and I'm sure you supporters will play your part in helping us to see the job through.

There was a profile of Wacko's favourite choices in music, food and films. Ironic or what? He'd been dropped. As Jake flipped through the pages the stats made uncomfortable reading – the photos of smiling fans, posing in replica shirts on sunny beaches, just a distant memory.

Jake walked onto the pitch. A few hardy fans had already taken their seats, offering good luck messages and requesting autographs. He went back inside the dressing room and started to get changed. His routine was always the same. T-shirt, jockstrap, ankles strapped. Socks on, boots.

It was a cold night, so he rubbed liniment on his legs and a chest rub that smelt awful. Half an hour before kick-off he trotted down the tunnel with the rest of the team for the warm-up session. Alex took them through some stretching and quick feet exercises at the side of the pitch and then a keep possession drill. Jake glanced over to the opposition who were going through exactly the same routines.

Whose night would it be?

Fifteen minutes before kick-off, they were back inside the dressing room. Jake held up his blue and white shirt. On the back – 'Watkins 36'. Goosebumps came over him. He was filled with pride. He tucked his shirt neatly inside his blue shorts and sat down. The gaffer had a final word.

'Be confident and look after each other. Don't leave your team-mates isolated. Take responsibility and always want the ball. Heads up and don't worry about mistakes. Good luck.'

The buzzer went. Every player made a beeline for Jake. High fives all round. The noise levels rose significantly as the clatter of studs thudded down on the tiled floors. There was an adrenalin rush.

The Dance of the Knights by Prokofiev welcomed them onto the pitch among a cacophony of cheering, singing, and flashlights. The gladiators had entered the arena.

The skipper shouted to nobody in particular. 'Hey, this is it. Let's do it.'

The rain began to fall and there was a cold feel to the night. Jake got into the game straightaway, but the move broke down and possession was lost. It was the visitors who took the early initiative and Burding found themselves defending their own 18-yard box.

It was all hands to the pump, but a rare break saw Willie streak clear and head for goal. His heels were clipped from behind, just yards outside the penalty area, and as he fell to the ground, the referee was already brandishing the red card. 'Boro were down to ten men. The home fans were ecstatic.

But, as so often happens in such situations, the ten men became inspired. Middlesbrough changed to a 3-4-2 formation and seemed to gain in strength and confidence. In fact, it looked like Burding who were a man short.

At the break with the score line blank, the boss decided to take action. He sent out sub Mark Booth to play at right back with Tommy coming off and Tibbo came in from his flank position to bolster up the back four. All the changes involved defensive positions.

Questions were being asked. Shouldn't Burding be looking for more attacking options?

'We need more zip and urgency,' said the gaffer. 'Pass the ball quicker and raise the tempo. If we do that, they won't be able to live with us. Make the extra man count. Come on.' He clapped his hands.

But the momentum was still with the visitors as the second half resumed and stifling the creativity of Downing was proving almost impossible. Everything was coming through him, now he'd switched to a more central role. The skipper told Jake to man mark him. Simmo made a couple of half-decent saves but mid way through the second period Burding got another break.

A clumsy foul brought Jake crashing down in the box and a penalty was awarded. 'Boro players went ballistic. They surrounded the referee and had two players cautioned. It looked a questionable decision but Burding weren't complaining.

It took an age to clear the area, but finally leading scorer Willie Short placed the ball deliberately on the spot. He was having an excellent game and was Burding's biggest threat. He stepped back. The 'keeper, trying to unnerve him, kept delaying the kick by turning his back and moving along the line, tapping both feet on the posts. The referee's patience became exhausted and another name was added to his ever-growing list.

A glance towards the dug-out would see Ged Marsh with his head buried in his hands.

The referee blew the whistle. Willie ran up to strike a right footer with tremendous power and it arrowed towards the top corner of the net. But Willie had leant backwards a fraction and the ball continued on its upward direction, missing the woodwork by inches and ending up high among the visiting 'Boro fans.

Hearts sank. The home crowd were devastated, the Burding players distraught. As Willie sank to his knees, Ged Marsh banged his head on the dug-out roof.

A general feeling of malaise hung over the team. But all was not lost. They could still salvage something out of the game. Jake had done well, limiting the star man to very few telling contributions, but five minutes from the end, Downing was again in possession. Jake saw his opportunity to get the ball out of play, but the 'Boro man was razor sharp and with a brilliant piece of individual skill, left Jake for dead.

Within seconds the ball was whipped across the six-yard box where Simmo could only parry and the Egyptian, former Roma and Tottenham striker, Mido, from no more than three yards out, gleefully prodded home into an empty net.

Disaster. Long balls were launched in a frantic attempt to retrieve the situation. All to no avail. The whistle blew for full time to end a wretched night. Another 1-0 defeat.

There were times when a manager just wanted to slide into his car and disappear without having to get in conversation with players, directors or press. This was one of them. Walking back from the dug-out, Marsh was subjected to a vitriolic tidal wave of abuse and criticism. His club jacket was covered in spittle. He entered the changing room firing from both barrels.

'That was the biggest load of crap I've seen for a very long time. Call yourself professional footballers? What I saw out there was pathetic. I tell you what, you're all so keen to come knocking on my door with your agents badgering me that every club is after you. Well I tell you what. They can have you. You lot couldn't tackle a fish supper. I'm looking for players with big hearts who are prepared to battle for this club and what do I get? Cheats. Not a semblance of moral fibre.

'Character? Forget it. But you've told me one thing I should already know. The shirt doesn't mean anything to you lot. We talked about it before the game but it's all bollocks. It goes right in one ear and out the other.

'All I'm looking for is you to play with pride and give one hundred per cent effort. But when the going gets tough you lot can't hack it. Well, if you don't want to do it on match days then I'll make sure you do it on the bloody training pitch.

'Don't make any arrangements for golf days or trips out shopping with the wife 'cos you'll be here every hour of the day and night until you show me how much it hurts.'

Marsh's blood pressure had risen to a dangerous level and if the club doctor had witnessed this latest outburst, immediate plans would have been made to visit intensive care.

He banged the dressing room door shut. After what seemed an age, Simmo eventually broke the ice.

'I take it it's not a good time to see the gaffer about a rise? Anyone fancy a fish supper?'

Jake met up with Marie and his parents in the players' lounge after the game.

'Well done, love,' said Linda. 'I thought you were very good.'

Leaving the dressing room Ged Marsh was fuming. After the morale-boosting display last week this was a real body blow to the experienced manager but he collected his thoughts and attempted to be upbeat in the press conference. At least there was some respite from what had been an awful night. The results affecting teams at the basement end of the division had gone their way.

Despite his mood Marsh had to speak to the press.

'We are now down to our last seven games and have points on the others. Survival is in our hands. I feel four victories will be enough. But we can't feel sorry for ourselves. We must put this one behind us and move forward. I must admit I was disappointed with certain aspects of our game but not with the effort they put in.'

'What things were you unhappy about?' asked the BBC radio reporter.

'I felt we were a little naïve after the sending off. The game was there to be won – nobody's died. We've lost a football match so let's get it in perspective. We'll come in tomorrow morning and prepare thoroughly for our next game.'

13

Ricky felt depressed as he left Hutchinson's room. Not only had his stash been discovered but he'd also been shamed in front of his mother. Now he was in for it. Explaining to his mum was one thing but if that cretin Ronnie found out he would really be in the brown stuff.

With hunched shoulders, he dragged his feet out of the school gates.

'Hey Ricky, fancy a kick about?' His schoolmates were organising a game in the schoolyard.

'Can't. I've got something on,' he lied. 'I'll see you tomorrow.'

It got them off his back.

He walked to the nearest coffee bar, got himself a can and sat at a dingy table, the only one vacant. It was covered with debris: half a sausage, a few crumpled chips all smeared in tomato sauce, ice cream leftovers melting to a milky white slush.

The waitress came over. 'You okay?'

'It's not been the best of days to be fair.'

'Like, what's the matter?' she asked, wiping the table.

'Just got a bollocking from my teacher,' said Ricky slumped over with head in hands.

'What for?' she said in a high-pitched voice.

'Ah you know, sort of nothing really.'

'I know what you mean. I was always getting it. They picked on me, thought I was lippy, you know, when there were others in class who could do no wrong.

'It was like so unfair. I copped the lot. I was well pleased when I left.'

Her team leader shouted over. 'Hey, mouth and co, remember you've got other tables to sort out.'

'Listen to that creep,' she said leaning over to Ricky. 'I've been on my feet all day and he's still moaning. If he has one more go I'll swing for him, I really will.'

'You'd better get back.'

Ricky waited till her back was turned and slipped through the automatic glass doors.

He ambled along the street, blankly staring through shop windows.

'Ricky mate.'

He looked up to see Joey and a lad he didn't know.

'How you doing?'

'Sound,' said Ricky unconvincingly.

'Hey listen, I've got some good gear. Fancy some? It won't cost you.'

'You've gotta be joking, haven't you? Let me tell you. They found the last lot I got from you. Laid it out in front of my mum.'

'No way.'

'Too right. Hutch had me in and found the lot.'

'Hutch?'

'Teacher.'

'What's he said?'

'Gives me all the spiel about drugs. They'll do your head in, that kind of stuff.'

'You expelled?'

'Don't know.'

'What you mean?'

'Well he's going to decide. I might have to go on a course or summat.'

'Bloody hell... and your mum was there?'

'She found them.'

'No way.'

'Hutch got some kid to get my bag and she opened it.'

'Shit. What you doing now?'

'Nothing. I'll have to go home sometime. If she tells Ronnie, I'm done for.'

'You think she will?'

'I don't know. She's having a bad time with him herself.'

'He's an alky isn't he?'

'And an evil bastard.'

'Bloody hell. Why don't you come with us?'

'Where you going?'

'Just hanging around with a few mates. Nothing heavy. Fancy it? Come on. Give you time to sort yourself out.'

They shuffled along the street until they came to a boarded up shop. Joey hopped over the wall at the back and eased through a window. The others followed. Inside it was pitch black.

Other kids were lying around on old mattresses. In the darkness Ricky didn't recognise anyone.

In the middle of the room was a large cardboard box. They gathered round in a circle like witches round a cooking pot. Various items were pulled out of containers and plastic bags.

Joey held the foil and struck a match. The white substance started to bubble into a little blob of brown.

'Go on Rick baby, it won't hurt,' said Joey egging him on. 'One sniff and you're off your head.'

'No way,' said Ricky backing off.

'Wot you 'ere for then, you ******* plonker? You're going to miss the chance of a lifetime. Feels fantastic. Better than you've ever felt before.'

Ricky wasn't ready to face the music back home. The thought of that bastard Ronnie made him sick. He'd treated them like dirt. Ruined their lives.

'You afraid or what?' laughed Joey.

'Joking aren't you?'

'Well then. Let's see it big man. What you got to lose?'

What was there to lose? His life was going nowhere. The moment was now. Right now. No danger. He could handle it. He'd tried other things and he'd been okay.

As long as he stayed cool, in control, no problem. Not like he was going to get hooked, was it? Old gits smoke fags and drink booze, don't they?

They roll about pissed. He had one like that at home. They're doing it, aren't they? What's the difference?

Suddenly all the crap started to disappear – like being wrapped up in a big ball of cotton wool. He floated away without a care in the world. This was it. It's what's happening. On a high like he'd never known before.

Ricky woke up feeling like his head was about to cave in. Bodies were crashed out all over the room. Only one was awake – a girl called Liza. She was spaced.

'Hi Rick, you okay?'

'Shite.'

'All the gear's gone,' she said combing her bleached blond tangled mess.

'Any money?'

'None. You short?' said Liza.

'Skint.'

'There's always a way,' she said removing a cracked mirror from her skirt pocket. 'I can make enough in twenty minutes to see me through.'

'Yeah, sure'

'Too right. There's always a punter ready to blow a few quid. Get my drift? Easy money. Just switch off then it's back to the real me. A nice looking lad like you, you'll have no problem.'

'Piss off.'

She laughed.

He ran out – blinked as the daylight hit him. He found the nearest 'phone box. With his last 10p he rang the number.

'Where are you?'

'Don't know.'

'In a 'phone box?'

'Yeah.'

'Look around. What's outside?'

'There's a church. St Thomas's.'

'Go in. I'll be there shortly.'

Tony Hutchinson sat next to Ricky on a pew in the middle of the empty building.

'It's all right son.'

'I've screwed up big time.' Ricky had his arms folded and was rocking from side to side.

'Hey don't beat yourself up,' said Hutchinson grabbing hold of his arm. 'You're a young lad and you've had lots to deal with. But there's people out there who'll get you through it.'

'Like who?'

'Like me for one. And your mum. You've made mistakes. So what? Who hasn't? The thing is, you've still got your whole life in front of you. But if you want to change, the time is now.'

Ricky let himself into the flat. 'Where've you been?' Ruth was distraught. ' I've been worried sick. I've been out of my mind.'

She hugged him while Hutchinson looked on.

'Just to go off like that without even letting me know. I was up all night, sick to the stomach. I thought all kinds of things had happened. Has he been with you?'

'Not exactly,' said Hutchinson.

'Come in, come in. Tell me what's been going on.'

Ricky went to the bathroom while Hutchinson told her about the 'phone call.

'I don't know exactly what Ricky's been up to but I've an idea. He's told me snippets but after the incident at school it seems like he was afraid of coming home.'

'Where did he go?'

'He met up with a group of boys. Stayed with them.'

'Taking drugs? Again? Oh my God.'

'Listen Ruth, I know what you must be going through, but kids do experiment with things. It's a phase they go through. Many go on to lead normal lives.'

'Not for others they don't,' said Ruth pacing up and down the room.

'Some find it difficult, I know. But we've all done something that we regret, haven't we?'

'Nothing like this. This is serious,' said Ruth taking a tissue from the box. 'I can't get my head round it. Who's to say he'll come through it all right?'

'It's tough, but I've got to say, most do. All we can do is give him support.'

81

'What can I do?'

'Talk to him. Try to find out more. Listen to what he has to say. Get a dialogue going. Point out the dangers and tell him he can always confide in you no matter what.'

'I might say the wrong thing,' she said blowing her nose. 'I feel so angry.'

'Don't worry about that. It's a natural reaction. I understand that. But there's a good chance you'll be able to solve the problem together.'

'I wish I was as confident.'

Hutchinson decided it was important to take the lead. 'Do you want me to talk to him?'

'Would you?'

'Of course.'

'You've been a great help. Thanks for bringing him back.'

'You know what, Ruth,' said Hutchinson trying to calm things down. 'No matter how bad it seems today, life does go on and it will be better tomorrow.'

Ricky came out and his mum gave him another hug. She squeezed him tightly and said, 'I love you so much.'

'I'll make a brew,' said Hutchinson.

'No no I'll do it,' said Ruth making her way into the kitchen.

Hutchinson took Ricky to one side. 'You've got a diamond of a mum there Ricky.'

'I know.'

'We understand what you've done Ricky. And why you've done it. But if you carry on it's just going to get worse. Affect the rest of your life. You do know that, don't you?'

'Yeah'

'And I'm not just talking about your health. I'm talking about everything.'

14

The result left Town tumbling into a relegation dogfight. They had a four-point cushion from the drop zone but with seven games to go it was going right to the wire and any one of a dozen sides could find themselves slipping through the trap door. The pressure was on. Jake could feel the tension in the dressing room but the older pros knew the score.

Skip pulled Jake to one side. 'Well done Jake, I thought you did well last night. Try not to take anything too personally. The gaffer was right to have a go, but I've been in this position before and we've got to stick together. Once the backbiting starts, then we've no chance.'

Ged Marsh was also in a positive mood the next day. It was as if he'd had a personality transplant overnight. He spoke to the players first thing.

'I said what I did after the game because that's how I felt. If we're going to get out of this mess then we need more from each individual. And that includes me. I'm the manager. I'll accept the responsibility because the buck stops with me but what I'm asking, no what I'm demanding, is just that little bit extra from you guys.

'Whether it's effort, courage or skill, it could make all the difference. You've all got your strengths; otherwise you wouldn't be playing for this fantastic football club. If you respond the right way, the fans will rally round. But it must come from us first.'

He took time out to collect his thoughts. He chose his words carefully.

'I have full confidence in you lads. I do get frustrated when I see things going wrong because I know you have it in you to challenge at the other end of the table. You're still learning as a group of players and that takes time. But this is when it matters.

'It's the business end of the season. It's no use us moaning about bad luck or decisions going against us. Let's face it, last night we got all the big calls. So it's up to us to make things go our way, starting on Saturday. Three points are vital and I want everybody thinking positively.'

From a folder he gave handouts to his assistant.

'Pass these around Alex,' he said.

When they'd all received one, he held up a copy and said, 'Here are the thoughts of one of the greatest players the game has ever seen. Some of you will not have heard of him but Alfredo di Stefano was a magnificent footballer.

'He played for Real Madrid when they dominated European football and won the European Cup five times on the bounce – Champions League as it is now. Di Stefano wanted to be the best. Obviously he had great ability, but he also knew that without dedication, determination and discipline it would count for nothing.

'He also maintained that whatever standard he achieved, he would never compromise on the one thing that, to him, was most important. And that was to play to the rules with no cheating. This guy set the standard for everyone else to follow.'

Jake, who was sitting next to Ivor, was deep in thought.

Every professional player owes maximum effort to his club. To hold anything back, even for a single moment, for the sake of comfort or convenience is a deception. It is a betrayal of the supporters who trust him. I can never understand non-triers. If they have no natural eagerness to play football, let them try something else rather than mock the game.

Football is a great game and when one is with a great club it should be a privilege to play and give of one's best, a privilege hard to sacrifice. If he has that enthusiasm he will not need anyone to tell him how satisfying a game of football can be. Nor that each match is an essay in brain, instinct and skill. If he does not recognise such things for himself, he is not the material for professional football.

One has to be wholehearted, for the capricious footballer never makes a consistently good one. Anything prejudicial to one's football, anything superfluous to one's career, must be avoided.

84

One must never become bored with training and match preparation, however great a burden it may seem at times. If a move is not mastered easily, then hours of work must follow and be accepted until it is perfect.

Every player makes mistakes, but every player does not need to repeat those mistakes. With will and hard work, almost anything can be achieved in football. It is fatal to sit back and be proud of our strengths.

Work will always produce the result wanted. A move on the pitch, to the crowd, can look a stroke of genius, as if the men concerned had spontaneously plucked that particular moment direct from heaven. The impression is that it must be awfully difficult, impossible to equal or even repeat. By and large it is not, far from it. Usually it will have been the product of patient work in training.

The buildup to the match against Blackburn Rovers was intense. 'All or Nothing' screamed one headline; 'Town on the Brink' was another. The pundits were having a field day and Town were many people's favourites to be playing lower division football next season.

Jake was back on the bench when the boss read out the team on Friday morning. He made two changes to the side with Wacko coming back into the starting line-up along with Juan Torres who had fully recovered from a hamstring injury.

Blackburn were handily placed in mid table and enjoying a good cup run and were looking forward to a successful finale to the season.

Understandably the Burding players were anxious with kick-off only an hour away but Ged Marsh had a beaming smile on his face.

'I feel good today boys, in fact, not felt this way since the missus told me I had the same eyes as Humphrey Bogart. "Here's looking at you kid". Problem is he's been dead over twenty years. Is she telling me something or what?'

Laughter echoed round the dressing room.

'There's a great atmosphere out there and it's good to be alive. Just think when we win we'll make thousands of our fans very happy bunnies.'

As the bell sounded his parting words were, 'Believe in yourselves and each other. It'll be okay.'

The players jogged onto the pitch and for a few seconds the home dressing room was silent. Ged Marsh wiped his sweaty forehead and placed an arm around his physio's shoulder. 'Well Jim, it's now in the lap of the gods. The next ninety minutes are going to be absolute ******* purgatory.'

Town failed to open their account early on because of their erratic finishing but they were having the better of the initial exchanges. It was all very comfortable at the back with only one snap shot from the edge of the box causing Simmo any concerns.

A tight game was anticipated and the team that scored first would undoubtedly have the edge. And so it proved. Skipper Jonesy met an inswinging corner, perfectly delivered by Torres from the right side, and he powered an unstoppable bullet header into the roof of the net to bring the stadium to its feet.

Inevitably, as time wore on, pressure was exerted on the home goal as the Rovers pushed forward looking for the equaliser. Town were hanging on to their slim lead.

There were a few scares and defensive mix ups which gave the spectators some nervy moments and when the fourth official signalled an extra four minutes of stoppage time would be added on, a groan echoed around the ground.

The boss called on Jake to get stripped. 'Sit in front of the back four Jake. Don't give them room to find the strikers. Okay son?'

Jake only had one thought in his mind. 'I hope I don't mess up.'

He sprinted on, the crowd responded; the noise was deafening.

Whistles screeched round the stadium, the tension was unbearable, but when the referee finally brought the game to an end the relief on the players' faces said it all. They went into a collective huddle. They knew the importance of the victory, and they'd given themselves a chance. Jake was happy to part of it – if only briefly. At least he was on the pitch. 'The Great Escape' theme blasted out over the tannoy system and the fans danced an impromptu conga.

Ged Marsh in his post-match press conference was upbeat.

'This was a massive victory because it gives us a little bit of breathing space. You know I was critical of our last performance but I'm full of praise for the efforts of the players today; the way they scrapped for each other.

'Every man jack of them did his bit. I was proud to be associated with such a courageous display. We are not out of the woods yet by any stretch of the imagination but we have given ourselves a huge lift for the remainder of the season. We have reversed the slide and are now looking forward to gaining the necessary points to maintain our position in the league. Thank you.'

In the next two away games, at Liverpool and Arsenal, they faced sides with Champions League expectations who had invested heavily in world-class players. Marsh was happy with the way the players had applied themselves, but the gulf in class was evident and two defeats kept them hanging by a thread.

'We will get our heads up and not feel sorry for ourselves,' said Marsh. 'Tomorrow is another day and we can take great encouragement from our performance.'

But the critics offered a slightly different slant on the Anfield defeat. One paper put it this way:

A fascinating match, full of strategy, high tempo and defining moments, changed significantly when the team conceded territory in the second half, compounded by the substitution of ace youngster Jake Watkins. Afterwards the manager defended his decision.

'Jake was magnificent, but he was absolutely shattered. He had covered every blade of grass and it is my responsibility to make sure that his development will not be impeded. I am very much aware that he is the future of this football club.'

The first goal exposed the folly of such a decision. Watkins had defended the near post magnificently for all set plays but after he was withdrawn, a poor challenge from a right wing corner resulted in the opening goal.

The manager complained of lack of communication and this

moment of madness obviously took the gloss off an otherwise
inspired performance.
'A dagger to the heart' was how the boss described it.
Before the game, the positive vibes coming from inside the club,
suggested the huge gap in quality and points between the two
sides, could be bridged. They were very nearly proved correct.
But returning with zero points must have been a shattering
experience. Whether it will have far reaching effects over
the final few matches remains to be seen. Clearly, similar
substitutions of key players at crucial times, could have a
significant bearing in the final analysis.

The next game against Reading was the biggest game of the season. Defeat would mean the teams swapping places but a victory would put them five points clear of danger with only three games left and survival very much a possibility.

In the buildup, the experts assessed the strengths and weaknesses of the teams and identified the key areas where the game would be won or lost. Jake hadn't known anything like it. He'd been struggling to sleep, waking up at some ungodly hour with thoughts of the game racing through his brain. At least it was a home fixture but with everything depending on the result would it prove too much of a burden?

During the training sessions Jake felt good, fit and confident but knew he had a lot more to offer. The press were saying some complimentary things after his brief appearances, which boosted his self-esteem. In most areas of his game he felt as good as everybody else and in others, better.

His shooting from distance had improved and his appetite for work was paying dividends. He'd had another growth spurt and had developed into a strapping six-footer. Everything – the weight work, diet and lifestyle – was coming together.

He would be very disappointed if he was overlooked for one of the most important matches in the club's history.

The boss didn't announce the team until two hours before kick-off. Maybe he wanted to keep the pressure off the lads, but Jake was named as one of the five subs. It hurt. He felt he deserved a place but he hid his disappointment.

The atmosphere at the packed ground was electric. Bunting and balloons greeted the players, the ground was awash with sunlight and noise. And colour – the ranks of the Reading supporters behind the cemetery end were bedecked in their away colours of claret and gold, the other three quarters of the ground showed their allegiance to the Town's blue and white. The boss had gone to the press urging the fans to raise the roof and sweep the boys on to victory. He felt they had a huge part to play and it could give them the edge on the day.

Jake took his seat alongside sub 'keeper Mika Hedersen and looked around the stadium.

'Hey Jake, look at that pillock. Tattoos all over 'is body. Ee's got the club crest on his titties. What's all that about?'

Jake nodded. He wasn't taking too much notice. This was it. Shit or bust. It could be curtains if they didn't win this one.

Burding forced two corners and several free kicks in the first ten minutes. Midway through the half they got the break when a long clearance caught the Reading defence napping and Jonah Sonsissko streaked clear.

The 'keeper raced out of his area and attempted to head the ball away but only presented it to the alert Willie Short who, from fully 30 yards out, lobbed into an empty net. One-nil. And there was more to follow. The best move of the game involved six Town players and culminated in Torres playing a neat one two at the edge of the box before slipping the ball past the 'keeper.

The fans were jubilant but within minutes the two goal lead was halved when Reading striker Leroy Lita evaded a weak challenge to let fly with a right foot strike which found the top corner. He couldn't have placed it any better. Two-one to Burding at halftime.

Sipping their isotonic drinks, Simmo shouted, 'What about that strike? They've never been in the game and he hits an Exocet.'

'Okay lads,' said Marsh. 'Sit down and listen. What you did out there was tremendous. Started the game brilliantly. I know you didn't deserve to concede that goal but you are the better side and have nothing to fear. Just keep playing the way you are. Don't go crazy at the back. If Holty joins in on the left flank make sure that someone sits in. Don't get stretched. Keep your shape, that's important.

'They are the ones who have to force the game and gaps will appear. When they do, get bodies forward quickly and attack with pace. But as soon as it breaks down, get your butts back behind the ball. Is that clear?'

Ten minutes after the restart, Shorty was bundled over clutching his leg. Physio Jim was called on. The prognosis wasn't good. 'It's a dead leg, boss. He doesn't want to come off. I've told him to give it another five minutes to see how it goes. But for me, I think he'll struggle.'

'Jake, get warmed up.'

Jake sprinted down the touchline and a great roar went up from the home supporters.

'There's only one Jakey Watkins, one Jakey W-a-t-k-i-n-s, there's only one...'

He hadn't come across that before. As he was stretching his hamstrings there was another lull in play as Willie went down again. Jake knew he was going on. He was ready.

He glanced up to the stands and picked out his mum and dad. Next to them was Marie. They waved encouragement.

'Jake get you arse back here!' Alex bellowed.

'You're going on... play centre mid. Clive is going to sit behind you so you've got the freedom to get forward and support the front two. But only when it's on. Get back alongside him when we haven't got the ball. Understand?'

'Yes boss.'

'Good luck son.'

The fourth official held up the board and the announcement came over the tannoy.

'Number 9, Willie Short, to be replaced by No 36, Jake Watkins.'

Jake spoke to Jonesy and then immediately won possession to knock a 30-yard pass out to the left flank. He'd made a good start. He felt sharp. The ball seemed attracted to him.

With a quarter of the game left and the score finely balanced at 2-1 Jake continued his run when the ball was delivered from the right flank. Kiddo leapt impressively to head it across the 18-yard box and without changing his stride Jake volleyed the ball spectacularly into the net from the edge of the area. The 'keeper was motionless as it whistled past him.

Jake ran, arms aloft, to acknowledge the applause of the home supporters. He was engulfed by jubilant teammates 'That'll do for me!' shouted Skip.

'Pick that out,' said Taffy.

'Magic.'

The fans went wild.

'Jakey Jakey give us a wave, Jakey give us a wave...'

Jogging back to the halfway line he felt like a million dollars.

The strike made the game safe and Burding took control. Jake helped himself to a second goal, a simple side foot from eight yards, to seal a famous victory. Fans rushed onto the pitch at the final whistle. In different circumstances the police would have been concerned. But not today.

The players returned to the sanctuary of the dressing room where the atmosphere was buoyant.

'You little beauty Jake.'

'Well done son,' was the gaffer's rather more subdued greeting. 'We only need a point now to be absolutely safe. We're almost over the finish line.'

They had three games left to secure their place in the top league for another season. In the very next game, a 2-2 draw against Fulham, they made sure.

After months of tension and anxiety, Burding Town had survived and there was a fantastic buzz in the dressing room on the Monday morning before the final match of the season. Most satisfying for the players was the fact they had silenced the many doom merchants. It had also been an eventful first season for Jake Watkins.

'Tonight we're down at the Wagon and Horses' shouted Skip who was struggling to get the attention of his noisy teammates. Simmo had his mobile glued to his ear, Willie had switched CDs and was playing the James Brown classic 'I feel good' and the rest were laughing and joking.

'Listen up, guys. Q and A with some of the fans followed by darts and pool. The landlord Pete is going to put on a bit of a spread so if the wives want to come then it's no problem.'

The first question on the night was directed towards the skipper.

'Dan, what was your highlight of the season?'

'For me it had to be the goal I scored against Blackburn. I don't score many and the gaffer is always banging on about me making it count at the other end. We needed a win and when I got on the end of that cross and hit the back of the net it was a great feeling.'

'What about all the criticism the team have received; especially from the media?'

The microphone was passed along to Jake.

'In many ways it gave us the determination to prove them wrong. It's been tough, and I suppose some doubts were around but the manager focused on the positive things and the experienced lads have been brilliant.'

'Must have been magic, scoring your first goal?'

'Fantastic. I caught it just right,' smiled Jake. 'Best moment of my career so far.'

'Who's the biggest joker in the pack?'

They laughed.

Tommy took over. 'As you know I've been out for a lot of the season and spent hours with the physio Jimmy Franks. If you ever come across Jimbo in the supermarket my advice is to get out of there fast. His jokes are the worst ever but the problem is he thinks they're funny.

'I went in for a strapping this morning and he said to me, "Hey Holty, when I was a young lad we were so poor we used to get our clothes from the Army and Navy stores. I tell you what, walking down the high street was an embarrassment with my dad dressed as a Japanese sniper and my mum a Ghurka".'

The fans laughed out loud.

'Hey don't encourage him. He'll think he should be on stage.'

'What about the one he told last week?' chipped in Simmo. 'The one about the chicken and the woodpecker.'

'What was it? I missed it.'

'A chicken and a woodpecker were having a chat and the chicken said to the woodpecker. "You lot are mad" "Why's that?" said the woodpecker "Well anything that bangs his head on a tree all day must be stark raving bonkers." "Well we're not as mad as you lot," replies the woodpecker "What'd you mean?" "Well, have you ever heard of a Kentucky Fried Woodpecker?" '

Once again the fans, perhaps out of embarrassment, cracked their sides.

'This is developing into a comedy bandbox.'

'We can take two more questions,' said Pete. 'Then we'll get into the darts, dominoes and pool competitions.'

'Dan, can you tell me why, at your age, you wear such tight-fitting shorts?'

The buffet of chicken legs, sandwiches and sausage rolls were wheeled through.

'Skip,' said Tim, devouring a pork pie, 'those shorts? Big enough for the lunch box then?'

'Don't you start.'

Jake was drawn to partner Tommy for the darts match against a husband and wife team of Betty and Geoff, both in their early 60's and originally from the Birmingham area.

Geoff was a keen supporter but Betty had never seen a game in her life. In her youthful days, she had been picked for the county darts team and was eager to show off her flights to the boys.

'I was twenty-one when I won these after getting through to the final of the All Ladies' Open tournament.'

Betty could certainly knock back her favourite tipple – brandy and coke. But as the night progressed she became unstable, wobbling from side to side.

'You okay Betty?' said Jake supporting her. 'Do you want to sit down?'

'No thanks love. One slight mishap. I'll soon be as right as rain.'

She took another slurp. The next flight hit the board but well clear of the mark. The last one hit the single ten.

'Who's moving that bloody board? This ochie isn't in right place.' She stumbled, knocking over a table of drinks and her false teeth jettisoned through the air, landing perfectly into a pint glass – the first decent shot she'd come up with in twenty minutes.

Betty was carefully placed in a chair alongside her husband and the players made a discreet exit.

15

Anne contacted her friend Jenny Miller, a retired psychiatrist, who for many years had worked for a special unit at the City Hospital, dealing with alcohol and drug abuse cases. Anne outlined her sister's dilemma.

'Listen, Anne, if you and your sister want to come and have a chat, I'm here. I won't have all the answers but if I can be of any help, don't hesitate to call me. Alan is always on the golf course these days, so it would be nice to have some visitors.'

'Thanks. Tell you what, let's pencil in Monday morning, around eleven. If there's a problem, I'll give you a bell. Bye.'

The three women settled down in Jenny's front room overlooking a large garden, which included an impressive water feature. Sparrows, robins and blackbirds were greedily pecking nuts from the bird table and a magnificent heron could be seen surveying all from the neighbour's roof.

All this activity passed Ruth by.

Jenny, a rotund figure, was a bundle of energy, a real chatterbox with a friendly manner.

'Now ladies, sugar and milk? Help yourself to the cakes. It's always nice to indulge in a few goodies, every now and then. Thanks for coming round, Ruth. I know it must be difficult but whatever is said, will be just between us. Anne has filled me in on one or two things, but perhaps you could tell me in your own words what's been worrying you.'

'Where to start? That's the thing,' said Ruth awkwardly. 'It's just been terrible. Ronnie's drinking for one and I've just found out that Ricky's been dabbling in drugs.'

'Oh my God, you never told me that,' said Anne, astonished.

'That's your boy?' said Jenny.

'He's sixteen. Ronnie and me aren't married. He's not the father.'

'Right. Well let's start with Ronnie. If that's all right with you?'

'I've seen him worsen over the last few months. He's drinking more. I always felt I could handle him but now he's getting more violent.'

Ruth told them he first hit her, after she'd put brown sauce on his bacon sandwich. He apologised, said he was sorry, but then got very possessive. He didn't like her talking to anybody, called her the most disgusting things, and even accused her of cheating on him.

'The first thing is,' said Jenny, slicing into a chocolate éclair, 'unless he recognises he has a problem then he is going to destroy himself and ruin your health and happiness. If he doesn't, the implications for your family are enormous. Just remember, it's Ronnie who has the problem. He must face the facts: he's the one who must change.'

'I suggested we get professional help – either see a doctor or go along to an AA meeting. But he didn't want to know,' said Ruth. 'In the end it was me who was prescribed tranquillisers.

'All of it has had a negative effect on Ricky and his schoolwork suffered. Ronnie had promised things, like taking Ricky to school football matches, but he never turned up. Ricky started losing interest, even though the teacher thought he had ability.'

Ruth excused herself and went to the bathroom. 'What I can't understand,' said Anne, 'is why women stay in this kind of relationship? He's obviously dangerous.'

'Battered wives make excuses for their partner's violence. When an incident ends, women get such a huge feeling of relief. She's often shell-shocked into believing that every horrible incident may be the last.'

'I still can't get my head around the fact that she doesn't leave.'

'Sometimes it's because they've become immune to the danger. No amount of logic can move a battered woman so persuasion requires emotional leverage, not statistics or moral arguments. In these types of relationships the abuser holds all the strings.

'He's the control freak so she may think by moving away she would lose what little possessions or influence she's had. He's usually the one who controls the money, has the bank accounts and the financial clout.'

'Surely it's better than losing your life?'

'Of course it is. But she thinks when everything settles down the worst is over. More often than not it turns out to be a false dawn. I can't force her to do anything, she must decide for herself.'

'I take it there's professional help out there?' asked Anne.

'You mean for Ronnie?'

'Yes.'

'There are lots of rehab programmes that he can go on but it takes a lot of guts to get through. But it's probably his best chance of survival.'

Ruth returned, and Jenny said, 'Ruth, we've just been discussing rehab programmes. Do you think that's a possibility for Ronnie?'

'Probably not. As I've said, he wouldn't go to the doctor.'

'Were you aware of any problems before you got together?'

'With his drinking?'

'That and any other personal problems.'

'Not really,' said Ruth flattening the creases on her skirt. 'When he was a young boy his parents died and his grandparents brought him up. Both are now dead.'

Jenny picked up that the situation had got worse, with Ruth sleeping in Ricky's room whenever Ronnie came home drunk.

'So you'd put yourself in between Ronnie and Ricky, as a barrier?'

'Yes.'

'But who's protecting you?' said Jenny, concerned. 'What's the difference between you and Ricky?'

'What do you mean?'

'Well, you're protecting Ricky – but who's protecting you?'

'I can look after myself.'

'Have you ever wondered what effect this is having on the boy?' said Jenny leaning forward. 'Kids learn from their experiences and if a son sees his mother being beaten then he considers it to be the norm. What are the chances Ricky will replicate his behaviour? Everyone needs a role model.

'You can't do everything yourself, Ruth. You said Ricky's been dabbling with drugs. It could be his way of coping with his problems, but he must be taught there are other ways to help him come through these difficult times.'

Ruth burst out crying. 'What kind of person am I? I'll tell you what – a failure, a complete and utter failure. I'm involved with a violent alcoholic and my son, who is the love of my life, is into drugs.'

Jenny got out of her chair and held her hand. 'Don't ever say that, Ruth. You are a very strong person and have shown tremendous courage. It will get better, believe me. It will.'

She asked her if she'd like to take a break.

'I'm all right,' said Ruth.

'Jenny, you mentioned about role models,' said Anne. 'What does that entail?'

'Someone who will find out why they're behaving badly and encourage them there's another way. Give them time. Try to channel their energies and teach them values. Take an interest in what they're doing and keep their enthusiasm going.

'Take the football thing, for instance. It seems like Ricky likes the game, but he's lost interest because of everything that's going on. If someone could encourage that talent then it's a starting point.'

'And I suppose trust is important.'

'Vital. When that trust is in place he will start to move on and begin to realise that going back to his former ways is unacceptable. As long as too much pressure isn't applied. Slowly is quickly – he's not going to change overnight.

'The people who are going to influence Ricky must remain strong to get him on the right road and keep him there. It's about being valued as an individual. Nothing is easy, but the end product will be worthwhile.'

After two hours Jenny suggested it was time to end the discussion. They said their goodbyes, and Ruth promised to 'phone in the next few days.

Anne reversed the car down the gravelled drive. They waved to Jenny standing by the front door.

'Do you think it's been of any help?'

'It's given me a lot to think about.'

'She's got loads of experience,' said Anne shifting through the gears. 'Some of the things she came across when she was at the unit were horrendous. Absolutely awful. She told me about one case where both parents had been in mental institutions. The father set fire to the caravan with his wife and child inside. The mind boggles. The child managed to escape and was brought to Jenny for safekeeping. The girl was emotionally out of control.'

'Did the wife survive?'

'She died in the fire, but the husband got off as there wasn't enough evidence to convict. You can only imagine what kind of childhood this kid went through. She was so disturbed. At the time she came into care she was only five years of age. It had a profound effect on Jenny and all the staff for a long time afterwards.

'The most important thing is, Ruth, we don't want anything happening to you or Ricky. It's not too late to get the lad back on track and keep you both out of harm's way.'

16

The awards dinner wasn't high on the agenda of every player but the upturn in performances and results towards the latter stages meant that the season had ended on a brighter note.

The fans had been quick to voice their frustrations during those long periods of failure. After all, wasn't it they who 'paid the wages of the so-called superstars?' So to have a 'pop' was perfectly acceptable. Some players would escape the snide comments but for others there was no hiding place.

Simmo, for one, had had his problems. He was usually a model of consistency, his preparation for games immaculate. Jake witnessed at first hand how thorough the 'keeper was after hitching a lift into town. Stationary at traffic lights, Hommie would imagine lining up the wall for free kicks, how many would be required and his own starting position.

He would then simulate the next option after catching the ball. Kick or throw?

'It's just mental preparation, Jake, so that when a situation happens on the field, nothing should take me by surprise. That's the theory anyway.'

But no matter how hard he worked, individual mistakes had cost him, and the team, dearly. The gaffer had considered a change between the sticks after Simmo had suffered the ultimate in professional embarrassment during the derby match against City.

Rolling the ball to the edge of the area, he failed to notice the City striker behind him, his shirt blending with the ranks of the away supporters in their replica kit. Within a split second, the ball was nicked away and stroked into an empty net.

How Simmo, with hands on hips, wanted the ground to open up and swallow him whole. The fact that he went on to produce one his finest performances was little consolation for the big man. There was no getting away from the clanger. It was there on video. Total humiliation.

The lads met up in The Crystal Glass wine bar. The wives and girlfriends looked gorgeous, designer labels and high stilettos, unquestionably stealing the thunder away from their loved ones even if at that time of the year the tans were fake.

They arrived at the hotel by mini-bus and mingled with other members of the football club staff; those from the commercial departments and administrative offices. The talk was low key and amusing. Around four hundred guests were seated before the players were introduced individually.

'Fifteen goals this season, a real icon at this football club, would you please put your hands together for Will-ie Short.'

'This guy missed games through injury and the team suffered because of his absence. A one-club player who has given outstanding service, please welcome Tom-my Holt.'

'He's going on too long,' called out Skip from the back. 'Tell him to get on with it or we'll be here all bleeding night.'

A few disparaging comments filtered through from the punters.

'He's ******* useless, wouldn't give him bleeding house room.'

One supporter slapped Jonno on the back and insulted him by saying, 'Don't worry son, I used to be shite at my job – then I got a new one, Ha! Ha!'

'Ladies and gentleman, please be upstanding for your top table.' The manager, chairman, sponsors and speakers took their places. The club chaplain the Revd. Mike Hughes said grace.

Jake and Marie were on the same table as Ivor Smeeten, Juan Torres, Mika Hedersen and Jonah Sonsissko and their partners. 'It's like the United Nations,' whispered Jake. The meal was excellent and the drinks flowed. The laughter grew louder. Cheese and biscuits and coffee followed.

There was a loud bang from the MC's gavel.

'Ladies and gentleman, could I have your attention please. Shush! The evening's entertainment will begin in ten minutes. Please replenish your drinks and be ready to return in a few minutes. Thank you.'

Autograph hunters surrounded the tables and the players were happy to oblige.

'Our main speaker this evening really needs no introduction. An outstanding player for us in the '70s, he won two championship medals. An England international, he went on to win forty-five caps and was the manager of the great team in the '80s. Let's give a warm welcome to the one and only Peter Sharp.'

'Ladies and gentlemen, thank you very much. I'm delighted to be here. I'm now living in Wischurch and I came over on the M92. I tell you what, whoever built that motorway must be a Town fan because every signpost I came across it said City 3 Burding 8, City 1 Burding 6. I thought, that'd do for me.

'As you know, I was a fullback and the 'keeper at the time was Neil 'The Cat' Forrest. Everybody assumed he'd got the nickname because of his reflexes and instincts in and around the eighteen-yard box...'

'Hey Juan, I'm going for a leak,' said Mika.
'Me too,' and they slunk off together.

'...not a bit of it. He was the only 'keeper in the Football League who could lick his own bollocks.'
'Not a bad night,' said Mika relieving himself.
'The fud was good. Ooz won playa of year?' said Juan.
'It's got to be between Joe and Willie, hasn't it? They've done it all season.'
The door opened and in strolled a thick-set man wearing a dark jacket, grey trousers, black open neck shirt. He had close-cropped hair and a pot belly.
He unzipped his trousers, looked up and recognised the two players. 'You lot are shite. You get shed loads of cash for doing **** all and I've lost thousands betting on yous.'
The teammates looked around. They were at the far end. They remained quiet.
'Are you listening to what I'm saying or are you deaf as well as ******* useless?'
'You've said what you think, so let's leave it,' said Mika zipping up his flies.
Another guy entered and Peter Sharp could be heard saying,

'I was just about to get into the bath after the game at Leeds and the gaffer took me back on the pitch. He says to me, "I want you to show me the hole". I didn't understand the question so I asked him to repeat it. "I want you to show me the hole". So I said "What hole's that boss?" "The hole you were bloody hiding in for the ninety minutes this afternoon".'

'What's going on Jimmy?'

'These two poncey gits are giving me bad time. They said I was a drunken pig.'

'Is that right?'

His mate was built like the proverbial brick-out house, 6ft 3ins tall, with muscles to match. There was an eagle tattooed on his forearm, and a ring pierced his broken nose. 'We'll see about that.'

In one movement he picked up Juan and sent him flying across the washroom, smashing his head on the tiles with a sickening thud. Mika leapt across to help and got a blow to the face, which made him keel over.

Several more blows rained down before the thugs disappeared. Blood was streaming from Juan's mouth, Mika was doubled over but he got to his feet to lay his Spanish colleague on one side. He then ran out to get Jimmy Franks.

The club doctor followed and examined Juan before contacting the emergency services. 'Ambulance quickly, River House Hotel. Head injury. I think he may have a broken jaw.'

'For the quarter-final against the Reds, I had a problem with my Achilles tendon and had to go onto the pitch to see if it was all right. The local radio man was keen as mustard and wanted an interview. But I had to get back to the dressing room for the team meeting so I put my thumb up to say I was okay. I could hear him telling the listeners. "Good news coming from the stadium. Peter Sharp has just pissed a late fatness test."'

Juan was lying motionless in the back of the ambulance with partner Rosa by his side – not knowing if he would ever pass a fitness test again.

A fractured jaw was confirmed. The thugs were identified, arrested and cautioned. They would be sentenced in due course.

Jake visited Juan in hospital.

'How you doing?'

'Berry zor. Eets brokin en too plezez.' he whispered.

'So what have they done?'

'Beeg opayrazion. Tay opayrate on crees line see? So dat no mark aftare.'

'It looks a mess.'

'Day ave poot a whyer eenside ant tied my teet together. Den day steetch u up wiz wan beeg peez of whyer. Zo I can't move.'

'You can't eat either?' said Jake.

'Day took out a tooz at back zo I can szlide a straw ant zuck op zom dreenks.'

'Does it work?'

'Ferst day I wok op. I waz ungree ant zerstee. But day tolt me to sock zlowlee coz eef I am zick, eet will com zroo my noze.'

'How long you in for?' asked Jake.

'Day set about a veek.'

'Afterwards just rest?'

'For seex weeks, den te why ers com out. I don't tink I weell be right for pree seezon.'

'They got the bastards who did it.'

'I know, Rosa told me. Day are bat men. But te doctor tolt me, don't woree. In time, I'll be ol right. I'm not as bat as som een ear. De man woo woz in te next room hat his fayz smasht een when a orse keekt eem. Is face cavet in. Day hat to do maykor work on eet. Ees ole botty waz covert een broozez.'

'Nasty. We'll make sure we don't bring in any animals on visiting days.'

'Goot.'

'Do you want anything?'

'No, Rosa as sortet tings.'

'We'll have to go for a paella when you can open your mouth.'

'Zat weell be goot. Enyzing appent at zee clob? Are we breenging een som players?'

104

'There's a lot of talk. You know rumours about coming and goings.'

'Cheerman get nervose. Cree-tee-cizm, not nice.'

'I know what you say, knee-jerk reaction. Get someone else in before they call for the chairman's head. But to be fair to the gaffer he hasn't been able to choose from a full squad all season, has he? Tim got that cruciate ligament injury early on and he's been missed and Jonno cracked a toe bone which put him out for months.'

'Zen Tomme's groin. Needed an opayrazion.'

'Never stopped did it? And all the niggly injuries and suspensions. When Smidgy got sent off it was a joke. I suppose it worked out right for me. I wouldn't have got a chance otherwise.'

'U deet well, Jake.'

'Everyone needs a break. Next season when everyone's fit, and that includes you Bully, we should be firing on all cylinders.'

'Seal-een-ders?'

'Just an expression mate,' smiled Jake. 'Anyway I'm off. If you're out next week I'll pop round to your place to see how it's going.'

'Zee you. Tanks for comeeng een.'

Leaving the hospital Jake saw a news billboard.

MARSH SACKED Boss exits Burding Town. Read the Post's exclusive report.

Jake bought a paper and read the statement.

The board very much regret the departure of manager Ged Marsh but feel this decision was taken in the best interests of the football club. The directors felt that Ged had taken them as far as he could and a change of direction was needed if the club was to move forward. We would like to thank Ged for his tireless work and wish him and his family the best of luck for the future.

When Jake arrived home he phoned coach Alex Pinder.

'Alex, what's going on?'

'I've no idea,' said Pinder, obviously saddened by the news. 'The boss told me yesterday he was leaving. Told me if I wanted to go for the position then he'd have no problem. In fact, he insisted. But nobody at the club has told me anything else so I'm a little in the dark. No doubt it will become clearer in the next few days.'

'Did the gaffer talk to you about me?'

'Nothing at all son.'

Jake then got a call from the secretary Harold Green. Nicknamed 'Hughie', he was popular with the players.

'Jake, can you drop in to see me?'

'No problem.'

What did he want? Jake tried not to overreact.

Until a permanent manager was appointed, Harold was asked to take on the job of discussing contractual agreements with the players. Harold looked jaded and harassed; his workload was horrendous, more so now Ged had been sacked.

His fondness for whisky and sodas and full strength cigarettes made him a certainty for a premature heart attack. Early retirement and a healthy pension looked a far better alternative to another five years behind his bulging desk.

'Jake, come in. How are you?'

'Not bad. Sorry to see the gaffer go,' Jake said.

'Yeah, he was a good guy, but that's football I suppose,' said Harold. 'I'm sure he'll get fixed up with another club, if that's what he wants. But let's get back to you. I've got some good news. The club is offering you a twelve-month professional contract after your scholarship agreement.'

'Thanks.' Jake could think of nothing else to say, but inside he was buzzing. This was what he'd always wanted.

'Don't thank me. Ged insisted that offers be made to certain players and the directors have been true to their word. Do you know that Davie and Tony have been given frees?'

'Yeah. They've taken it badly.'

'I'll get the forms drawn up and when they're ready I'll give you a call,' said Harold shuffling some papers. 'Are you going on holiday?'

'I've booked a couple of weeks with my girlfriend. We're off to the Greek islands, Skiathos. Get a bit of sunshine.'

'Have a great trip and I'll see you when you get back.'

Jake had only been in football for five minutes and things were happening all over the place. What else could he expect?

17

Ricky woke up. He felt thirsty. He got out of bed and headed towards the bathroom when he heard voices. Raised voices. Angry voices. He was afraid and cowered in the hallway.

'Come one step closer and I'll kill you!' His mother's distinctive tones reverberated through the flat.

'I'm warning you; one step and I'll use it!'

Ricky was shaking.

Mum was in trouble. Was there a burglar in the flat? He needed to get help. He tiptoed towards his mother's bedroom but Ronnie wasn't there.

His brain was working overtime. Frantic, Ricky went back to his bedroom. He found what he was looking for and returned.

'You might think I haven't got the guts but just try me. Come on, just try me.'

Ricky eased forward. His mum came into view. For a split second there was an eerie silence. She held a large kitchen knife. The table was overturned and pieces of broken glass were scattered all over the floor. She lunged towards the intruder.

There was a scream.

'You bitch!'

Ricky peered around the corner. He saw his mother kneeling over the victim attempting to stop the flow of blood oozing from the open wound. Ricky was in for a shock. The person on the floor was Ronnie.

'I've had enough, son,' said Ruth clinging to Ricky after the ambulance had taken Ronnie away. 'He's a pig and it's all through drink. He came in tonight and was completely off his trolley. Threatened us both. Something must have happened to set him off. But I've had enough.'

The wound was around the shoulder blade. It had missed the vital organs. It would heal but the relationship wouldn't. Ruth had already decided.

The police took a statement.

Ricky picked up the baseball bat and returned it to his bedroom. He hadn't had the pleasure of using it.

18

The games at the end of the previous season had whetted Jake's appetite, and he arrived for the first day of pre-season training full of enthusiasm. All the senior staff loyal to Ged Marsh, with the exception of physio Jimmy Franks, had departed and Jake was particularly disappointed for Alex Pinder who had supported him during their brief time together.

He had no similar feelings for youth coach Matt Downie. His exit was universally approved. Jake was learning a very important lesson. There was no sentiment in professional football. A new manager had been installed and the slate was clean.

First team regulars, sitting on fat contracts, even those with international appearances under their belts, would have to impress. Jake believed he could build on the few appearances he'd made and felt confident of making an impact. The atmosphere in the dressing room was electric. On a gloriously sunny day in the middle of July, the smell of new paint wafted through the corridors of the training ground mixing with the scent of newly cut grass.

New faces had been drafted into the squad. Irish international, Sean O'Connor, a 23-year-old midfield player, had arrived for a fee of £1.5m. Craig Hennessey, a 29-year-old Scottish centre back, had come on a Bosman and experienced Italian, Marco Cornelio, had signed a 12-month loan deal from Italian giants Milan to add competition for the striking positions.

The conversations were lighthearted.

'Where did you get to, Skip?' enquired Jake peeling off his casual shirt to display a bronzed, burgeoning physique.

'Couple of weeks on the Algarve. What about yourself?'

'Skiathos, one of the Greek islands. Pretty basic really but plenty of sunshine. Did you know that you can't put the bog paper down the loo? You've got to put it in a bin. Eh, I tell you what, I had a curry one night and you wouldn't believe how much I stuffed into it. England's not that bad when you think about it.'

'Yeah, that's what put me off when we went over a few years ago. They were always unblocking the drains after the Brits bunged everything up. Nightmare, we've never been back.'

Similar nondescript chats were breaking out in groups of twos and threes. Jake headed off to the gym.

Willie was already in there, stretching his hamstrings.

'All right son?' said Willie slapping him on the back. 'How you doing?'

'Fine thanks. Have you met the new gaffer?'

'No. But I had a word with Jazzy Spence. He's played under him and I got the lowdown,' said Willie doing some sit-ups. 'Looks a flash bastard but strong on discipline and gets results.'

Jake programmed the running machine, set the timer and glanced through the window. The sun was streaming through the windows and sweat was beginning to break out on his forehead. A squirrel dashed into the woods at the back of the training ground.

Smooth as silk, fifty grand's worth of polished metal glided into the car park, to rest in the no parking zone. A sign had even been erected in big bold letters. DON'T PARK HERE.

A dark haired man, in a short sleeved Armani shirt, white trousers and matching shoes got out. He checked a large Rolex before walking over to the main entrance. His whole demeanour shrieked of self-importance and indulgence. The sweat on Jake's forehead increased significantly.

The pitches looked immaculate and an air of anticipation among the players greeted another football season. The equipment, including balls, bibs, cones and water bottles, was already in place.

'Just a loosener. Twice around the field jogging. Exercises on route. Then back to me,' barked Frank Hart, the new first team coach. 'It's a running day so forget about the balls. We've got to get a decent standard of fitness first.'

This would be a testing season for a 17-year-old, but the monotonous laps, backbreaking hills and conditioned fartleks had to be faced. Jake's general fitness was good and he was determined to keep up with the leading group. The stragglers involved the 'keepers and to see them trailing off at the back was an invitation for relentless abuse.

'Hey, Hommie, fancy a greasy bacon butty? Lovely mate. Lots of brown sauce.'

The first day back was agony for the big man.

'Piss off you bastards!' was his non-too-subtle response.

An hour into the session the players took in their quota of fluids, overseen by the physios. During the break, pulse rates were monitored. The manager, kitted out in a brand new tracksuit with the initials LW emblazoned in bold letters, walked over to his assistant.

They were deep in conversation and the manager's arms gesticulated like overworked pistons. Hart strolled over and told the players to sit down. Only the gentle breeze wafting through the trees broke the silence. The track-suited LW took over.

'You know who I am. Les Whitehead, the new manager. You can call me boss.' Originally from the Bristol area, he stood six-foot tall, spoke in a West Country accent and looked confident and assured.

'I've always been involved at the top level, as a player, coach and manager. I'm here because you lot let the other guy down. I'm here to change the mentality of you players so that we become a winning, successful team. You will all get your chance. It's up to you whether you take it or not.'

After the day's session Jake went home completely knackered. Mum had made his favourite meal. Jake squirmed. A new diet sheet had been issued to all the young pros and, looking down on the list, meat and potato pie wasn't on it. Pasta, water, fresh fruit and vegetables were. Jake decided to have a word in his mum's ear later on but for now, the pie looked too appetising to turn down.

He crawled onto the settee and flaked out.

19

Ronnie was lying in bed with a white dressing covering the wound. 'Where am I?'

'You're at a drug and alcohol facility. I'm Dr David. I will be looking after you. You were admitted this morning. Do you remember anything about last night?'

'No.'

'It may become clearer in time but for now just listen. I am part of a qualified team who are here to help you. We need to assess you both physically and mentally. Do you understand?'

'Yes.'

'No alcohol is allowed on the premises,' pointed out Dr David. 'No drugs either unless a member of staff prescribes them.' He walked round to the other side of the bed. 'How do you feel right now?'

'Like crap.'

'I've got to tell you it isn't going to be easy. A lot of hard work is required to make a full recovery – and during the time you spend with us, it's essential you respect the other patients and staff. Is that clear?'

Ronnie nodded.

There was a knock on the door. A nurse entered with a tray.

'I'm leaving now,' said Dr David, 'but the nurse is here to do a few tests.'

'Hello, Ronnie. I'm Kelly.' She brought over a chair and sat by his bed. 'I need to ask you some questions as well as do some tests.'

The questions related to his drinking habits – what he drank, how much and when. Then his drug taking and smoking. Had he taken either, and if so, in what quantities?

She got out a stethoscope and asked if it was all right to lift his nightshirt. She was careful not to touch the dressing. She'd been told that twenty-one stitches had been inserted into a deep wound.

'Breathe deeply. And again.'

She wrote something down on a clipboard. She then took his

blood pressure. She did some enzyme tests to ascertain if there were any signs of liver or kidney damage.

'Ronnie, we must do this survey in order to identify your specific problems. Alcohol is a killer. At this rehab facility we classify alcohol abuse in the same category as cocaine or heroin addiction.'

He started to shiver. He fell on the floor and curled up rocking backwards and forwards. His whole body started shaking. The dressing became bloodstained. The nurse rang for emergency backup and a man in an orange jacket rushed in and put him back on the bed. Ronnie was given some Librium tablets. His anxiety subsided.

Ronnie was prescribed a course of pills to keep his blood pressure down, stabilise his heart and help him through his withdrawal. He had to take them every four hours. The problem for Ronnie was getting his medication – those precious red and yellow tablets known as 'bumble bees' – which became the epicentre of his entire world.

Queuing for his regular dose with other patients feigning illness or pushing others aside to get to the front, became a major balls-ache. Ronnie had never bothered to join the rat race for the New Year's Day sales bargains. Now he knew what it felt like – he flexed his muscles.

Ronnie had been in for two days. He went to the bathroom and was sick. He started pacing up and down the room. He got the shivers and started rubbing his body. He shit himself. He thought about running away.

He was escorted along the passageway to the far end of the unit, where he entered a small room. Inside were a table and two chairs. Ronnie sat down. Dr David closed the door and sat opposite.

'We need more information, then we can decide what is the best way to treat you.' Dr David opened a booklet. 'I'm going to ask you some questions and all I want you to do is answer yes or no. Take as long as you want. If you want me to repeat the question just ask. There is no time period. Is that clear?'

'Yes.'

'Okay, let's get started. The first question is – I like myself. Yes or No.'

First question and it was a stinker. Ronnie deliberated. This was going to take forever.

Ronnie was gagging for an alcoholic drink.

Hundreds of questions. At the end Ronnie felt exhausted. He sank his head into his hands.

Ronnie's digestive system was shattered – his nervous system defective. He found walking difficult and his co-ordination clumsy.

Ronnie got up. He went to the toilet. He was sick.

The rain battered the window pains and the wind howled. It was 2.15 in the morning. Ronnie put on his clothes and he paced the landing. At home he would open himself a can of strong ale – maybe two. He needed some fresh air, but the doors were locked. The rehab centre was, in essence, a psychiatric facility and, as such, a secure unit.

Only when he had shown some resolve and self-control would certain restrictions be lifted.

The rain became heavier and the wind deafening. How he longed to amble along the gravel path, his broken body swept away to the nearest boozer.

Instead, he walked slowly back to his room alongside a guy in a white jacket – to reflect on his life.

The following day Ronnie attended a lecture in the main meeting room where a Dr Joe Reed, an imposing figure – over six-foot tall, broad shoulders, dark suit, white shirt and bowtie – was introduced. Dr Reed took off his jacket to reveal red braces.

'My name is Joe Reed and I'm an alcoholic. I now work for the AA. Alcoholics Anonymous. Alcoholism is basically incurable. AA is the only organisation from my experience that will keep an alcoholic sober. I am here to tell you how it was founded.'

Ronnie's mind was drifting. This guy was going on about a man called Bill who had a chance meeting with an old pal and had seen the light. It all became blurred to Ronnie.

'He decided there and then to turn his life over to God. He never drank again. He developed the twelve steps and the concept of AA and devoted his life to spreading the word.'

Ronnie was finding it hard to concentrate. Did this guy Bill sort out the twelve steps or was it Joe? What the hell. Who cared? He wanted a drink.

He got up and started to walk out of the room.

'Sit down tosspot,' shouted a guy with long wispy side burns, piercing eyes and a menacing sneer. 'If we've got to listen so have you, so get your arse down there and don't move.'

The days before being admitted had been a blur but now certain things were beginning to surface. The scar would be a permanent reminder of the breakdown of his relationship with Ruth. He couldn't remember arriving home that night or how he'd got there. It was a total blank.

Who's this guy with the braces? What's he on about? Is he some kind of celebrity? Ronnie slumped to the floor.

20

Jake was buzzing and couldn't have been better prepared for the new season. His technical ability and athleticism had come on in leaps and bounds during the pre-season training and the hard graft was paying off.

Ged Marsh had given him the chance by easing him into the senior squad but now was the time to push on. The game had changed dramatically, and Les Whitehead and Frank Hart had already shown the necessary knowledge and expertise to be successful in the modern game.

Advancement in diet, psychology and team awareness, involving innovative strategies and tactics, were very much to the fore and it was all a massive learning curve for Jake.

A sports psychologist, Phil Easton, had been employed to formulate profiles of each player and identify factors to help them achieve high levels of consistency. Training and coaching programmes were then implemented, taking the club onto another level.

There was a lot to absorb. But Jake was receptive. He wanted to be the best and he knew, even at his tender age, it was vital to learn quickly. In discussions with Easton he was asked to pinpoint his own weaknesses.

Jake felt there was room for improvement with his left foot and that he needed to be more effective with his runs from deep positions. He laughed during one session when Easton talked about how things used to be.

'Light years away,' he informed Jake. 'It's advanced so much. You used to hear about players coming back from injury, being told to kick medicine balls to test their fitness. Probably put them out of action for another six weeks. And the eating habits were a joke. They used to stop off at the nearest fish and chip shop after an away game.

'Can you imagine it? The kit man popping in for twenty-six fish and chips? Those in the queue behind must have been well-pleased. All washed down with a few cans of lager.'

'The mind boggles,' said Jake. 'But the players must have had the same passion?'

'Of course. Since the year dot players have had to be fully committed and that's what develops team spirit. There'll always be room for the clenched fist and the verbals but we've moved on from there.

'Remember those black and white film clips of players in baggy shorts drinking sherry and raw eggs before cup ties? Is it any wonder they spewed their guts up?'

'I suppose managers will try anything to get results.'

'I understand that,' agreed Easton. 'They'll do something different or throw a wobbler. It gets players out of the comfort zone.'

Whitehead hadn't said a great deal to Jake but he'd been included in most of the first team sessions. Now and then Jake was recalled to the junior ranks but it was obvious he was head and shoulders above anyone in his peer group and those sessions were curtailing his development.

He'd never felt so good. He was purring like a finely-tuned engine. In one practice game he lined up for the reserves against the first team but was so impressive during the first forty-five minutes, the manager switched him to the senior side after the break. He was loving every minute of the whole experience.

Word was getting around. Jake was included in the England under-18 squad for their friendly against Austria.

The last pre-season friendly was away at Preston North End and it was assumed that the team selected would start the opening league fixture. Jake was in centre midfield.

The game was into its second quarter when he was caught on the halfway line with an innocuous looking tackle. The groundsman had left that little bit of extra growth on the pitch and Jake caught his studs in the lush turf.

He fell awkwardly, landing on his back. He wasn't aware of any major problem until he looked at his right foot – then he realised the seriousness of the situation. His foot was pointing at a ninety-degree angle.

The referee blew his whistle and frantically signalled to the bench.

Physio Jimmy was quickly at the scene and immediately gestured to the paramedics. A stretcher was called for.

'It's all right son,' said Jimmy, trying to comfort him. 'We'll get you sorted.'

But Jake looked directly into his eyes. It told him everything. Jimmy couldn't disguise his distress.

The opposing player was apologetic.

'Oh my God! Sorry mate.'

From their reactions Jake knew it was serious. Players from both sides gathered round. One was physically sick.

Jake was stretchered off to a sympathetic round of applause and carried to the physiotherapist's room. Frank, Jimmy and the club doctor, Dr Pierce, followed.

Jake was lifted onto the medical couch as the doctor made an initial diagnosis. 'It looks nasty, Jake,' he said. 'You've certainly dislocated your ankle but there's a good chance you haven't broken your leg. I am going to try to put the foot back in position. Is that all right?'

Jake nodded.

The doctor laid his hands on Jake's foot and in one swift movement manoeuvred it back in place. For a split second the pain was excruciating.

'Jake, you will need to go to the hospital for an X-ray to see if there is any other damage.'

He was still wearing his Burding kit – his blue and white number 36 shirt, his blue shorts and one white sock. He was proud to wear that jersey. It had always been his ambition – he had never wanted anything else. But now he was sweaty, frightened and vulnerable. How bad was it? Had he misinterpreted the reactions of the players or could this injury, indeed, mean a premature end to his career?

'Now then Jake lad, what have you been up to? My old man's a footie fan, can't stand it myself but it gets him out of the house.'

Ellen Whitlow, wearing a crisp white uniform over her small squat figure, was a sister at the hospital. 'We'll look after you, good and proper. You'll be as right as rain before you know it. No airs or graces about me. I tell it as it is and if it upsets people, so be it. I haven't got time to mess about. First things first. Let's get this looked at.'

Jake was wheeled down to the X-ray department and awaited the results in his private room.

'Good news and bad news Jake,' said Mr Martin, the orthopaedic surgeon. 'The bad news is; you have broken your leg. The good news is it's the bone at the back, the fibula. The tibia, the one at the front, the main weight bearing bone, is fine. It's a straight fracture, no complications, so an operation isn't necessary. All being well you should be out of plaster in six weeks.'

'Will I play again?' said Jake clearly worried.

'I don't see why not,' said Mr Martin reassuringly. 'It's just a matter of time before you're fully recovered.'

'How long will I be in here?'

'Just a few days. We'd like to see everything settle down. You'll be in good hands and the staff will look after you.'

The plaster came up to just below his knee and a rubber heel was fitted so that he could potter about with aid of the crutches. That first night he was given sleeping tablets and awoke the next morning hungry and thirsty.

'How are you feeling this morning?' asked Sister Ellen, holding a newspaper.

'Not bad.'

'Well you've hit all the papers,' said Ellen turning to the back page. 'Look at this "Burding's Break. Watkins' Woe". They've been ringing up all morning. I've told all my staff to say nowt. That gets rid of them.

'Photographers have been trying to find out which ward you're on. If they come within hundred yards, I'll string 'em up by their goolies.'

She wrote something on a clip chart at the end of the bed.

'Anybody coming in to see you today?' she said popping her pen into her top pocket. –

'My girlfriend and parents.'

'That'll be nice. When they get here, if there's anything they want, then press that button.'

'Thanks'

'I'm sure you'll be a good patient. We get all sorts you know. Well, nobody likes being in hospital, do they? Sometimes it seems like the whole world's gone mad. One time, I was on night duty and one of our patients smashed all the windows on the ward. No reason, he just blew a fuse. Out of his tree.'

'Are there a lot like that?'

'Not too many I'm glad to say. But there are some special ones as well. Many years ago when I worked as a volunteer I got to know a little girl named Sue who was suffering from a rare disease. Her only chance of recovery was a blood transfusion from her 5-year-old brother who had survived the same disease and had developed the antibodies needed to combat the illness.

'Well, the doctor explained the situation and asked the little boy if he would give his blood to his sister. He hesitated for a moment and then said "Yes, I'll do it if it will save her." As the transfusion progressed he lay in bed next to his sister and smiled as he saw the colour return to her cheeks.

'Then his face grew pale and his smile faded. He looked at the doctor and asked with a trembling voice, "Will I start to die straightaway?" Being young he had misunderstood. He thought he would die for her to live. What a magic moment that was.'

'Brilliant. What about life or death situations?' asked Jake. 'You know the kind of thing. If you don't do the right thing, there and then, the patient could die.'

'There was one time when a doctor told a nurse to put some blood into the ice. She instructed me and although I was new and thought it was an odd way to do it, I squirted the blood into the bag of ice.

'A few minutes later she comes back and said the doctors said, "what the hell is that – a slush puppy?" I twigged what I should have done – put the syringe in the ice bag not the blood!

'I said, "Oh my God!" I took the rap. What a cock up! Thinking about it afterwards it was so funny.'

'The guy didn't cop it, did he?'

'No. But that's what we're dealing with every day. Sometimes you don't have time to consult a senior colleague. You've got to fly by the seat of your pants. Anyway, I'll have to get on. Are you comfy, love?'

'Fine.'

'That's grand. I've been told that you're a good 'un. One for the future. So we'd better get you right, hadn't we?'

'How are you?' Marie leaned over to give him a kiss and put the grapes and magazines on the side table.

'I've no pain but the plaster feels a bit funny.'

'Just when everything seemed to be going so well, this happens,' said Marie sitting on the bed.

'The specialist said there's a chance I'll be back playing within three months. It depends on how the bone knits together.'

'You're going home tomorrow, aren't you?' asked Ellen, two days after Jake was first admitted. 'Has the physio had a word?'

'He's coming round to my place next week,' said Jake who had just finished shaving. He'd found bathing with one leg over the side of the bath a little awkward. 'We're going to do some upper body exercises.'

'It's important that you keep as fit as possible, 'cos you're going to be sat around for a few weeks. Any ideas on how you'll fill your time?'

'I've got college work – plenty of reading there.'

'What you studying?'

'Sport and Leisure.'

'Like it?'

'It's good. It's taken a bit of a back seat lately but now I'll be able to get on with it.

21

'You've a lot of damage to your liver, your heart and your stomach. Carry on drinking and it's odds on you'll die.'

Ronnie laughed after hearing the assessment from counsellor Norman East.

'Now tell me the good news.'

'You're a very violent man. Reckless, vindictive and disrespectful.'

Ronnie sipped his black coffee.

'I'm a dead man.' He stretched out his arms and had a resigned look on his face.

'You've been given a chance,' said East. 'I think we can find the reasons for your anger, which will go a long way towards solving your problems. And, for me, the best way is through the twelve steps programme.'

'No way.'

'I'm an alcoholic myself and from my experience, it's the only thing that works.'

'How long you been sober?' said Ronnie, head down facing the table.

'Nine years. You can do it too. It's up to you. But you have to make two decisions,' said East, attempting to make eye contact. 'First one is, do you want to live? The second is, are you willing to knuckle down and do whatever it takes to see it through? Only you can decide.'

'That's heavy,' said Ronnie shuffling in his seat.

'What have you got to lose? You're at rock bottom now. Ronnie's way has got you here,' said East. 'Your life's a mess. You've been stabbed by your missus, your jobs on the line, you've got a GBH charge pending, you live in a shit hole – and it's all because of the booze.

'So it's time to change. Us alcoholics are anarchists, Ronnie. Rebels. "My Way" is all about us, isn't it? I know how you feel – I've been there. Whatever you say I've heard it all before. You can't blag a blagger. So it's time to listen.

'The world doesn't change – it's us who's got to change. When I came in here I took things too personally. I thought life's against blokes like you and me. I wore my heart on my sleeve. Other people seemed to be able to brush off little problems but I couldn't.

'I didn't use alcohol for pleasure; I used it to get drunk so I didn't have any feelings. I don't know one alcoholic who's good with feelings. It's a big ask Ronnie. For the first time in your life you'll have to face life without alcohol.'

Ronnie stared impassively.

'Have you any spiritual beliefs?' asked East, folding his arms and leaning back into his chair.

'What? Religion?' grunted Ronnie. 'I've never believed in God.'

'Think of it another way,' said East. 'Some of my group think of God as a "Group of Drunks" all coming together to help each other. They could be your higher power. They could be your God. I've seen them develop the feelgood factor, which nobody can explain.

'It's a spiritual thing; it happens within the group. They call it a "spiritual phenomenon" – and it works. The alcoholic by himself has no chance – believe me. He needs the support from others; otherwise he will wallow in his own self pity until the day he dies.'

Every so often the unit invited members of the family to sit in on group sessions. Ruth wondered whether it was worth attending, knowing that she and Ronnie would never be an item again.

'He's brought it on himself, mum. You couldn't have done anymore,' said Ricky. 'We both know what a pig he is. I don't want to go anywhere near him.'

'I know what you're saying love, but he's got nobody else,' said Ruth mulling it over. 'What if we just sat through the meeting? We don't have to say anything, do we?

'Just be there and listen. Maybe we'd find out why he behaved like he did. There must be others who are just like him. I wonder if their families support them?'

'He's nothing to do with me, is he? He's not like my dad, or anything, is he? The further I'm away from him the better. If I don't ever see him again it'd be too soon.'

'Nobody wants to be labelled an alcoholic, Ronnie. They all think they are coming in here to learn how to drink. But the reality is, this is not a halfway house. People try controlled drinking but I've got to tell you it doesn't work.

'I met a bloke once who said he was trying the controlled drinking method. He told me he'd only had one drink the previous day. Then he admitted to me afterwards – it was a gallon of beer!'

Ruth and Ricky were tense as they got into the car. As they made their way slowly out of the car park, she asked Ricky what he wanted to do.

'You know my feelings, mum. But if you want to go it's okay with me. Whether I'll be able to get out the other end, I don't know.'

The route to the rehab facility took them past Maple Park. 'I used to take you there as a little kid. Can you remember?'

'Bird sanctuary with all the peacocks.'

'That's right,' said Ruth. 'Haven't been for there for ages. Fancy popping in? We've got a bit of time to spare. Unless you think it's uncool to be out with your old mum.'

'Well, you are knocking on a bit, aren't you?'

'Hey, cheeky monkey. You're not too big to go over my knee.'

Ruth attempted to turn round but the traffic was heavy – she felt uncomfortable. She'd only passed her test a few weeks before and everything had gone well – mirrors, indicators, first gear, handbrake. But while turning right, she stalled. Irate drivers flashed lights, honked horns, gesticulated. She stalled again.

'Mum, you're in third gear.'

Tears welled up. It had all got too much.

Chairs were placed in a circle. Family members sat alongside the addicts.

Norman East stood up. 'Welcome to the first group session of the family programme. Ask whatever you want but please remember the feelings of others.'

One by one they went round the circle and introduced themselves.

One was a heroin addict. Another was the wife of an alcoholic. Next came the mother of a crack cocaine addict.

After the introductions there was a painful silence. Everybody looked at the floor. Unable to face each other or make eye contact.

Then the mother of one of the group wanted to know what crack was.

'Crack is cocaine mixed with bicarbonate of soda and water and heated on a spoon,' said East. 'What's produced is skimmed off and that's what's called rock or crack. You smoke it with a pipe.'

They asked about ecstasy, heroin, amphetamines and marijuana and why some were called class A drugs.

Then the son of an alcoholic asked, 'How does it feel to be addicted to something?'

'I'll answer that. I'm Mark. It's terrible because we know what we're doing and we can't stop doing it. It's a need and when we get it we feel relieved. But then it's followed by anxiety because we need more.'

'If I can come in here,' said Julie, another counsellor. 'It's been confirmed that alcoholics and addicts are born with a gene that, when stimulated, controls that individual. It's now recognised that alcoholism is a disease as is addiction.'

She talked about the drinking culture of modern society, the influence of friends, the availability of alcohol and drugs. She said it was important to remove as many triggers as possible.

She told a story of how one man reacted aggressively to another just because he was wearing a rugby shirt advertising a beer sponsor. He kicked the lad and made him take the shirt off. His tolerance levels were so small – he was in such a state of anxiety and paranoia – all because his body was suffering.

'Can you imagine five guys all wearing the same shirt? So in a home environment it is something we can control.' Julie then gave a frightening statistic. 'Twenty per cent of the addicts in our area are under fourteen years of age.'

Turning into Maple Park; Ruth turned off the engine. At the far end of the grassed area were the swings, slides and bouncy castles and the smiles on the toddlers' faces said everything. Nothing better than grappling up the steps 'all on my ownsome' and feeling the thrill of sliding down the Mickey Mouse chute.

Ruth and Ricky walked along the tree-lined path. Ruth's stress had disappeared and she warmed in the bright sunlight.

Ricky broke away to retrieve a football that had blown over. He flicked it up, kept it on the back of his neck for what seemed an age and then in one movement volleyed it straight into its owner's hands.

'Eh, that was good Ricky,' said his mother.

After the bowling green they came to the bird sanctuary. Ducks were paddling, cockerels and pheasants were making a racket and guinea pigs and hamsters were being fed.

'How are you doing anyway?' said Ruth placing an arm round his shoulder. 'You okay?'

'I'm all right.'

'It's not been easy.'

'Just going through a phase I suppose. Nothing's clear at the moment.'

'Confused?'

'Sort of.'

They wandered out of the park gates, looking for a café.

'Come on we're going in here.'

'Church?' said Ricky, surprised.

Ruth crossed herself. They sat near the altar.

One woman asked: 'I've heard of pills that you can take to help you stop drinking.'

'They are called antabuse. They make you sick, if you have alcohol.'

One man asked about relapse and why the disease returned with greater strength.

Julie told them: 'If I stopped drinking two years ago on the 14th March at 10 pm, whatever state of paranoia or anxiety I was in, either physically or mentally, if I had a drink now, I would be right back to where I started.

'You don't go back to the so-called good old days when you went out with your mates to have a good laugh and a few drinks. When the clock stops that when you start from. That's a fact.'

One mother and father felt responsible for their boy's plight. The boy was an alcoholic. They reckoned they should have seen the signs and done something about it. But the son did not blame them. The general consensus was, addicts were responsible for their own actions – nobody else.

A few isolated parishioners were scattered around the lovely church. Ricky sat there, quietly, looking around at the sculptures and the stained glass windows.

His whole body seemed heavy – as if he was stumbling around in the dark. He felt vulnerable and exposed. Naked. He was relieved to share his uncertainties. He took in the moment – the sense of peace.

In the pew he picked up a leaflet. On it was a message written by Pope John Paul II.

Remember the past with gratitude, live the present with enthusiasm and look forward to the future with confidence. The new Millennium is opening before the Church like a vast ocean upon which we shall venture, relying on the help of Christ.

He came out a little humbled. Religion had never been at the top of his priorities. His mum had never forced it on him. But she had always been there for him even when he was threatening to destroy his own life.

He owed everything to his mum. How could he criticise her? Just then. In the car. Wrong gear. So what?

What quality of life had she had? Single mum who'd been out there, scrimping and saving to put clothes on his back, wipe his dirty arse and keep him safe.

What had she got to look forward to? It was time for her to enjoy the good things in life.

'Thanks mum.'

'What for?'

'For that. For taking me in there. For today.'

'You know what love, I needed it just as much as you.'

She held his hand.

The addicts and alcoholics didn't ask any questions themselves. They knew they were everybody's worst nightmare.

'You know what Ricky I was very lucky to have two parents who loved me.'

'I wish I'd known them.'

'So do I. Perhaps it was best they died together. I don't think either one of them would have been able to carry on without the other. They were that close,' said Ruth crossing her fingers.

'I do miss them. I used to go with mum to Mass first thing every Sunday morning. We called it "our time". Whatever people say it's still a good moral code. It teaches the difference between right and wrong. I still think it's a good grounding for later on and what life throws at you.'

'Have you seen the time?' said Ricky checking his watch.

'I know,' she said quietly. 'Let's just say, it wasn't to be. Come on, love. Let's go home.'

'If you can find that first gear.'

'You little horror, come here and give me a kiss.'

'Mum!'

Norman asked the group to join hands. He said a prayer.

'God grant me the serenity to accept the things I cannot change, the courage to change the things I can and the wisdom to know the difference.' He then brought the meeting to a close. 'Thank you all for coming. I think we have done some great work today.'

The group filed out of the room, some in better shape than when they entered.

Ronnie stood up. The chairs, either side of him, had been vacant throughout.

22

Most players recovered from serious injuries, but it didn't stop the nagging doubts at the back of Jake's mind. He'd never had an injury before – a slight strain or a pull, stitches for a head wound or an ingrowing toenail – not even a bloody nose. He'd always been fit and he was finding it hard to deal with.

The team had started the season well. After five games they had nine points under their belts, and were well placed in the top half of the division. The big guns – Chelsea, Manchester United, Liverpool and Arsenal – were again leading the way with Everton on their coat tails.

Jake got on with his college work but it was a poor substitute.

When Jake had his plaster removed he expected to pick up where he left off but he soon realised it wasn't that simple. The break had healed successfully but the ligaments and tendons around the ankle joint had been wrenched so badly that regaining the flexibility would be a major obstacle. He had to learn how to walk without a limp, jog through the pain.

Jimmy's repetitive 'Heel toe, heel toe, rotate the foot' was beginning to get on his nerves. It was a slow and painful process and seemed to go on for an eternity. Weeks would go by without any significant improvement. 'Dig deep, son, it'll happen. Just keep at it.'

Jake's eighteenth birthday coincided with a dramatic change in circumstances. The months of exercises and treatment had eventually paid dividends and there were positive signs of improvement.

He was running without pain or discomfort and he was finally given the go ahead to resume full time training. The relief was indescribable, and he came through that first session without any reaction.

He'd also decided it was time to get mobile. He took driving lessons and started scouring the papers and local car showrooms for a suitable vehicle. The lads in the dressing room had contacts for exclusive models with ten grand stereo systems but he was targeting a slightly different market.

And his relationship with Marie was also going well. She was gorgeous and they were happy to spend all their spare time together.

But there was one thing they failed to agree on: Jake's dress sense. Marie reckoned that Jake was the worst-dressed footballer in the world. Nothing matched.

He wore the first thing that fell out of the wardrobe. Occasionally he made an effort but usually jeans and T-shirt were the sum total of his fashion sense.

'Hey I'm not as bad as Holty, the lads give him plenty of stick.'

'And you'll be the next one if you don't get yourself sorted,' said Marie grabbing his arm.

'That's why I like you loads. You look after me.'

'Like all men, you have to have someone fetching and carrying for you.'

'What do you mean, all men?'

'Come on,' she said taking control. 'We're going shopping and no moaning.'

He passed his test and bought a 3-year-old 1.4 litre bog-standard saloon, although if truth be known, colour was the first thing that attracted him to that particular model. It was blue. His first car, his pride and joy.

On the Sunday they had a day out in Blackpool. They spent the time holding hands, walking along the prom, eating candyfloss and knocking over cans at the funfair.

The flash attendant on the dodgem ride kept leaping onto Marie's car in an attempt to win favour. They laughed all the way to the top of the tower and into the amusement arcade.

'How come these pennies don't fall off?' said Jake irritably.

'They're glued on. Come on, let's go bowling.'

They jumped on a tram and huddled together on the top deck looking at the bright lights of the illuminations. They kissed. Long lingering kisses.

'Have we to stay over?' said Jake.

131

'What about training tomorrow? And I've got to get to work,' said Marie spotting a giant Christmas tree.

'We'll set off first thing, get away early. Come on let's go for it. It'll be cool.'

'We haven't brought anything,' pointed out Marie.

'All we need is a toothbrush. It's not like we need pyjamas, is it?' he said laughing.

They found a modest bed and breakfast place and the woman at the desk asked for cash up front.

A sign stating 'No Cheques' in big bold letters left them in no doubt.

The room looked clean but they didn't move the bed in case something suspicious was lurking underneath.

'Fancy seeing a film?' suggested Jake.

'I'll have a shower,' said Marie. 'Then we'll decide.'

She made her way into the bathroom and Jake switched on the kettle. He shouted to see whether she wanted a drink but couldn't make himself heard so he opened the shower door...

The film was put on hold for another day.

After several youth and reserve games Jake showed no ill-effects and early in the new year he was back involved with the first team, and although the team's performances had levelled off since the good early season form they still well placed without any relegation fears.

Les Whitehead wasn't afraid to experiment with different systems and his knowledge of the game was vast. He instilled in the players an adventurous approach and insisted they play with panache and spirit. Unlike a lot of football managers he embraced the media attention and saw it as a way of promoting himself, not only the football club.

He wasn't afraid of negative comments that came his way, totally confident in his own ability. The club was heading into a new era with an inventive, forward-thinking manager who continually asked more of his players in an effort to improve them as individuals.

He was in the results business. Every victory enhanced his reputation and the sceptics were fading away like the morning mist. Whitehead's man-management skills were his greatest strength.

He knew every one of his players inside and out. In Jake, he soon recognised, he had one of the game's most talented young players. Whitehead was devastated when Jake was injured but his young star was now back and available.

As far as the manager was concerned, there was nothing this young man could not achieve. He had everything: strength, pace, height, ability, attitude, his bludgeoning style could dominate the game for years to come and his influence on the team would be enormous.

But he was still only eighteen years old and would have to be managed correctly. No burnout for this lad. He would be brought through patiently. Whitehead wanted him involved in every game but that wasn't going to be possible. He must be looked after properly.

It was frustrating for Jake. He'd already missed many games through injury and wanted to make up for lost time. Being told he was on the bench or to watch from the stands was baffling to the young man. He became a little angry.

He took out his frustration in the next game by rampaging around the field, covering every blade of grass and dominating the entire ninety minutes.

Returning home after the match, Jake switched off the radio and the engine idled to a stop. The manager had been delighted with his performance in his first game back. 'Keep playing like that Jake and things are going to happen pretty quickly.'

He was establishing himself in the team and felt comfortable with the players. His injury had recovered completely and there was nothing to hold him back.

Whitehead used the remaining games as an opportunity to build for the following season. Jake was very much to the forefront of his plans. In between rest periods the manager gave him specific responsibilities, sometimes playing him in the holding role in front of the back four, then switching him to a more advanced position, giving him licence to get forward – getting into the opposition faces and not letting them rest for a split second. He adapted brilliantly.

There was one major disappointment. The anticipated FA Cup run didn't materialise after Burding were comprehensively beaten

3-0 by Everton in the fourth round, scuppering any hopes of an exciting climax to the season.

Jake didn't want the season to end. After the final game he felt deflated. He had energy to burn but nowhere to channel it. The other players were desperate for a break to recharge their batteries but Jake's only required the slightest top up. He'd have to be patient before the action was resumed.

At the awards dinner he was voted 'Young Player of the Year' by a distance even though he had missed large chunks of the season and was placed just behind Sean O'Connor for the main prize of 'Player of the Year'.

These two were the engine room of the team. They complemented each other so well and had an understanding that was almost telepathic.

'Thanks very much for this award. It makes me feel very proud. I couldn't have done it without my teammates who have been absolutely brilliant. I hope next season will be even better. I'd like to thank the fans who voted for me. Thanks again. Enjoy the night.'

A packed house stood to applaud the gifted youngster. When he returned to the table, Marie gave him a huge smacker, grabbed his tie and whisked him onto the dance floor.

'Come on Young Player of The Year,' she said laughing. 'Let's see if those million dollar legs are as good as John Travolta's.'

'Night fever, night fever... . We don't have to do it... '

'What's wrong with that left foot? It's the same one that flashed a 20-yarder into the Arsenal net isn't it? Well it seems like it's stuck in concrete right now. Loosen up.'

Jake and Marie enjoyed a two-week holiday in Spain. On the last day Marie booked a table at the Haven Restaurant overlooking the magnificent harbour in the port of Moraira. She looked ravishing in her white linen outfit, highlighting her deep golden tan and on a warm balmy evening they enjoyed a delicious meal of red mullet and fresh vegetables. Coffee was being served and she held Jake's hand.

'I've got something to tell you,' she said quietly.

'What is it?' said Jake feeling totally relaxed.

With only the sound of crickets scurrying away in the undergrowth she whispered, 'I'm trekking round the world for a year.'

23

Hutchinson bumped into Ricky during the morning break. 'You're back in the football squad I hear?'

'Played the last two matches, sir,' said Ricky, heaving his bag over his shoulder. 'I'm still a long way off being as fit as the rest of them.'

'Well you've missed so many matches with one thing and another. Can you pop in and see me before you disappear tonight?'

'Yep, no sweat.'

Music was the last lesson of the afternoon and it bored the class. 'What's wrong with garage or rap?' the boys demanded. 'Part of the twenty-first-century. This classical stuff is for coffin dodgers. Give us a break.'

Ricky made his way over to Hutchinson's room, knocked on the door but there was no answer.

Should he hang around? Six months ago it wouldn't have been an issue. He would have been straight out of there, no messing, but things had changed. Hutchinson had given him a fair crack. Head teacher Collette Smyth came out of the room opposite.

'Do you want something Grant?' she asked, obviously in a hurry.

'I'm waiting for Mr. Hutchinson, miss.'

'I'll check to see where he is.'

'Ricky,' said Hutchinson appearing round the corner. 'Upper 5th exam and I've had to fill in. Come in.'

Hutchinson placed his bag on the floor as he answered his 'phone.

'Yes Dorothy I have spoken to the Head about next year's syllabus. It's all in hand thank you. Anything else? Fine. Would you hold my calls for the next ten minutes?' He put the 'phone down. 'I'm making myself a brew Ricky, do you want one?'

'I'll have a can if you've got one.'

'Help yourself. They're over in the corner,' said Hutchinson switching on his kettle. 'How are the exams going?'

'Tough.'

'I can understand that. And things at home?'

'Ronnie's in that drying-out place and it's a lot better.'

'Just you and your mum?'

'Yeah.'

'And your own situation?' said Hutchinson motioning Ricky to sit down.

'I've managed to stay clean. I've been talking more. So far I've kept off the stuff.'

'Good for you,' said Hutchinson, adding milk and sugar to his coffee mug.

'Any thoughts about what you're going to do when you get out of here?'

'For a job?'

'Yes. With the rest of your life?'

'I'll get down to the job centre I suppose,' said Ricky gulping from the can.

'Have you seen the school's careers officer?'

'No.'

'What about this football bit? Mr. Spencer's been telling me you've shown a lot of promise lately.'

'I enjoy it. Something to focus on.'

'Nobody shown any interest?'

'Other teams you mean? I haven't played enough. Don't suppose anybody's seen me.'

'Well you might be interested in this. The reason I've got you in is to tell you about the school's development programme. In the last few years we've sent boys over to the States – it's been an exchange arrangement.

'This year they've offered us a place on a soccer camp. I've got to be honest, you weren't the first choice, but a couple of lads have cried off and after talking to Mr Spencer we wondered whether you'd fancy it.'

'Sounds good.'

'You don't think your mum will mind?'

'I'll ask her but it should be okay.'

'Right then. I'll find out a bit more and let you know.'

'Thanks sir.'

24

'I don't believe it,' said a furious Jake, 'I thought we had something special.'

'We do,' insisted Marie.

'How can we if you're bunking off?' said Jake, slipping on his top. It was beginning to feel distinctly cooler.

'I made a promise,' she explained.

'Who to?' he demanded.

'Helen.'

'Your friend from school?' said Jake, pouring himself a glass of wine. He felt he needed it.

'Yeah.'

'You're going together?' he asked.

Looking directly at him she said, 'You didn't think I'd be going on my own, did you?'

'I don't know what to think anymore,' Jake said, disappointed.

'It's something we agreed years ago.'

'But that was before we knew each other,' Jake pointed out.

'I know,' Marie said, stroking his right hand. 'But it doesn't change anything,'

Suddenly he raised his voice. 'What? It changes everything. For a year we won't see each other. I would have thought that's a massive change.'

'But our relationship can survive,' she said, trying to reassure him.

For a moment he was flustered. 'Long distance relationships don't. They just don't. How can they?'

'We're still young,' said Marie.

'But we know what we want,' said Jake, moving his chair a little nearer.

'Do we?'

'Well I know what I want. That's you,' he said.

'What, forever?'

'Maybe.'

'But we've never talked about it.' Marie said, lowering her voice. 'We've had dates, we've had a great holiday but we've never sat down to discuss our futures together, have we?'

'No.'

'Why's that then?' asked Marie.

'I thought that's what you wanted. Day at a time. No big deal. But it looks like you were just stringing me along,' said Jake, frowning.

'When I made that promise, you weren't in my life,' she explained.

'But I am now. Don't you love me?'

'Jake, I'm only nineteen, you're eighteen. How do I know? Do you love me?' she asked.

'I think so.'

'Are you just saying that because of what's happened?'

'Well I've never felt this way before,' he said, honestly.

'I know, I'm the same. Since that first day I haven't thought about anyone else.'

'But now you're bound to meet other guys.'

Marie agreed. 'And you'll meet other girls.'

'Then what's going to happen?'

'Sorry?'

Jake explained his concerns. 'Well if either of us meets someone, it's got to lead somewhere hasn't it? How would you feel if I was seeing someone else?'

'Right now I wouldn't be happy,' Marie said grabbing hold of Jake's hands.

'Neither would I. But traipsing around the world, a great looking girl like you, every guy you meet will fancy you.'

'I think you're getting a bit carried away here.' She smiled. 'Don't you trust me?'

'I'd like to think so. But come on, we weren't born yesterday.'

'Jake, let's get one thing clear. There is nobody I want to be with more than you. When I return and if we still feel the same way about each other then maybe we do have something very special to hold onto.'

'I can't help feeling the way I do.'

'I know. But you haven't had any other girlfriends. Come on, there's millions out there. Do you honestly think you've found the one girl to spend the rest of your life with, two miles away from your own doorstep?'

Jake was hurt. 'Sounds like I'm getting dumped.'

'Of course you're not. Answer the question,' demanded Marie.

'Yes I do.'

'Are you just saying that?'

'No I'm not. That's how I feel. But tell me one thing. There's something I don't understand.'

'What's that?'

'If you were thinking about doing this crazy thing, why didn't you go last year?'

'Maybe you've forgotten, dumbo,' she pointed out, 'but you broke your leg. How would it look if I scooted off and left you in the mire just when you were at your lowest ebb? You were just making a name for yourself and then wallop. Disaster. I couldn't leave then. I had to be there to support you through all the months of doubt.'

'But during that time my feelings for you have grown even stronger.'

'Mine too. If it's meant to be then we'll come through it.'

At that moment, she looked very beautiful. 'I don't want to lose you, Marie.'

'And I don't want to lose you.'

'But you might. Are you prepared to risk it for a silly jaunt?' argued Jake. 'Something you could easily cancel. Tell Helen to go with someone else. I'll pay for it.'

Marie wasn't convinced. 'She won't go if I don't.'

'Is there nothing that'll change your mind?'

'No, I've decided. That's it. But I tell you what. When we get back we'll have the biggest party ever,' she said laughing.

The atmosphere was warming. 'How we going to keep in touch?'

'Emails. There's internet cafes all over the world. I'll be sending you stuff from everywhere.'

'I won't know where to send your birthday present.'

'Ha! Ha! I might be in the jungle in South America so a mosquito spray will come in handy.' She leaned over and gave him a kiss.

'When do you leave?'

'In a month – 4th of July.'

'That's the day after we start pre-season training,' he told her.

'Well then, you can get fully focused on the season with no distractions. And I want to hear about some great wins when I tune in. Burding Town top of the league and winning the Champions League. If you don't, I'll hold you personally responsible.'

'Does Helen know you were going to spill the beans?'

Marie took her 'phone out of her bag. 'Shall we ring her?'

'What now?' said a flummoxed Jake.

'Why not?'

'Go on then,' he agreed.

As Marie dialled the number Jake glanced over to see a small sailing boat making its way slowly to a mooring point. As the vessel drew to a halt Marie said, 'Helen, guess what? I've told him.

'She wants to know how you took it.'

'Brilliantly,' he lied.

'Fibber. Do you know what she's just said? If Jake was my boyfriend there's no way I would be dashing off around the world.'

'Give me that 'phone.'

'Helen, whatever I'd have said, it wouldn't have made the slightest bit of difference. Just promise me one thing. You look after each other and come back safe.'

'I'll make sure she doesn't marry an Elvis impersonator in Vegas,' said Helen, laughing down the 'phone.

'Thanks for that,' replied Jake. ' I'll put your sneaky mate back on.'

With one hand covering the 'phone, Marie said, 'what did she say?'

Jake picked up his glass and downed the contents. 'That's for me to know, my little honey bunch, and you to find out.'

'You horror.'

'Excuse me, I'm not the one gallivanting around the world, am I?' reasoned Jake.

'We'll just have to a make it a night to remember won't we?' she said seductively.

'Your place or mine?'

25

Hutchinson told Ricky: 'You'll be based in Boston staying with an Irish family. Their kids are involved with a soccer club called Green Isles and it's all arranged. That's if you're interested?'

'Too right,' said Ricky.

Buttoning up his cardigan, Hutchinson asked, 'Have you got a passport?'

'No.'

'Well that's the first thing to sort out,' he pointed out.

The final exams were a real bind. Ricky struggled. But in maths, history, metalwork and PE he thought he'd done pretty well.

With the regular training routines and extra gym sessions Ricky's physical development was improving. At 5 foot 9 inches, he was maturing well, and his dark flowing hair and olive complexion were finding many new admirers. He also had another great asset: a cultured left foot.

But survival was still the number one priority. Even though Ricky's lifestyle had changed dramatically since Ronnie had left the scene he still faced plenty of intimidation from other kids on the block.

'Hey Wicky, you plonker, what's that you wearing? Get yourself some wight gear mate. You ponce.' It was a bind but he was becoming streetwise and was able to resist the insults without too much hassle. Other residents wouldn't leave their flats but that wasn't going to happen to Ricky. Only sixteen, he didn't say a lot. He'd developed inner steel.

After seeing Hutchinson, he was about to climb the steps to the flat and they were waiting. 'Hey Wicky you ******. Just 'eard your muvver's on the game. Wight little hussy.'

The disaffected bolshy youths had attitude. Worried about the law? Do me a favour. Respect? Forget it. Violence will get them what they want. There was no thought about destroying lives. Live for today. Tomorrow? Leave it out!

Ricky put his bag on the floor, walked calmly over to the trio of thugs and with a perfectly executed volley, kicked the ringleader squarely in the groin. The others were downed with successive punches. All three were on the ground. Ricky leaned over the 'main man' who was squealing like a demented mule holding what was left of his manhood.

'If there's any more aggro, I will find you no matter what. There'll be no hiding place. Understand?'

He mumbled.

'Is that clear?' warned Ricky.

'Yeah.'

Ricky picked up his bag. He walked up the steps, got the key out of his pocket and entered the flat.

His whole body was shaking.

Ricky's flight was scheduled for the Friday lunchtime. The security at the airport was intense. Ricky sat with his mum as Hutchinson joined the queue for refreshments.

'I'm proud of you Ricky, you know that,' she said, patting his cheek.

'I know.'

'Just enjoy yourself.'

'I'm looking forward to it,' said Ricky knowing it was important to be positive. 'What would I do if I stayed here?'

Hutchinson came over with a tray of toasted sandwiches and hot drinks.

'All set Ricky?'

'I might stay over there and get a Yankee accent.'

Eventually it was time to go through into the departure lounge.

'Don't worry, mum.' For a brief moment he felt awkward.

'I love you very much,' said Ruth hugging her boy. She slipped a note into his pocket.

It was a tender moment. 'And I love you too mum.' He'd never said that before.

He shook Hutchinson's hand. 'Thanks, sir. I'll always remember what you've done for me.'

'Get out of here.' Hutchinson took some money out of his wallet and stuffed it in Ricky's hand. 'Just take it all in and enjoy it.'

One last turn, a wave and Ricky was gone. He was nervous but excited.

He bought himself a cola and a magazine and sat down. The noise coming from the adjacent bar was deafening; stag parties heading for the sunny climes of Spain's Costa coastlines. The blokes revealed pot bellies and hideous tattoos and knocked back large quantities of draught lager. Giant TV screens were locked onto silent sports channels – basketball on one, cricket another. Rock music blasted out over the speakers.

Sayings were chalked on a notice board outside.

All you need is love
Or failing that – alcohol
Candy is dandy
But liquor is quicker
The right honourable was a tubby little chap
Who looked as if he had been poured into his clothes-
And had forgotten to say 'When'.
It was a woman that first tempted man to eat but he took to
drink on his own!

The sayings were meant to amuse. But Ricky had experienced the darker side.

Inside, the guys, wearing replica soccer strips, were all trying to out shout each other.

Mobile 'phones were making annoying ring tones, all demanding attention, getting louder and louder every second they went unanswered.

A hen party made its way through to the bar. Around a dozen girls all dressed in red T-shirts informed the rest of the airport, 'I'm a virgin'.

'Flight number BA551 to Boston, now boarding. Will all passengers please make their way to gate number 32.'

Ricky dumped the mag, sipped his drink and strolled to the gate.

He had a window seat and sat next to an older couple. It was a long trip and whether he wanted it or not they were determined to strike up a conversation.

'I'm Richard, and this is my wife Susan. Our son met his future wife on holiday in Italy and before you knew it, they'd gone over to the States and got married. It's the first time we'll see our grandson.'

'Good on you,' said Ricky.

'Are you on your own?'

'Yes.'

'Have you flown before?'

'Never,' said Ricky, glancing through the window and taking in the marvellous view.

'What you think?'

'The take off was a little scary 'cos I didn't know what to expect. You see all these things on screen or TV but to be on one, well it's mega.'

'Please return to your seats. We will soon be arriving at Logan Airport. Make sure your seats are in the upright position and your seat belts are securely fastened.'

The lights dimmed and Ricky looked out of his window. The engines slowed.

He felt in his pocket for some chewing gum and brought out an envelope. He opened it and started to read.

Hi Ricky
Hope you have a great time in the States. I would have loved to be there with you. Make the most of it son. It's a great opportunity so don't let it pass without enjoying it. It may never happen again. I love you very much. Don't forget to thank the people you are staying with. And make sure you keep your room tidy!
Lots of love, Mum.
PS I've enclosed something written by a parish Priest – Daniel J O'Leary.

Some months ago a friend asked me to write down a few thoughts for his teenage child. If I had a child of my own my blessing would be like this:

Allow yourself to dream, to hold onto your childhood vision and however old you are, always try to follow that vision. And every time you lose it, because in today's hard world you will often forget it, then begin again and try to make that dream come true.

Give yourself permission to make mistakes. There is no other way to grow. Forgive yourself – easily and often. There are enough people out there who will condemn you. Until you begin to accept and even love your own weakness and vulnerability you will never know the meaning of God's power and love.

Allow yourself joy. The world can be a demanding place with relentless expectations. Some people feel guilty about loving themselves, about enjoying the pleasures of life. They grow very serious. Learn to laugh at yourself. Let your inner child come out to play, to be free, to wonder, to live in the present moment.

Ricky read on. It mentioned about believing in your own ability, being proud of who you are and not wanting to be anybody else. About the pressure in life.

So be careful about the people and the messages you follow. Learn to accept the disappointments of life. It's a slow and painful lesson. Without some form of suffering, you'll never become passionate.

Let go of the mental baggage that can weigh you down. So much time is wasted in useless worry. Live in the present moment. You will never walk alone. There is nothing to fear but fear itself.

Ricky folded his arms and closed his eyes. The aircraft landed safely, screeched to a halt and then taxied to the far side of the terminal.

146

As the engines shut down the passengers were on their feet, opening the hatches and collecting their belongings. They stood motionless for what seemed an age. Ricky didn't move.

He was the last one to leave the jumbo jet. He made his way over to the conveyor belt, where he said his goodbyes to his travelling companions before squeezing through the exit doors into the arrival lounge.

RICKY GRANT

Up there in bold letters. He felt embarrassed.

'Ricky, great to see you,' said a guy wearing colourful shorts and a casual shirt. 'I'm Terry and this is my son Pat. Welcome to the States.'

'Good to see you,' said Ricky shaking hands.

Pat was tanned, with a crew cut and was the same age as Ricky. Sixteen.

'Good flight?' asked Terry picking up Ricky's bag.

'Great, thanks.'

'Right let's get you out of here. Is this everything? Any more?'

'No that's the lot.'

'Right then follow me. Let's go.'

In the back seat Ricky and Pat struck up an instant rapport. After half an hour the people carrier swung left into the driveway and a detached timber built house – painted cream – came into view. Ricky took everything in.

A blue Chrysler family saloon was parked alongside the double garage and nearby a basketball stand stood tall and erect as if on sentry duty.

The gardens stretched out on either side of the drive. A tent nestled next to a giant tree and the nets of the small-sided football goals gobbled up a variety of coloured balls.

A welcoming, bright red door opened and Terry's wife Carole came out to greet them.

'Oh to be sure he's a handsome lad.' She gave him a hug. 'Come on kids and welcome Ricky. This is Megan and this is Kieran, show Ricky his room.'

'See that Ricky,' said Terry laughing. 'I never get a word in edgeways when my wife's about.'

'We'll have none of that kind of talk. The lad will be hungry and tired so get yourself up there and settle in.'

'Thanks.'

'No, thank you for coming to visit us.'

Ricky couldn't take everything in. Their home was a mansion.

His room was something else. Three times the size of his bedroom at home. And it had everything – TV, CD player and radio, computer with stacks of video games, double bed and its own bathroom.

He couldn't get his head around all this stuff. It was like being transported in a time warp to a surreal world. He dropped his bags on the floor and walked down the long sweeping wooden stairway into the dining room.

'Everything all right Rick?' said Terry. 'Good. Well you sit next to Pat; Kieran you on the other side and Megan next to me.'

Carole served the food.

'Let's get it sorted right from the off. Is it Rick or Ricky or Ricardo? Which do you prefer?'

'Ricky.'

'Right. Ricky it is,' said Terry.

'If there's anything you don't like, leave it,' said Carole. 'Hope you'll enjoy your stay.'

Ricky awoke early. At home in England it would have been ten o'clock and his mother would have been badgering him to get up. But in Boston it was 5 a.m. and although the sun was streaming through his window the house was quiet.

He wandered around the house, still unable to believe how big it was, before returning to his room to listen to his iPod.

At last he heard movement and, going downstairs found Carole picking up the linen basket.

'Ah Ricky. Good night?' she asked.

'Woke up really early,' he replied. 'Jet lag.'

'Of course,' she said. 'You'll be hungry. Don't wait for the others. The cereals and toast are out on the table but if you want anything else I can easily rustle it up. Pancakes or omelette?'

'No, cereals are fine.'

'Well sit yourself down and I'll get you some orange juice.'

Pat arrived yawning to sit next to him. 'We're going to the beach today Ricky. It's the best around and the sea is brilliant – giant breakers. Have you done any surfing?'

Ricky laughed. Surfing down the stairs of his tenement flat when it was lashing down, was the nearest he'd come to riding the white horses.

'No, but I can swim,' – pouring milk on his cereals.

'Good to hear.'

They packed the people carrier with iceboxes, sunshades, folding chairs, blankets, beach balls, rackets, footballs, frisbees and headed off down the freeway.

'I'll drop all the stuff by the road and then park the car,' said Terry. 'Fairly quiet; looks like we're in for a great day.'

Loaded up, they shuffled across the sand.

'This area looks fine,' said Terry sweating profusely. 'What you think, mother?'

'As long as the sun shades are in place I'll be well pleased,' came the reply.

Everybody busied themselves. Ricky helped Pat with the blankets and then after stripping off wandered down to the sea front.

'Do you do this every weekend?' asked Ricky.

'Not that often. Usually we're involved in soccer tournaments.'

'Where at?' said Ricky throwing a pebble.

'Could be anywhere. But next week's matches are nearby at the Four Oaks Centre. Best pitches around. There's about a dozen, all in great nick. We played well last season but lost in the final.'

'How many teams are there?' said Ricky switching his baseball cap the American way.

'Eight, split into two groups of four. The four teams play against each other on Saturday morning and afternoon and again on Sunday morning.

'Whoever comes through will play in the final on Sunday afternoon.'

'Fancy a swim?'

'Come on.'

'That's bloody cold,' said Ricky, thrashing around in an attempt to get the blood circulating.

'Ha Ha, I bet you didn't expect that,' said Pat.

They didn't hang around for long. They went back for their towels and picked up the frisbees.

Rubbing himself down Pat shouted, 'Come on you two. Off your butts.' Kieran and Megan put down their MP3 players.

'Hey. That was my favourite Artic Monkey's track – When the Sun Goes Down,' said Megan.

'You've heard of the Artic Monkeys over here?'

'Nobody like them.'

'Brilliant, they've got an edge. Seen them live?'

'No but my dad took me to The Coors. We were somewhere at the back of this massive theatre.'

Kieran's attempts at frisbee throwing were an embarrassment; nearly decapitating an elderly man shading under a Panama hat.

'What about a game of volleyball?' suggested Pat. 'Megs, get that stick and I'll mark out the court. You guys get rid of all the stones and seaweed. Ricky, you and Kieran against me and Megs; first to ten.' There were plenty of disputed calls.

The soccer ball replaced the volleyball. The younger kids returned to their music.

'How many keepy uppies can you do?'

'Haven't counted,' replied Ricky.

'Let's have a comp then,' said a confident Pat. 'Best of three.'

'Okay, you first.'

Pat did a straight dozen. Ricky dropped it at five.

Second go – Pat 39 – Ricky 24.

'Right I'm leading. Whoever loses has to go back in the sea and do twenty-five strokes and five under water.'

'Without shorts,' added Ricky.

'You're on.'

Pat couldn't better his second attempt. Ricky took off his trainers.

'It'll be harder without sneakers,' said Pat.

When Ricky reached the one hundred mark he went through his

party pieces – held the ball on his neck, top of the foot, then on the forehead. To finish, he smashed it out to sea.

'Right Pat, go and fetch and I'll be counting those strokes,' he said smiling.

Pat ran off and dived in. Right behind him was Ricky. They started laughing, swinging their shorts above their heads.

'Right boys help yourselves,' said Carole taking charge. 'We've tuna and mayo or cheese and tomato sandwiches. Chicken legs in that box and the chips are over there. Terry, would you sort out the drinks and Patrick stick to the sodas. Where's Megan?'

A feast.

'So who do you play for, Ricky?' said Terry tucking into a tuna sandwich.

'Just school,' said Ricky handing round the potato chips.

'I understand they're big over there in developing youth schemes.'

'I haven't played many games,' said Ricky, skirting around the subject. 'Missed school a bit and the coaches haven't picked me.'

Terry was sprinkling salt onto a chicken leg when he said, 'Remember boys, the session starts at ten thirty tomorrow. On Tuesday it's five thirty in the evening but I'll give you the full lowdown when we get back. The following week we've got an ex-pro coming over from England. Simon Howarth. Have you heard of him?'

'No, who did he play for?' said Ricky opening a can.

'Played in the top division with Mexter City. Played for England as well. Qualified coach. Came over to help us last year.'

'Ricky have you had enough?' said Carole.

'Yes thanks.'

'Right then. If you feel peckish later on just help yourself. You know where everything is. Listen up you lot. Your father and me are going for a walk, so keep out of mischief. Terry get your hat on and cover that bald patch. I'll get the water bottle. See you all in a bit.'

'She fusses so much. Thinks we're kids or something,' said Pat.

'I heard that,' said Carole laughing.

The kids were lucky to have two parents who loved them. They took it for granted. They hadn't experienced anything else.

Ricky was introduced to the squad and coach Brad had 'gotten' them into pairs for a passing drill. It was only mid-morning but the sun was belting down. After the first of many water breaks Brad barked out new instructions.

'Right this time control with the right and pass with the left. Go. Strike through the ball and keep your head over the ball.'

Shooting was the next session but accuracy had deserted the youngsters.

'Listen, don't try and break the back of the net. All that power is wasted if you don't hit the target. You know where the 'keeper is so just try and hit him first before going for power. Make sure the lay-offs are good.'

Ricky's strike rate was impressive, each one being on target.

'Ricky, out you come. Right boys look at Ricky, the angle he approaches the ball, where his feet are and how nicely balanced he is. Some of you are coming from the wrong angle, sometimes too straight. Okay feed one in, Dave.'

With a short back lift, Ricky's shot skimmed over the grass but the 'keeper produced a fantastic save low down to his right side. The next one though whipped past him before he moved.

'Great Ricky. Right who's next? Chris?'

The session finished with a five-a-side, 'scrimmage'.

'Tomorrow it's a 5.30 start. Anybody who can't make it see me before you go. And a bit of advance warning guys, the tournament is at Four Oaks this weekend. Again if you're going to miss it I want to know today. If you're unsure, talk to your folks tonight and ring me at home. Remember we're in a strong group and everybody must be at their best if we're going to do well. I'll see you tomorrow. Have a good day.'

'Coach seems to know his stuff,' said Ricky, walking back to the car.

'Played for a college side and had trials for the US National team. Fancy hanging out at Andy's house this afternoon? He's got a pool and games room. Said we could come over.'

'Sounds cool.' Ricky was already picking up the lingo.

After lunch Ricky watched a replay of the weekend baseball games. He said to Pat, 'Goes on forever, doesn't it? Ever been to a game?'

'I haven't, but dad goes a lot. Kieran, are you coming with us? We're going to Andy's for a swim? What about you Megs?'

'No Kate's coming round this afternoon and Kieran doesn't want to.'

'Okay we'll see you later.'

For the weekend tournament Terry told the boys to be ready to leave at 8.30. 'We have to report at Four Oaks for 9.30 so I expect you guys out of your pits and bags packed, ready for the off.'

Military operation.

'Mum, where's my socks?' cried Pat.

'Where they usually are.'

'Not my blue ones, the green and white striped ones.'

'Keep looking.'

'Found them,' said Pat. 'Ricky you got everything?'

'Trainers stink. I should have left them out by the back door last night. Think anyone will notice?'

'You're not joking. They miff. Here, I've got some spray. Give them the once over otherwise they won't let you near the place. "Ricky the tricky" has now gone to "Ricky the stinky."'

'Hey, at least I don't fart in the changing room.'

'No way. That wasn't me!'

'SBD. Funny how everybody fled through the door except you,' said Ricky stuffing his towel into his bag.

'What?' said Pat, innocently.

'Are you two ready? Down now,' shouted Terry. 'Or we'll be late for the first game.'

'Coming. Why do they get so stressed?' said Pat.

'Tell me about it.'

The opener for Ricky and Pat was against Leamington Juniors, and it turned out to be a comfortable 5-0 win. Ricky scored the third goal and was replaced ten minutes from the end, when the score was

4-0. Pat was very steady at the heart of the defence. Not much got past him.

'Nice one Pat,' said Ricky after the game.

'Good game. We did well, but it's going to get harder.'

'Right guys, I was pleased with the way you went about your jobs, although we did get a bit casual when the game was won,' said Brad handing round the water bottles.

'Our passing started to get a little sloppy so remember to concentrate throughout the game; see it through to the end. But generally well done.

'Get changed and we'll meet back at field number eleven at two o'clock. The kick-off against Scorson is at three.'

'Ricky, do you fancy watching some of the other games,' said Pat.

'Sounds good.'

'Dad, we're going to do a bit of spying. We'll catch you later.'

'Don't forget the next game is on field eleven.'

The week had passed quickly and Ricky had bonded closely with his Irish friend.

'When did you first come over to the States?' said Ricky.

'When I was five. Dad was working in Ireland for this big company but got the chance to move over here. Better prospects. He said things were tailing off back home so we all moved.'

'Was it tough for you?' said Ricky as they sat on the touchline.

'Early on. Megan was only a baby and Kieran hadn't been born. I didn't really know what was happening being so young.'

'That was a great goal!' shouted Ricky. 'See that number ten – he's got a lot of ability. If we play them in the final we'll have to keep an eye on him. Do you see the games from England on the box?'

'The highlights are on every weekend. Do you play tournaments back in the UK?'

'No.'

'You're not being picked up 'cos of your smelly feet.'

'Hey, what smellies? You can talk.'

The afternoon fixture was a tight affair with Green Isles coming out on top 2-1. The free flowing football of the previous game was missing with plenty of mistakes from both sides.

'Right guys listen up,' said Brad. 'If we get a draw tomorrow morning against Fradling then we're in the final. So no messing about tonight. Get yourself something to eat, stay in and rest. Same kick-off tomorrow morning, 10.30, so report usual time. I take it everybody is feeling good, no injuries? Good. Well done and I'll see you tomorrow.'

In the back of the truck the boys switched on the Playstation. Ricky got a 1600 score and Pat took over.

'No way. Like that monkey has just leapt off the bridge. How did that happen?'

'Pressed the wrong button, you divvy.'

'Pizzas tonight boys,' said Carole interrupting. 'I'll drop you two off at Leo's Pizzeria. We've got to pick up Megan so we'll see you back home. Pat have you got your key?'

'Yes, mum.'

'Get your dad and me a vegetarian medium sized and some French fries. Kieran what do you want?'

'Margarita.'

'That's a small margarita for Kieran and get Megan the same. No – get one medium between them. Here's thirty bucks. We'll see you at home.'

'Hey Pat ow you doin' ma frienda? You playa soccer today? How you go on?' Luigi at the pizza place was obviously pleased to see the boys.

'Won both games. We play again tomorrow.'

'Good for you. And this your frienda?'

'Yes this is Ricky. He's from England.'

'England. Man United, Liverpool, Arsenal. But listen to me Ricky. My club is Milano. Here's team photo; that bootiful side that won European Cup in 1994 against Barcelona. Magnifico. What can I get you guys?'

During the ten-minute walk back from the takeaway, the boys passed some fabulous houses.

Beautifully manicured lawns with exotic flowering borders. Neighbours lounging by the pool, the smell of barbequed chicken filling the air.

'Funny age this, isn't it Pat?' said Ricky nicking a chip.

'What'd you mean?'

'Well we're in between. We're not kids anymore but we're not grown up.'

'Yeah. You know what, I looked at a photo and I had this sweater on which I thought was ace. But it's the pits. What did I ever see in it?'

'What about spots on the boat race?' said Ricky.

'Boat race?'

'Face. Cockney rhyming,' explained Ricky.

'Where'd you get that from?'

'There was a kid at our school. Came from London. That's how he'd talk all day.'

'Give us another,' said Pat.

'These spots on the face. Splattered 'em all over. Mum went Radio Rental.'

'Radio Rental? What's that, for feck's sake?'

'Mental.'

'Radio rental–mental? No way. Give me a sentence and I'll try to work it out.'

'Not easy putting 'em together. They're just words. What's dustbins?'

'Dustbins? Err – Tins? Sins? Gins?' suggested Pat.

'No. You're pony and trap.'

'Crap?' said Pat, obviously pleased with himself.

'Yeah.'

'So what's dustbins?'

'I should have said dustbin lids.'

'Dustbin lids? Bids? Sids?'

'Sids?' said Ricky laughing. 'I'll give you a clue. What we are.'

'What we are? The business,' said Pat clutching at straws.

'Come on you've got to get that.'

'Dustbin lids? KIDS.'

'Yeah, cool.'

'Give us another.'

'After the games today I'm cream crackered.'

'Knackered.'

'Correct. Did you drop an apple tart in the car today?'

'Fart.'

'Yeah.'

'And no, I didn't. It must have been your feet.'

'No way. Another one. That number five today, had an Aunty Nelly.'

'Belly.'

'Right on. I went into your room this morning and the pen and ink was unbelievable'

'Stink.'

'It was so bad I thought someone was brown bread.'

'Dead.'

'Over here in the States we can't go to the battle cruiser until we're twenty one.'

'Battle cruiser? Loser?'

'No – pubs in England.'

'Pubs don't rhyme with battle cruiser,' said a puzzled Pat.

'Another word for pubs. Give up?'

'Yeah.'

'Boozer.'

'Boozer? I'd never have got that.'

'What about Brahms and Liszt?'

'Pissed. Even I know that.'

'You'll never get this. It's getting a little George and Zippy.'

'No idea.'

'Kids' TV programme in England – nippy.'

Pat opened the front door and whispered, 'Ricky you take 'em in. I need a Donald Trump!'

'Ricky, I want you to start at left wing back today. We're going to change the formation to a 3-5-2 so that means Chris, Pat and Ed will be the three at the back and Brian will be on the right.

'Try and pick up your game quickly today. Yesterday in the second game, we couldn't string two passes together. Remember, plenty of movement and if you need that extra touch take it. Right, get warmed up and good luck.'

The teams cancelled each other out in the first thirty-five minutes. Nil-nil at halftime, but after the interval Green Isles stepped up the pace. Pat fed Ricky on the left flank; he played a one-two and scampered down the touchline before delivering a perfect cross to where Brian arrived at the far post. A simple nod of the head was all that was required. A perfectly executed goal.

'Go! Go! Go! Greens! Go! Go! Go!' came the chant from the sidelines.

The one was enough. A place awaited them in the final.

Hollers and cheers and lots of high fives.

'Magic guys, you deserved that win. Tight, but I thought you just about edged it. And what a goal! A great team effort. Just before you disappear, we play Parish in the final. The kick-off is 2.30. It's going to be a scorcher so try to keep in the shade.'

'Well done boys,' said Terry as the lads came over.

'Great game,' added Carole. 'How you feeling?'

'Not bad but I tired towards the end,' said Pat.

'Well that's three games in two days and there's another one to come. Ricky how are you?'

Ricky was looking a little groggy. He was shaking. The medics were called over.

'Looks like he might have gotten a bit of sunstroke,' said Carole concerned.

'Is he going to be okay for this afternoon?'

'Only time will tell,' said the medic. 'If we get his temperature down it's still going to be touch and go. What time's the kick-off?'

'Two thirty.'

'We'll keep our fingers crossed.'

Ricky wasn't one hundred per cent so he started on the bench. They took the lead but Parish equalised within minutes. At the break it was anybody's game.

Both teams had periods where they could have won but chances were spurned and fatigue was beginning to set in. Who had the strength to see it through?

Brad made numerous changes in an attempt to revitalise the team but in the final minutes when Sam went down with cramp, there was only one option. He signalled Ricky to get ready.

'Can you see it through Ricky for the final ten minutes? If it's a draw it goes to penalties.'

'Yeah I'm okay.'

'Good on you Ricky. Play at left back. Don't venture too far forward. Keep it tight.'

He felt awful. His legs were like lead weights. The sun was blazing down. Green Isles lost possession and a dangerous situation was developing down their right flank. Ricky moved into a covering position alongside Pat as the ball was floated over to the far stick.

Goalkeeper Nick shouted, but in that split second Ricky decided to head clear. They clattered into each other, and the ball dropped invitingly at the Parish striker's feet. It was impossible to miss.

The ref blew the final whistle straight after the restart. The boys sunk to their knees.

Ricky fainted. He woke up with water being splashed on his face.

'Ricky, your mum's on the 'phone,' shouted Carole.

'Hi mum, how are you?' Ricky stretched out on the bed.

'Fine love. How are things going?'

'Great, apart from dropping a ricket last week-end.'

'What was the problem?'

'We got to the final of this tournament but I felt a bit rough. We'd already played in the morning and the temperature was boiling. They reckon I got a bit of sunstroke. I got in the way of our 'keeper and we lost the game. I fainted.'

'Are you all right now?'

'No problem. Next day I was fine.'

'So you've settled in with the family?'

'They're magic. Pat is my age and we get on great, play in the same team and do things together. They have a fabulous house. You know what mum, I've got my own bathroom. Yeah shower, bath the lot.'

'Sounds nice.'

'Terry, that's Pat's dad, let me cut the grass yesterday. They have one of those machines you sit on; drive up and down. How's things with you?'

'Got a call about Ronnie last week. They don't think he's going to make it.'

26

Jake returned home from training, switched on his computer and opened his emails. There was one from Marie.

Hi Jake or should I say 'Peg'?
How you doing? Everything is going well with the old travelling.
Helen's friend Anna picked us up at the airport in LA. We had
a great night at the local Irish bar before we headed off to Costa
Rica. I tried to speak Spanish (could have done with Bully)
– ended up asking the hotel receptionist if they had a 'taxi
reservation system'. She had no idea what I was on about!
Peru is brilliant. We flew to Lima first of all and have since
been on a couple of long bus journeys, which were surprisingly
good, and we are now in place called Arqueipa. We have booked
onto the Inca Trail. Helen saw a bloke in a Burding top – turns
out he's the chairman of the Norwegian branch of the Burding
Town supporters' club! I couldn't believe it either! Guess who he
thinks is going to be the next superstar? Lots of love Marie.

Jake tapped on his keypad.

Nice to know I've got one fan! Most of them disappear and jet
off around the world! Not mentioning any names, of course!
'Things are going well over here. We played a few pre-season
matches and I've been involved in all of them. I'm feeling
strong and fit but don't worry. I've got my feet on the deck. I
don't want another broken leg and be out for 4 months! So I'm
looking out for dodgy pavements and quickening up in any
50/50's involving 'Scotty' (Craig Hennessey). He's a nutter
– one hundred per center in training, goes right through with
the tackles. He'd kick his own grandmother.
We start the season with an away fixture at Bolton. It'll be
tough but if we get something we'll be on our way.

Mum's been feeling a bit iffy last few days so I did the supermarket run. Went early – 6.30 am. Nice and quiet. I wore a baseball cap. Well you don't want some fan asking what the gaffer has for breakfast, do you? I looked like a young kid with 'attitude'. All I need now is an asbo. They are the best things around for street cred! Anyone without one is minging! It's also good at that time, 'cos you don't get whacked up the backside by too many blue rinses pushing their trolleys!
Look after yourself. Missing you. Love Jake.

27

'Right lads, I'm Simon Howarth.' The ex-international introduced himself on the Monday morning. 'I'll be taking a few sessions and all I ask from you guys is that you listen and do your best. I'm here to try to improve you. We'll have fun, I promise you that, but no messing about. Right, on your feet and follow me. Last one on somebody's back.

'What's your name? Josh? Right Josh give me five knee jumps and don't be last next time. I'm looking for the last one... wait for it... sitting down... Last group of... threes. You guys ten press-ups. Get yourselves in... twos. What's your name? Nick? Give me ten squat thrusts.

'How you feeling?' said Pat grabbing hold of Ricky.

'Thighs are a bit tight,' – hands on hips, ready for the next stretch.

Tying up his laces, Pat said, 'Could have done with an extra hour in bed.'

'That's you all over. You like your pit, don't you?'

'Hey, don't you talk. You were zonked by nine o'clock last night. Missed most of that movie.'

'Right get in lines and jog around the field. Side to side, twists and turns. Hey, bit of balance at the back. Last two from the back, in and out of the lines. Go.

'Wait for it next two – go. Jogging for the rest of you. When I blow the whistle change direction. Hey Dozey, get your brain into gear. Keep jogging... this time we're doing opposites so when I shout "heads" you touch the ground and when I shout "tails" you head it. Got it? Heads ... . Got out of bed the wrong side today, did we? Or in your case, Jed, didn't get into bed at all? Okay stop and rest.

'Next exercise, take a nice long stride, both feet on the deck and ease forward. Feel your calf muscles – and again. Don't overstretch but hold for ten and relax. Okay fellas, pay attention. You two, what's your names?'

'Pat.'

'Ricky.'

'Okay guys, out you come. This session is all about passing and movement in this ten-metre square. Pat you stand at that corner and Ricky at that one. With this exercise you can only pass the ball along the outside of the square. The three of us are playing together and it's two touches max. So, Pat, if the ball is with you, who can you pass it to from that position?'

'Ricky.'

'Right. Because I'm diagonally opposite, you can't pass the ball inside the square. So at the moment I'm not involved. What do I need to do to help you?'

'Get along the line.'

'Correct,' said Simon. 'By moving, I make myself available for a pass. So now Pat has an option. He can either pass the ball to me or to Ricky. In other words he has options. Okay Pat, pass the ball to me. Right guys what options have I got?'

'You can pass it back to Pat.'

'That's right, so what does Ricky need to do?'

'Make the run.'

'Good. It's about helping the man on the ball. What's the best position for me to be in to receive a pass? Right let it flow. Good pass; don't forget to call a name and demand the ball. Pass down the sides.

'Well done, good touch Ricky, pass it, good. Pat move. Okay hold it there. Just before the rest of you get involved, let's remind ourselves of the important things when doing this drill.'

'Shouting for the ball,' called out Jed.

'That's right. Good communication. What else?'

'Accurate passing.'

'Good. Anything else?' said Simon, picking up the bibs.

'First touch.'

'Spot on. Don't allow the ball to bounce off. And remember, timing is very important,' said Simon, walking away from the corner of the square. 'If I leave my post too early what problems will that cause?'

'Ricky may want to pass to you but you've already gone,' Jed said.

'That's right. Okay guys, get yourself in threes and make your way over to the squares. Don't begin until I blow the whistle.'

At the end of the session Simon told the boys to sit down. 'You've worked hard fellas. Get your water bottles and have a drink. Did anyone see the game last night on TV? What about that second goal?'

'Top corner but it did get a slight deflection which put the 'keeper off,' said Tod.

'There were some decent players on view. What qualities are needed to reach the very top level?'

'Skill, right attitude,' said Matt.

'You've got to be an athlete these days,' Pat said.

'That's true. In my day we could have a breather but now the game's so quick.'

'Confidence.'

'Right. Belief in what you're doing. You've mentioned a few there but there are others and, of course, you need luck.'

'You need to be competitive as well coach. Aggressive. Everybody wants to win.'

'But it's got to be controlled, that's something we all have to learn.'

'Even you?'

'Yeah, of course. Early in my career if I felt hard done by I'd take out the frustration by kicking somebody. But you learn from experience.'

'What's the best way of handling it then?' jumped in Pat.

'Take time out as you guys say,' said Simon. 'Count to ten; don't do anything stupid because if you get yourself sent off, it ain't good for the team is it? And don't do what one of my teammates used to do.'

'What's that?'

'We had a player called Andy Rock who'd say, "Leave it to me, son". The ball would be at the other end of the pitch and there'd be a player laid out fifty yards away from the action. Andy had his hands on his hips in a kind of "who me?" pose. He'd nailed him.'

'And got away with it?'

'More often than not, because everybody would be following the ball. These days cameras pick up every incident… Right lads, on your feet. I'll see you all tomorrow. Matt, you take the warm-down.'

'Sure coach.'

'Anyone got a spare bottle?' asked Simon.

Ricky handed his over. 'Thanks, son… You looked good today.'

'I enjoyed it.'

'And you can look after yourself. Your tackling was spot on. Lots of players are good when they're in possession but switch off when they have to defend. I know 'cos I was one of them.'

'That part has always been easy for me.'

'I tell you what Ricky, you've got some ability,' said Simon. 'Pace, great left peg, dribbling skills. I can't understand for the life of me why you haven't been picked up back home.'

'I've had a few problems,' said Ricky, lowering his voice.

'Anything I can help with?' Simon said, having another drink. 'Sorry, don't want to nosey into your private life.'

'Most of the worst stuff is over.'

'There's been a few things?'

'You could say that. There's lots of aggro where we live.'

'Not a safe place?'

'I'm dealing with it.'

'But it's put pressure on you?'

'Yeah, I got involved,' said Ricky glancing around. 'Took some stuff. With all that was going on in my life I couldn't cope. Felt really low and my life was a mess. It seemed like an easy way out. Just get away from all the crap that was going on.'

'But it's better now?'

'Back at school I felt like a right balloon. But one of the teachers has been mega. He's helped me through and got me on this trip.'

'Taught you a lesson?'

'Too right. No way do I want to go through that again.'

At the end of the Friday session the guys were gathering in the balls, cones and bibs when Simon caught up with Ricky on the far side of the field.

'How's it going?' said Simon. 'Enjoyed it?'

'Cool.'

'Ricky I've been thinking. What if I tried to get you a trial?'

'Too late, isn't it?'

'Never too late for talented players. I can vouch for that,' said Simon.

'But you played for Mexter. I know they're in the Championship now but then they were a top club. And England.'

'Yeah, but I was given the boot from my first club Winton United,' explained Simon.

'No way.'

'It's true. I was absolutely gutted.'

'How long had you been with them?'

'I joined as a kid at twelve but then at sixteen I was released. They didn't even tell me to my face. I got a letter through the post. I was ready to pack it in but my dad talked me round. He believed in me, said I deserved another chance, so he started ringing round a few clubs to get me a trial.'

'City?'

'They had a great reputation for bringing on kids and I wasn't going to let the opportunity pass me by. Made me realise what I had to do. After the trial they offered me an apprenticeship. The wages were small but I would have played for nothing. They believed in me and I wasn't going to let them down. You've got a lot of potential. It would be sad if you weren't given a chance to prove yourself.'

'You think so?' said Ricky, unused to compliments.

'Absolutely. Listen don't get carried away. I just feel you've the ability to take that first step. Then it's up to you.'

Ricky picked up the last cone and red bib and he and Simon made their way back to the car park.

'Leave me your number and I'll be in touch. I'm not promising anything but I'll do my best.'

28

12 August
Hi good looking
Good to hear you're doing your bit for your mum. Tell her I was asking about her and send my love to all the family. Hope she's a lot better now. Chile was a bit chilly so we are now in Bolivia. We met a nice English couple on our last night in Peru and somehow ended up in a Peruvian karaoke bar until 4 am. I must have been drunk as I was singing, 'Killing me softly' while swaying with 6 Germans, 4 Peruvians and a man called Les-os. Helen did a fine rendition of 'Say a little prayer' and if all else fails we can make a living singing in tube stations. We then went to Northern Chile and visited the National Park. It was amazing – loads of lakes, volcanoes, and wildlife. We took hundreds of pictures of flowering cactuses or is it cacti? We are now in the capital of Bolivia – La Paz which is a fantastic city. When we arrived we were a bit scared, as there are thousands of people, street markets everywhere and mental taxi and bus drivers hooting the whole time! But it is a very laidback city and there's no stress whatsoever.

Yesterday we did a very stupid thing – we signed up for a mountain bike ride down the world's most dangerous road. 76 kms down a dirt track alongside a very steep mountain cliff, with no barriers! Everyone went bombing down but we decided to be like Lou and Andy from Little Britain and take it nice and easy. We wanted to live! Glad we did 'cos the food and drink afterwards was the best ever.

We watched a match on TV. Violent or what? 4 sendings off! And that was only in the first half. Today we are going to watch a live game in La Paz. The kick-off could be any time 1, 2 or 3 o'clock – nobody is really sure! A bit different from back home. Keep at it. Hope things are going well. Miss you. Lots of Love Marie

29

'Ricky? It's Simon. Simon Haworth.'

'Hi!'

'No problems coming back?' asked Simon.

'An hour delay at Boston but the flight was cool.'

'No terrorists on board?'

'Just a little old lady who was going mental.'

'Couldn't find her false teeth eh?'

'She wanted to smoke a pipe. Would you believe it?'

'You always get one. Listen up, 'cos I've got some good news. I've been in touch with Mexter City and they'd like to have a look at you.'

'That's magic.'

'Fitness wise, you won't have missed out too much. They're just back in training.'

'I feel good.'

'I'll tell them you're home. It'll mean staying in digs but that won't be a problem, will it?'

'No way.'

'Right leave it with me. Either Bernie Bradshaw or Bryan Lewis will be in touch. Give me ring when everything's set up.'

'Sure.'

It was Bernie who rang and offered Ricky a two-week trial. Brief and to the point.

Ruth and Ricky sat together on the battered old settee. 'You deserve this chance son. But if it doesn't go right then it's not meant to be. Something else will come along.'

'I'm in good shape mum. Going to the States has helped me and I feel confident. I can't explain it anymore than that but getting away was just what I needed. I know I nearly screwed up big style but I've changed. I feel different. I'm going to give it my best shot.'

'Good for you love. You've had a lot to deal with and maybe it came at just the right time .'

'Oh, I've just remembered, I'd better give Simon a ring.'

He jumped up and dialled the number. 'Simes, I'm going tomorrow. They want me for two weeks.'

'Cleaned your boots?'

'Polished!'

'Feeling nervous?'

'A bit. When he told me, I couldn't believe it.'

'Just enjoy it. Do your best. Get the basics right and everything will fall into place.'

'Don't they want to see something special?' asked Ricky.

'All they're looking for early on is to see if you can handle the ball, that you're a decent athlete and you've plenty of enthusiasm. That's all.'

'Thanks for what you've done.'

'No problem. When you play your first international match, I'll be after a ticket.'

'You've got it.'

'Give me a ring if you want to talk, otherwise I won't bother you. You'll have too much on your plate for the next few days.'

'I'll keep in touch.'

'Enjoy it and remember.'

'What?'

'Smile.'

Ricky sat on a bench at the railway station on a beautiful English summer's day. All was peaceful and quiet – a far cry from the blood and guts of the professional game.

The stillness was broken by a group of screaming schoolgirls running onto the platform, looking expectantly for the incoming train. A sharp blast signalled its arrival.

Ricky opened the door to the last carriage. He picked a middle seat, unzipped the holdall and got out his iPod. He adjusted the volume and settled back for the two-hour journey.

He got out his football magazine and browsed through the fixtures for the coming season. Mexter were in the Championship, having been relegated from the top division four seasons ago and, according to the predictions, were unlikely to regain their previous status this time around.

He read an article about top international player, Mickey Poulster, who had wrecked his career through drink and gambling addictions. Poulster had lost his wife and family, was ruined financially and had even thought about taking his own life. He had sunk that low.

Ricky took it all in. Here was a guy who had everything going for him – talent, recognition, idolised by millions but was now spiralling to a bottomless pit. Ricky ripped out the page, folded it and stuffed it in his pocket.

At Mexter station, Eric Jenkins was there to meet him. In a previous life Eric had been a player, coach and trainer and was even now, way past retirement age, still very much involved with the football club.

'What would I do if I packed it in lad? Rot that's what. I love it. Keeps me young and the gaffer's great. Lets me run around in his Merc. Should have picked you up in the mini-bus today but it's in dock – needs a new exhaust – so that's why you've got the special treatment. Don't get used to this son, it's a one off. Where are you from anyway?'

'Place called Crixton – near Nottingham,' said Ricky fastening his seat belt.

'Hope you do well,' said Eric, messing about with the air conditioning. 'What position do you play?'

'Left midfield.'

'Left footer eh? Not many of them about. Good ones that is. Have you been to the stadium before?'

'No,' said Ricky, watching a motorcyclist giving Eric a two fingered salute.

'It's showing its age,' said Eric, oblivious to the gesture. 'We're looking to move but the local council knocked it back. Typical isn't it? You'd have thought they would have been well pleased with the chance of bringing more people to the area.'

Eric rabbitted on about the old days; how things were when he was a player.

'Don't get me going son. They don't know they're born these

170

days. Bloody millionaires. I ask you. We had to go down t'pit during week and then play on a Sat'day in bleeding steel toe cap boots.'

He took a sharp left.

'Here we are. Didn't take long, lad, did it? Get your bag and I'll take you in.'

Ricky followed Eric through the front doors of the stadium and was seated in the reception area.

'Ricky? I'm Bernie. I'm the youth scout. I spoke to you on the 'phone. Come on through.'

In his office Ricky was introduced to youth coach Bryan Lewis.

'You met Simon in the States, didn't you?"

'Yes.'

'He was impressed by what he saw out there,' said Lewis. 'We'd like to have a good look at you and then we'll see what happens. We won't mess you about. Once we've made a decision we'll let you know straightaway. First thing is, let's get you settled.

'You're staying with a lovely couple Mary and Fred Bullard who are big City supporters. Billy Pointer is also there. He's a second-year scholar and he's done well so maybe there's something in the grub they serve up. Give us your train ticket and we'll get your expenses sorted out. Come on, let's go.'

Ricky and Billy reported to the training ground at 9am the following day and met up with the other junior players. The first team stars didn't show for another hour but their kit, boots and other bits and pieces had to be ready.

'Stay with me, pal,' said Billy. 'You'll soon get the hang of it. Most trialists sit around in the dressing room until it's time to get out but it's better if you do a few things to help pass the time.'

'What do you want me to do?'

'We've got to get the training kit laid out for six first team players – numbered fourteen to nineteen. If anything goes missing they get a real strop on.

'They all have their little quirks. For instance, Mickey, who's got dodgy ankles, always wants ankle protectors even in training. Got to be washed every day.

171

'A manufacturer sponsors him. You've probably seen him on TV spouting on about how good they are.

'Last season he missed twelve games, all with ankle injuries. Can't be that bloody good can they? Boots are another thing. You never know what footwear they want, so we put them all out – trainers, moulded rubbers, studs. They can't moan then, can they?'

'Have I to do the boots then? Where are they?'

'Along the corridor. First right. Pegged up in numbers.'

Ricky found his way to the boot room. The other lads were scurrying around collecting footwear.

'Need any help?' asked one of the boys. 'Billy's got you doing his donkey work, has he? They're on that wall. You've got Phil Speak in your bunch. He's great. Top player and treats the lads great. Different class. But some of the others are selfish gits. Do their own grandmothers.'

Ricky collected numbers fourteen and fifteen and took them back to Billy. 'That's fine. Put them under their strips, in a line. Good, now get the rest.'

Pristine kit, laid out immaculately. The smell of fabric conditioner filled the room. The equipment was next. The footballs had to be cleaned and tested for correct air pressure, the bibs, cones and water bottles sorted out for each group.

The youngsters then went into their own dressing room.

'There's two sessions today,' moaned Billy. 'So straight after we've finished we've got to get the second batch out for this afternoon. We're supposed to be future football stars; more like bleeding laundry women.'

Ricky was handed his kit. Blue shirt, white shorts, slip, blue socks and track suit top.

'Don't even think about putting on the top. Lewy'll go spare.'

Ricky looked like a proper player. Like the rest, part of the club. He didn't look out of place.

A blast of the whistle and the lads made their way outside.

Bright sunshine, mowed pitches, players' banter – it reminded him of his time in the States.

The first team squad grouped together on the far field where the surface looked magnificent. The manager, his assistant, fitness trainer and physio all stood and watched as the coach took the first warm-up session.

The juniors knocked the balls about on an adjacent pitch before Bryan Lewis shouted. 'Right lads, in you come.'

The goalkeeper was a lad called Oswald John. He was last to make his way over.

'Down you go Ossie, son. Ten press-ups and make sure you're tuned in for the rest of the session. First of all, let me introduce the new lad here. You'll get to know the lads pretty quickly Ricky but just a word of warning, watch out for this one, he's a right piss-taker.'

'Piss-taker, me coach? No way.'

Lewis gave him a clip around the head.

'Can't do that coach,' said Ossie. 'I'll sue.'

'Sue? I'll tell you what Ossie; if you play crap this season I'll sue you for impersonating a professional footballer. Get my drift?'

'Steady. You know the doc told you not to get too excited,' said Ossie backing off. 'At your age.'

At the end of the session Ricky was peeling off his sweaty top when Billy pointed out that the pros room had to be cleaned and the kit changed, before they got showered.

Jobs done they drifted over to the canteen for lunch. Self-service. Salads with cold meats, orange juice and water.

Ricky's body was glowing, his face had caught the sun and he was buzzing.

Come 4.30pm they'd cleaned the dressing rooms, washed two lots of kit and made sure that everything was ready for morning.

They got back to the digs and were met by Fred.

'How's it gone boys? You look shattered, Ricky.'

'Didn't realise how tough it would be. Thought it would just be playing the game.'

'Mary is making tea and it'll be ready soon. Why don't you two go in the living room and watch a bit of TV?'

'Good shout.'

They settled in the armchairs. Within minutes both were asleep.

Ricky was due to play his first game on the Friday, four days into the trial. He'd fitted in well and was used to the set up. But he was under pressure: if he didn't impress by next weekend he'd be out on his arse. Nobody would give two figs. Some other kid would be in his place and Ricky would be yesterday's news.

On the Thursday night he rang Simon.

'I'm playing tomorrow,' Ricky told him.

'Looking forward to it?'

'Yeah. I'm on from the kick-off but I don't know where. The lad who usually plays centre mid picked up a knock this morning so I might play there. Otherwise I'll be out on the left flank.'

'Will that bother you?' asked Simon.

'Not really,' said Ricky, sounding confident. 'I've played both in the last few days and I've felt okay.'

'How you going to approach it?'

'Get on the ball and do something positive.'

'Like what?' asked Simon.

'Beat a man. Get some crosses in.'

'And if you play centre mid?'

'Keep things ticking over and don't give the ball away.'

'That's it,' said Simon. 'And show them you're prepared to get hurt. Don't whack players but be aggressive. Don't be bullied.'

'Anything else?'

'Shoot – just let fly. Get it out of your feet and welly it. Anything within shooting range, twenty yards out. Have confidence and remember that smile. Shows you're enjoying it.'

'Thanks Simes. I probably won't sleep tonight.'

'That's okay. You're ready. Adrenalin will be pumping tomorrow. For what it's worth, I think you'll do great.'

30

Hi Marie.
Sounds like you're really behaving yourselves!! Clubbing till 4am? And who are all these Germans? And the guy called Les-os? It's not a woman is it and the b is missing? As you see 'I'm just a jealous guy' as Lennon would say. Well, it's not easy knowing that your top bird is doing adrenalin bike rides down mountainsides and knocking back Peruvian cocktails, is it? It conjures up all kinds of things. I know you've only been away for a month but I miss you like mad. I'll tell you one thing. I'm really fired up in training. I get rid of all this aggression by steaming into everybody. The coach has had a word. I just nodded. But tomorrow I'll do exactly the same. Everybody sends their love especially me. Pegleg

Jake.
Sorry about that. It must have sounded like we were on the pull but it couldn't have further from the truth. It was just a load of mates. Let me tell you about Les-os. He was a 66-year-old guy with a stubbly beard, who smoked the foulest ciggies you've ever come across. He was sat in the corner on his own and we dragged him up in front of the mike. He didn't know what was happening, couldn't speak a word of English but when we did 'My Way', he hummed along. Anyway we are now back in the Lake District in Chile, which is very much like our own, except there are lots of stray dogs. Completely harmless but too many of them. We started off with only one mutt following us but by the end of the walk there were ten! A guy was shouting at us to get them on leads. We wanted to scream at him and tell him they weren't ours! We are now sat in a café and they're sitting outside, so we'll have to either order a few more pork chops or sneak out the back door! We've done so much walking our feet are killing us. We'll have to get some cream. Love from Marie

Hey! Acquired a few 4-legged friends have you? Well they sell a mean pooper-scooper at the local pet shop. Have I to send one over? Longer you stay in the Chile and Bolivia regions and all points west, they could end up in the slow cooker! Just add a few veg and spices and walla-Boxer Bourguignon! Watch out 'cos all the locals will want a leg!

I suppose you've seen we've had a great start to the season. Picked up 10 points from 5 games which means were well placed. 5th in the League. Nosebleed time. Everybody is enjoying it and last week when Marco scored a hat-trick the atmosphere was fantastic.

Well done Jakey. Keep it going. We pick up the results regularly and when we saw that Burding was near the top we jumped for joy. Everybody around us thought we were a little crazy – hopping around like schoolgirls.

Since we left the dogs behind we have travelled 6 hours on a bus, got a ferry for 4 days, walked 8 hours in another park, got 3 more buses and are now in Ushuaia in Argentina which is apparently the southernmost city in the world.

The only problem here in Argentina is the food. It's too good! In Chile most meals had chips and rice, were a bit cold and heavily featured Alpaca (a type of Llama), which was a bit chewy, and not my cup of tea.

Here in Argentina, Helen ordered the set menu. Sounded good. Anyway we were given one piece of chicken, which tasted nice but there was not much of it. The waiter then whisked the plates away and served us with big pieces of steak, lamb, sausages, pork and black puddings! We asked for doggy bags. Could have fed all our old friends in Chile ten times over! Have we got time to nip back? Maybe not! Lots of love and kisses and keep up the good work. Marie

Hi Marie. With all that grub inside there's no way you'll be able to do the Inca Trail! Talking about food, I've just read an autobiography about a footie player who was caught up in a betting scam. He was sent down and his wife visited him in prison. He looked so thin she decided to cook him a steak and take it with her on the next visit. To keep it warm she rolled it up and put it inside a thermos flask! Problem was, when she got there she couldn't get the damn thing out! The guy is so hungry it's untrue and there she is poking about but it wouldn't come out! They didn't know whether to laugh or cry.

31

'Boss, have you got a minute?'

Bryan Lewis nabbed manager Tim Ward at the end of the training session as he was about to go into his office. 'Hold on Bri.' Ward, tall and slim with receding hair, picked up his messages from his secretary and asked her to sort out a round of sandwiches and a pot of tea.

'What do you fancy?'

'Anything apart from beef. If they've cheese and ham, that'll do. Come in Bryan.'

Ward's ambitions, after a fairly modest playing career, had always been on the coaching side – that part of the game excited the 41-year-old – and his thirst for knowledge had seen him advance rapidly through the coaching levels.

It was his innovative ideas, successful in the lower divisions, which gave him his first managerial position at Mexter City. The directors were hopeful that the appointment would revive City's fortunes and see the club back in the Premier League.

Ward was very much 'hands on' and respected by the players. He told them what was expected and treated them like adults. It wasn't his style to berate them in the heated atmosphere of the dressing room straight after a highly charged ninety minutes, much preferring to analyse the game thoroughly before speaking to individuals on a one to one basis.

It was an approach that was clearly working. The players were responding and steady progress was being made.

He took off his boots, put on his trainers and sat behind his desk. The 'phone was ringing but he diverted it to voicemail. His mobile went and he was about to do the same when he saw it was from his wife.

'Hi love. How are you?' They had a dinner appointment that night. 'I'll be there.' He turned it off. 'Sit down, Bryan.'

'Can I bring in Bernie? He's waiting outside.'

'Yeah, course.'

Bradshaw and Lewis removed coaching manuals from the chairs and sat down in the cramped office.

'Right lads, what's the problem?'

'No problem Tim. In fact, just the opposite,' said Lewis smiling.

'That's the type of news I want to hear.'

'It's about a trialist we brought in this week. He's been recommended by Simon Howarth who did some coaching in the States this summer.'

'An American?'

'No, no. He's from the Midlands,' said Bradshaw. 'He was over there on a soccer course.'

'What's his name?'

'Ricky Grant,' said Lewis. 'He's been with us a few days and played in a game today.'

'And this lad was unbelievable,' said Bradshaw.

'He showed some fantastic ability,' added Lewis. 'Head and shoulders above anything else on the pitch.'

'That good?' said a rather dubious manager.

'You'd better believe it, Tim. It was a pleasure to watch him,' said an excited Bradshaw. 'Every time he got the ball there was a buzz. You knew he was going to do something special. Real class.'

'Where does he play?'

'Started in centre mid. He's left-footed and he goes past people like they're not there. He's got balance, pace. The lot.'

'Big lad?'

'Not really,' said Lewis. 'Around five foot nine but strong upper body, low centre of gravity. Physically, very mature for his age.'

'How old is he?'

'Sixteen.'

'Just left school then? And he hasn't been anywhere else?' questioned Ward.

'Not that we're aware of,' said Bradshaw.

'Sounds a bit dodgy, doesn't it?' said Ward with a hint of cynicism. 'The fact that he hasn't been picked up before? A kid with all that ability?'

179

'I know what you're saying, boss,' said Lewis, becoming a little agitated. 'But he's been with us a week and so far so good. There's been no problems. He's knuckled down in training, just got on with it, settled in with the lads. His landlady tells me he's no trouble. Does the washing up without being asked.'

'I'll have to get him to stay at our place. My missus is always nagging me about emptying the rubbish bins.'

'I wished you'd have seen him, Tim,' said Bradshaw. 'He lit up the place. Everything about him. His whole body language. He just loves playing. A natural. Some of the things he was doing you just couldn't coach. That left foot of his opens up the old tin can.'

'So where are we up to with the lad?'

'He's here for a fortnight. After that we'll have to decide what to do. But I've got to say, if we hang about too long, he's going to be snapped up somewhere else. You know how word gets around and if any of the big fish start sniffing we're knackered,' said Bradshaw.

'What's his date of birth?' asked the manager.

'It's on my desk,' said Bradshaw. 'I'll nip out and get it.'

Ward turned to Lewis. 'What are the alternatives, Bri? What could we offer the lad?'

'We could put him on a non-contract form, or keep him on trial I suppose for a few more weeks. Pay him exes.'

'That it?'

'Put him on a scholarship. Maybe a guarantee of a pro contact after that,' added Lewis.

'I'll have to take a look but from what you've said there'll be nothing lost if we get him on board. First of all would you do something for me?'

'Course.'

'I want you to check up on his background. Find out which school he was at. Talk to his headmaster. Arrange to get his parents in. You know the drill better than I do. He may be able to play but he could be a wrong 'un.'

Bradshaw came back in. 'He's seventeen on the 5th September.'

'Only a couple of weeks then?'

'Two weeks on Monday,' said Lewis looking at the calendar.

'Right this is what we'll do. You say he's still got a week to go on trial?'

'Yeah.'

'Keep him on that and keep him sweet. We'll talk more after I've taken a look.'

'Thanks Tim. I think we've got a gem.'

'How often have I heard that?' he said, laughing, as his secretary arrived with his lunch.

The first team squad were limbering up, ready for the warming up session with the fitness coach. 'Aidy, have you seen this kid play?' said Ward to his assistant Aidan Newton.

'The trialist?' said Newton folding his arms. 'Took in the last ten minutes. Couldn't fail to notice him.'

'That good?'

'Well from what I saw, he had everything.'

'Eh don't take the piss, there must be something he's weak at,' said Ward. 'Bobby Charlton wasn't the greatest tackler in the world was he? But what a player.'

'All right. He's not the best header, I grant you that. Coming up against a six-foot two centre back, he ain't going to dominate in the air – that's for sure.'

'I get your point. But on the ball?'

'Different class. It's like it's glued to his feet. Picks out people, range of passing is great. The thing is, he always wants the ball and knows where to go to get it.'

'Bryan was telling me he went past defenders as though they were dead men.'

'It's his speed off the mark,' enthused Newton.

'Way you're talking it sounds like he should be in the first team.'

'I tell you what, Tim, from what I saw, that wouldn't surprise me one little bit.'

'The next Wayne Rooney?' said Ward, placing some cones around the halfway line.

'Who's to say? Anything's possible.'

'I've told Bryan to find out about his background,' said Ward pointing to the bag of balls.

Newton emptied the bag and rolled the balls into the 18-yard box. 'You think there's a few skeletons hidden away?'

'Makes you wonder doesn't it? A lad with all that talent, not being picked up.'

'At sixteen?' said Newton sorting out the coloured bibs. 'Can't be too many can there? Maybe he's murdered his parents? Or burnt the school down?'

'More like he's been bonking his maths teacher.'

'Seems to be the in thing these days.'

'Listen, Aidy, I'm not going to be in tomorrow. There's a board meeting. Chairman's going through the budget for the season. If I get fifty grand to spend I'll be lucky. He'll probably tell me I've got to bring in half a million to break even.'

'Or get in the Prem,' said Newton, sarcastically.

'That's right. Totally unrealistic. I reckon we need another three or four players to make a fist of it this season.'

'And that's not allowing for injuries.'

'You know as well as I do the squad is wafer thin,' said Ward, glancing over to see the squad doing a sprint session. 'If we have a couple of serious injuries then we're in big trouble.'

'Well up to now boss, the lads are looking the business. I don't want to get carried away but I tell you what, we'll give most teams a run for their money this season. They're improving all the time and we've started well.'

'It's just that extra bit of quality we need.'

Newton agreed. 'It'll make all the difference.'

The day after Ricky's seventeenth birthday, Tim Ward arranged for Ruth and Ricky to meet him at the stadium. It meant Ruth taking time off work.

'Come in. Nice to see you. I'm Tim Ward. Good journey?'

'Yes, thank you,' said Ruth, wearing a white blouse and dark grey pencil-style skirt.

'Please take a seat.'

'I've got you in because I've got some good news. The club would like to offer Ricky a professional contract.'

'Oh, my Lord,' said Ruth jumping up and down and grabbing her boy. Ricky had a big beaming smile.

'You knew already?' she said looking into her son's face.

'I was told this morning,' Ricky said.

'I can't believe it. It's happened so quickly. Thank you very much Mr Ward. I can't thank you enough.'

'Don't even think about it. We're pleased that Ricky's come to us.'

'What does all this mean?' said Ruth taking out a tissue to dry her eyes while she sat down.

'Ricky's got a two-year contract, so he's full-time as from today. His basic wages will be £300 per week. If he plays for the first team he will be on appearance money and bonuses.'

'£300 a week? That's marvellous, isn't it Ricky?'

'Brilliant, mum.'

'It's only the beginning. The real work starts now,' said Ward. 'Ricky seems happy with his digs so I don't see any reason to move from there for the time being. You get on well with your landlady, don't you?'

'Both Mary and Fred. They're nice people,' said Ricky.

'I'm sure you'd like to meet them Ruth. I'll get one of my staff to take you round.'

'Ricky's told me all about them,' she said.

'Good. And don't forget, anytime you'd like to come and watch a first team game, just let Ricky know and we'll sort it out.'

'Thank you.'

'I know it's all come as a bit of a shock but is there anything you'd like to ask me?' said Ward.

'I don't think so but I'm not thinking straight right now,' said Ruth emotionally. 'But I'm thrilled to bits. And I know my Ricky won't let you down.'

'Well if he carries on like he's started, everybody'll be well pleased.' Ward stood up and walked round his desk. 'I wonder if you'd mind waiting in the next room, Ruth?

'There's a coffee machine in there. I'd just like to have a few words with Ricky.'

'Of course.'

Ruth was shown through into a lounge area, which had a large table, five chairs and a window that looked out onto the pitch. The ground was empty but she was full of anticipation. What would it be like to see her son out there in front of thousands of people?

'How you feeling son?' said the manager walking back to his desk.

'Fantastic Mr Ward.'

'From now on it's boss or gaffer. Maybe they'll be a few other names you'll call me but as long as I don't hear them I won't mind,' said Ward taking a seat.

Ricky smiled self-consciously.

'Now then, Ricky, I've got something important to say to you. I asked one of my staff to find out a little more about you. What do you think he came up with?'

'Dunno boss.'

'Think again Ricky.'

'That I ducked out of some of my school lessons.'

'It was mentioned.'

'I wasn't the brightest kid in school.'

'But you had your strong subjects.'

'Not that many.'

'Didn't have too many friends, did you?' said Ward. 'A bit of a loner.'

'Liked my own company I suppose.'

'Got into a few bad habits?'

Ricky fell silent and he stared at the floor.

'If we're going to get off on the right foot then you've got to be honest with me. I need to know everything. It won't go any further. Take your time and tell me in your own words.'

It took an age for Ricky to raise his head. 'I got into bad company. My life was going nowhere and there was a bit of trouble.'

'It all started when Ronnie moved in?'

'You know about him? He was a nightmare. Mum stuck by him

184

but even she couldn't sort him out. It got to the stage I didn't want to go home.'

Ricky was finding it difficult to talk about it. 'When I did, he'd be laid out on the settee drunk. All he'd do was swear at me. Knocked me about a bit. Mum didn't know. He was a thug so I kept away from the flat.'

'Where'd you go?'

'Met up with some other kids.'

'Drugs?'

'I thought "what the hell", said Ricky, deciding to come clean. 'I'd nothing to lose. But I've not touched anything since the day I rang for help.'

'That's when Mr Hutchinson got involved?'

'That's right. He was a diamond. I was in a right state but he had time for me. Some days I stayed at his house. Him and his missus looked after me.'

'He helped you a lot?'

'Sound bloke. But nothing heavy. Told me I wasn't giving myself a chance. Said there was another way. He didn't preach to me. We had fun as well. Took me fishing. We sat talking most of the time.

'Didn't catch anything mind but over time I knew I couldn't go on doing what I was doing. I'd screwed up and I'd hurt my mum badly. That was the worst bit. She'd done everything for me. She had all these problems herself. I just added to them.'

'It was a tough time?' said Ward, mellowing.

'Yeah, but then I went on that football trip and things got better.'

'Mr. Hutchinson arranged that, didn't he?'

'That's right. I stayed with a great Irish family. Had a real cool time and that's when it dawned on me how much I enjoyed playing.'

'I'm going to ask you again, Ricky, and it's important you think about it before you answer. Have you dabbled in drugs since then?'

'No way.'

'Never touched them or had any cravings?'

'I don't know a lot, gaffer, but I know one thing. All that's in the past. I'll never go anywhere near them ever again.'

'You've been through a lot.'

'Maybe more than some kids.'

'It looks like you're on the right road now. But I've got to tell you. We'll be checking up on you on a regular basis and if we do find you're back to your old ways then you'll be out of here so quick, your feet won't touch the ground. Is that clear?'

'Yes boss.'

'Right then, this is the deal. As far as I'm concerned the slate is clean. You've been honest with me. It's what I wanted to hear. If you have any more problems, it's important that you come and see me.'

'I will.'

'Good. All we want now is to get you fully fit and maybe you'll be knocking on the first team door.'

'I'll do my best. You can count on that.'

32

Is that story true? The one about the flask? Or are you making it up? One thing's for real – we're back in Peru and have just finished the 4-day Inca Trail to Machu Picchu, which was absolutely amazing but very hard work. The sausages kept us going! We had 8 Canadians, 3 Kiwis and an Irish girl in our group. All great people. Luckily the Canadians decided to carry ridiculously heavy rucksacks, which meant we could keep up with everybody.

The guide was a guy called Paolo who led us at a gentle pace until the last day. We had to get up at 4am to make sure we got to Machu Picchu before all the crowds and I think Paolo had had enough of us by then because we practically ran the 2 hours to get there. But it was worth it. The view was magnificent. Not surprisingly, we are taking it easy today and indulging ourselves. We have found a restaurant that does Sunday roasts. Sadly no black puddings!

Well done with the walk. Paolo sounds like a bit of a sadist. Lashing down back over here in the UK. People are taking precautions. The next door neighbours are building an ark! Won our last two games. I got on the end of one at Spurs. Prodded over the line from 3 yards. I like those kind. We're still up there – 6th at the moment. Everybody sends their love. Chloe is nagging me to get a date for her with one of the young players who she fancies. I've told her to keep away from football players!

I'll have a word with your sister when I get home. Too right – they are bad news! Hope you had a great birthday – 19 already. Did you celebrate on Bonfire night? I was thinking of sending over a lamb chop now that we're over here in New Zealand. Seen a bit of the north island and then got a ferry *over to the south. You'll be glad to hear I haven't done any bungee jumping (have seen it and it made me feel sick). We are going to stay in NZ for Christmas. Helen has a friend called Samantha who lives in Auckland and has kindly invited us to spend Christmas Day with her. I'm downloading some photos. The first one is of us at the top of a mountain that took 5 hours to climb but was worth it. Another is us having a hot drink by the side of a glacier and then there's the view from our tents on the Inca Trail.*

Went out with the lads after the game to celebrate my birthday. I wanted to go out with my girlfriend – but she's thousands of miles away on the other side of the world! Went to the Fireball disco. Got a taxi home with Taffy. After the game with Chelsea I presented the trophies at an awards do at the local snooker club. Really got into the '70s music they played that night. Went along with mum, dad and Chloe. Pete Rogers, the lad who Chloe fancies, just happened to be there! Should have seen her face! She went bright red! Love J.

33

'Lots of games to get through,' said Les Whitehead, 'so look after yourselves and no partying. We'll have our Christmas in July.'

It was a heavy schedule but Burding came out with a decent return of four points from the three games and made it through to the fourth round of the FA Cup, defeating Wrexham away.

One of those tricky ties – the match was on TV and an upset was on the cards – until Jake put them 3-1 up with a cracking finish.

The only dampener was a knee ligament injury picked up by skipper Dan Jones in the Boxing Day fixture against Liverpool. It was a bad one.

Grandad didn't have the best of good fortunes either – he broke his hip. Popped out to the shops and insisted on walking even though there'd been a heavy fall of snow. He was operated on – screwed and pinned. Jake got the job of taking Max out every morning.

The manager wanted a word with Jake. Alarm bells rang. His performances had been good and he hadn't got into any scrapes off the pitch but it didn't stop him feeling anxious. He showered, got his mail, checked his mobile and confirmed the next training session before heading off to the manager's office. He knocked on the door.

'Come in.'

Whitehead, still in his training kit from the morning session, and drinking tea from a Town beaker – bearing the words 'Flying High With The Burds' – was on the 'phone. He signalled to Jake to sit down. Videos were all neatly stacked on the shelves behind, alongside coaching manuals. A computer was positioned on the far corner of his desk.

'The next game is so important but after last week's result we are confident of producing a similar performance and getting the points. But it won't be easy. Birmingham have had a good run themselves but home advantage could sway it in our favour.'

He was talking to a reporter. The boss reacted angrily to the next question.

'Look, when I've decided what course of action to take, I will let the player know, then I will inform the media. But first, I will have to wait for the referee's report, look at the video evidence and talk to the player to establish exactly what went on.

'Was he provoked or did something go on immediately before the incident, which nobody is aware of? You know what I'm about, Len. If I find that the ref was justified in giving him a red card, then I'll jump on Jackson from a great height.'

Jake knew what the discussion was about. Wacko had reacted violently to a nasty foul by throwing a punch and getting himself sent off. It was totally out of character. In the dressing room after the game, Clive said the guy spat at him, one of the vilest acts inflicted on any professional. The tribunal could rescind the red card if video evidence showed it to be the case.

He put the 'phone down. 'Now, young man, sorry to keep you waiting.'

'No problem, boss.'

'I'll come straight to the point. We're having a problem with the captaincy. As you know, Dan picked up a serious injury and he's going to be out for a long time. Ivor's taken over but it's affecting his game. So I've decided to make a change. I want you to be captain.'

This took Jake completely off guard. Of all the things he'd mulled over before the meeting, being offered the captaincy wasn't one of them.

'I don't know what to say. It's a big shock.' Jake was floundering and initially had doubts. 'The thing is I'm only nineteen and just started my career. There's lots of older players in the side and I'm bound to find it difficult telling them what to do.'

'Don't worry about that, Jake,' Whitehead assured him. 'It's an important role, I know, but the tactics are my responsibility. I'll deal with all that. I just want you to carry on playing the way you are. Nothing else. Toss the coin, decide which end and let your football do the talking. Inspire others by the way you play the game.

'I know the lads rate you very highly. You're a good player and an important member of the side and I think the time's right. What I'd like you to do, though, is think it over.

'Talk to your family. Have a chat with a former captain to see if he can give you any tips. I think Bill Johnson is still living in the area. He was well respected when he skippered the side in the late '70s and I've got a feeling Dave Harwood is also local. He did the job in the '80s.

But when you're ready come back and tell me what you've decided. Whatever that decision is I'll respect it. Okay?'

'Fine.'

'Anything else?'

'No, apart from thanks for considering me.'

'See you tomorrow and, by the way, get your haircut. You look like a right ponce!'

Jake left the manager's office and sprinted out of the club. He felt light-headed. Bloody hell! The gaffer must think he was a half-decent player to even think about offering him the captaincy. He shifted through the gears and before he knew it, he was doing fifty in a built-up area. He slowed to a crawl and pulled over.

Jake was keen to take up the offer. There was no way he was going to turn it down, but he had to consider all the responsibilities. The prospect of being the spokesman for the squad didn't exactly thrill him but he had never shied away from anything before and he wasn't going to start now. But he needed some advice. He got on the 'phone to the secretary.

'Okay Jake?' said Harold Green.

'Yes thanks. Bill Johnson? Have you got his number and do you know if he's still living in Burding?'

'I know he moved but only locally. Hold on, I'll find out.' Jake could hear a rustling of papers.

Green came back on.

'Here it is. Bill's number is 415890. Sorry, I haven't got his address.'

'Cheers, Harry. See you later.'

Jake dialled the number.

'Bill?'

'Yes.'

'It's Jake. Jake Watkins. How are you?'

'Fine thanks, son. And you?'

'Good. The results have gone all right. I don't know whether you've seen any games this season?'

'I haven't. I was hoping to get down but the knees aren't what they were and a couple of hours sitting in the same place really does me in. Especially when that cold wind whistles through the main stand.'

'I understand. Bill, I'm looking for a bit of advice. Any chance of popping round to see you?'

'Of course.'

'Tomorrow? Around two o'clock?'

'Fine with me. Have you got my address?'

'No.'

'Well it's 2 Clifton Road. First left by the Jolly Pigeon pub. You know it?'

'I'll find it. I'll see you then.'

'Look forward to it.'

The boss sidled up to Jake during the next training session. Was he coming the heavy sell? Not a bit of it. He told Jake to tighten up with his tackling. 'Don't dive in son, hold your ground.'

Jake arrived at Bill's house and the ex-skipper and former international welcomed him with a cheery smile and a strong handshake. He was a little unsteady and was carrying a few extra pounds from his prime playing days but generally seemed in good health.

'Come in. Good to see you.'

'Thanks. Nice place you've got here,' said Jake glancing around.

'Yeah we like it and it's quiet which is what the wife and I like,' said Bill closing the door. 'She's just popped out to the shops but shouldn't be very long.'

Jake was shown into the living room where a collection of black and white photographs adorned the walls.

'This one was when we won the Second Division championship

– too many years ago. The photo is fading now but not the memories. Good days. This is when I made my first international appearance against Yugoslavia.' Pride was etched on his face. 'All black and white but we had a decent team and won a few games. Fancy a brew?'

'Thanks. Tea please, one sugar.'

'Right come on through into the kitchen, I think I can manage that. I'm a de-caff man now. The wife gets me these low fat biscuits. They taste crap but she's cutting down the calories. She's even giving me broccoli and chicken with all the fat drained away. I think it's a lost cause. But she's a love.'

Bill poured the hot water, added the milk and found a teaspoon. 'Come on through,' he said. 'Sit yourself down. How can I help?'

'The thing is, the manager's asked me to be skipper. It's a great honour but I'm wondering whether to take it.'

'Well, good for you. I was a little older when I took it on but it's something I always wanted. I was a bit bullish and cocky like.'

'Did it affect your relationship with the other players?' asked Jake.

'No, not one bit. There was a bit of mickey taking early on, just what you'd expect but if the manager has chosen the right man, he'll already have the respect of his teammates. Just keep doing the things you're doing now.'

'That's what the boss said. Don't change your style.'

'I know what he means,' said Bill, biting into a biscuit. 'Other things will come into it when you've got a bit more experience. Funny that. You know what lad, experience is the quality you have, just after you most need it.

'You'll make some mistakes but things are going well for you right now and from what I've read the manager rates you highly. Are you happy at the Town?'

'Very,' replied Jake.

'That's good. Local lad and the fans like you. They know you are totally committed. So it will be a popular choice as far as they're concerned.'

'What other things can I expect?'

'Presentations. In our day we had a players' list. There was a rota and everybody took it in turn. It was shared out. And I sorted out the fines. If players were late for training or got booked for silly things it would go into a fund to help local charities.

'Some clubs put the money towards a piss up at the end of the season, don't they? Not much of a punishment that, is it? In those days it wasn't a lot of cash but it gave the club good publicity and many charities benefited, so we developed a good community spirit.'

'We did a panto last year,' said Jake. 'Raised funds for the hospital.'

'That's the way. Another thing. Get used to saying a few words. Thank people. Try to include a funny line. It always helps to relax everybody and the more you do, the easier it becomes.'

'Good shout.'

'But basically don't change. Just grow into the position. The most important thing is to concentrate on your own game. Get that right and gradually you'll be able to take the other things in your stride.'

'Should I talk to the players individually?' asked Jake.

'No way – that's the manager's job. He may have a word with you about a certain player. You know the kind of thing – what are your thoughts about the balance of the side? Has such a player got a problem? Don't try to take on any more. You've enough to do. If a player wants to talk to you about his own game that's different. Listen to what he has to say and if it's in confidence, then you must respect it.'

'I see.'

'And one other thing. When I got the job I made sure I knew all the names of the staff at the club. I went around one afternoon and introduced myself, shook their hands and told them I'd been given the captaincy. Everybody's got a part to play if the club is going to be successful.

'Nobody is more important than anybody else, apart from the manager or the chairman that is, but if you see the cleaning lady and you know her name – great. It brings everybody together.'

'Thanks Bill. I've already decided I'm going to take it on,' said Jake confidently. 'What you've told me is all brilliant stuff.'

'Makes this old git seem useful again,' smiled Bill. 'You might want to talk about other things later on.'

'Like what?'

'Fans thinking they own you. They buy their season tickets so they think it's okay to have a pop at you. Off the field as well.'

'We had an incident at the club do. Juan was put in hospital.'

'Read about it,' said Bill, slurping his coffee. 'Nasty. Drives you bonkers. So just be aware.'

'I must admit I haven't come across it myself,' said Jake.

'I'm not getting cynical, lad. Just trying to let you know what might happen so you can deal with it. Keep to your beliefs, remember what's important. The values. Pick your friends carefully. Are you married?'

'No, but I've got a girlfriend. She's away at the moment.'

'On holiday?'

'Sort of. She's taking a year out, backpacking around the world,' explained Jake.

'Bloody hell, that'll test you.'

'I know.'

'Where is she now?' asked Bill.

'Australia.'

'Beats a weekend in Bridlington don't it?'

'Just a bit.'

'Well I hope it works out for you, Jake. Get in touch any time.'

Jake finished his tea and was about to leave when he saw Bill's wife, Veronica, walking up the driveway carrying a supermarket bag.

Bill levered himself off the settee and opened the front door. 'Give that to me love. Jake's just leaving.'

'Hello Jake, has the old fool looked after you?'

'Yes thanks. He's been a great help.'

'Well he's going to be great help to me this afternoon,' said Veronica. 'He's about to clean out the drains and the guttering.'

An expletive came out of Bill's mouth. Followed by a huge smile.

'Thanks Bill, look after yourself. All the best Veronica... those biscuits were top class.'

She smiled.

Many things had already happened in his young life. Many more would undoubtedly follow. But today was a pivotal day in the career of Jake Watkins. Burding Town had found their new skipper.

34

The responsibility of the captaincy certainly didn't affect Jake's performances. He was playing some brilliant stuff – really focusing on his game – but as the long winter months set in, he was missing Marie, desperately. He'd emailed her about the news and also texted. To fill the time, he accepted every invitation that came his way.

He was contacted by the organising committee responsible for raising £1.5m towards completion of the new hospital extension. Would he like to be involved?

The chairman was a retired army brigadier, Ralf Goodson – perfect for the position. Didn't know anything about the game but was interested to hear Jake's views as a young professional. 'As far as I'm concerned, Jakey lad, it's got way out of hand. All this dosh sloshing around. Not good for these young whippersnappers.

'Tell them to tip their wads over to us. We'll put it to a good cause and even name a private room after them.' Forthright and belligerent, he opened one meeting with the words, 'Let's get cracking. No time to mess about chaps – and chapesses. Onwards and upwards. This building won't wait and neither will I.'

He began with news of a summer musical extravaganza, on 6th June. A black tie audience would enjoy vintage champagne and the finest cuisine, while being serenaded by a classical orchestra. He was hopeful that the auction alone would raise in the region of a quarter of a million pounds. According to the chairman – and he had it on good authority – already in place was a chance to bid for a luxury 12-berth yacht, which included its own staff, to cruise around the Med for fourteen days.

Another fantastic offer was a helicopter ride to any destination in the UK to spend a week at a five star hotel. And the guests could even bid for a sports car, which would be on view on the night.

'With so many months to go,' said the chairman placing his monocle on the table, 'I don't think it's a bad start. Well done to you all.'

When Jake suggested the club might agree to one of their hospitality boxes being auctioned for a Premier League match, it was greeted with much enthusiasm. A journalist on the committee was willing to take someone to a major event, with the paper promising to publish the lucky winner's account of the day. By way of an aside he whispered to Jake, 'Should you ever have a problem with bad publicity, give me a call.'

The person responsible for marketing the events was Tess Nugent, a very attractive blonde in her early thirties, who had been drafted in by the board to deal with communication problems. She asked Jake if he wouldn't mind staying behind for a few minutes.

The chairman brought the meeting to a close and Tess and Jake made their way through to her office, which was covered with glossy pictures and leaflets – all relating to the construction of the new hospital wing.

'We get dozens of inquiries every day from businesses wanting to help,' she told Jake, placing leaflets into a folder. 'But of course they want a huge say in how their company is going to be marketed. We don't get a monopoly on the media. That's the problem. We can only go so far.'

'I can understand that,' said Jake, switching off his mobile.

'But I tell you what, Jake, since you and the boys did that panto, the interest in the project has been fantastic. Even now, after all this time.'

'At first, we wondered what we were letting ourselves in for. But you know what? – we're all well pleased we've done it. We probably made a pig's ear of it but it didn't matter, did it?'

'You wouldn't have got me doing anything like that. On that stage? No way. But you guys looked so professional.'

'I think you're being very kind. I'm sure any drama critic would think differently. If they did, they kept quiet,' said Jake, glancing up at the clock.

'Sorry, I'm keeping you. Oh – and congratulations on the captaincy. I'm sure you have a dozen other things you've got to get on with – but you know when you said the club might be willing to offer a box? – well, it gave me an idea. What about one of the very poorly kids, being a mascot for a first team game? Do you think it's a possibility? I didn't raise it in front of the others because if word gets out and we can't do it then it would be a major disappointment.'

'I'll have a word with the commercial department. Let's see if they can come up with something. Leave it with me. I'll be in touch.' For a split second, there was an awkward silence. Shaking hands seemed a little formal so he bent forward and kissed her on the cheek. Her perfume enveloped him. She smiled and kissed him back. Jake rang two days later to give her the good news.

'Come in Jake, don't stand on ceremony.' Tess, wearing a short leather skirt, white blouse and ankle boots, met him at the door. She showed him through to the lounge, which had a full-sized piano situated at the far end and a collection of expensive pictures on the wall. Jake asked about the one of an exotic dancer.

'To be honest I can't tell you who painted it. Just not my scene. My husband buys all the paintings – he's a real buff and he's the one who likes the classical music. He's been drafted in to help with that do the chairman was on about. Problem is he's away on business such a lot. Down in London this week. It's getting ridiculous. Enough of that, can I get you a drink?'

Jake made himself comfortable on the settee and was impressed with the place. It was class. No money worries here. She returned with a bottle of beer.

'Okay? Do you want a glass? No?'

Jake placed the bottle on the table. 'Before I forget,' he said,' here's all the info about the mascot thing. I've managed to get four tickets for the match and they've also invited the party to have a meal before the game. They said they'd fill you in with the details later on. The person to speak to is Liz. Liz Curry. The contact numbers are all there.'

'Great,' said Tess sitting next to him and crossing her shapely legs.

'The other thing is – it's for the Man United game.'

'Brilliant. That's just fantastic, Jake,' said a delighted Tess.

'I take it you'll be coming?' asked Jake, feeling very relaxed.

'I hope so. We're going to ask Sally who's had a setback. This will give her a real boost – she's only ten but is such a big fan of Burding. I can't thank you enough for what you've done.'

She leant across and kissed him. Full on. Her tongue darting in and out of his mouth. Her hands in his hair. Jake responded. 'Come on,' said Tess as she held his hand and led him up the staircase. By the time they reached the bedroom they were half undressed. Jake was in overdrive.

'Not so quickly, Jakey. Please, slow down. You're going way too fast. Let's both enjoy the moment.' She gently pushed him onto the bed and stripped off the remainder of his clothes.

35

Ricky got on well with his digs-mate, Billy Pointer, a big, imposing defender. Both were enjoying a lot of success in the under-18 team. They played with invention and passion and were growing in confidence every day. Laughter filled the dressing room. They felt invincible.

Bryan Lewis was delighted with their progress but repeatedly stressed the importance of maintaining those high standards. They had excelled in everything asked of them in the first six months of the season.

That was on the pitch. They still had to learn off it.

Lewis made them aware that everything they did away from the ground would be scrutinised. It was an honour to play for Mexter City, something that should never be taken for granted. If they stepped out of line there would be no hiding place – it only took a second to switch off and the consequences could be devastating.

Dave Swift found himself in such a position after being caught up in a serious police investigation. The young Sheffield lad had left a nightclub in the early hours of the morning and was waiting for a taxi when he heard a cry for help coming from the side of the club.

He decided to take a look and made his way over to the darkened passageway where he found a young girl in obvious distress. She was crying and her clothes were ripped. Swift tried to comfort her but the girl became hysterical and when others arrived at the scene, the police were called.

The girl had been raped and Dave Swift was suddenly the prime suspect. He was interviewed and kept in cells overnight. Lewis was hauled out of his bed and the story found its way into the nationals.

After his DNA was taken, Swift was completely exonerated but the incident caused him terrible personal problems. He became withdrawn, his performances dipped and he took months to recover.

After being cleared he was left to reflect if he would act in the same way again

Another thing Lewis kept harping on about was that 'cars and professional footballers don't mix. When you pass your test, get yourself a small run-around.' But to the players that was almost as bad as travelling on public transport.

They wanted the speed, the thrill, the excitement. Diminutive full back, Joel Low, found out the wisdom of Lewis's advice, soon after he'd thrown away his L-plates. The following week his 2.5litre top of the range sports saloon clipped an articulated lorry on the motorway and ended up crashing through the boundary fence into a field. Luckily, no physical damage was done. Just a bruised ego.

Childish pranks in the dressing room were part and parcel of any footballer's routine. Itching powder liberally sprinkled in underwear or deep heat massage cream had to be laughed off, embarrassing comments taken on the chin.

Lewis, himself, wasn't exempt from the jokey behaviour. After giving an interview for the matchday programme, he was quoted as saying, 'Ossie was caught on the head and concussed but he'll be okay for next week's game. He went to the hospital for a brain scan and the specialist didn't find anything'.

Ossie was nicknamed 'Thicko' the following week.

They had to chuckle when striker Sid Milne, the joker in the pack, was getting his kit on and the lads noticed his highly distinctive underwear.

'Hey Siddo, nice thong mate. Pink your colour or what?' The dressing room fell about.

'Shit. The bird's wearing me boxers!'

Ricky kept his head down and got on with the job. He trained hard, played the games, went home, got his rest. Got out his Playstation back at the digs and watched TV. Boring, mind blowing, professional.

A simple life. Did what was asked of him, listened to his r and b music and got himself some decent clothes. Not only was he clean from drugs, he steered away from other distractions.

He was determined to make the football thing work. He'd

promised to give it his best shot – and failure wasn't going to be for the want of trying. If he didn't make it, then he wasn't good enough. Nothing else. Other obstacles had gone.

Ricky had a few girlfriends and like any good-looking professional footballer was top of the list for gold diggers who made their intentions clear. The pound signs were flashing and they wanted a piece of the action.

On the odd off day he and Billy would go into Mexter. The city was situated just on the edge of the magnificent Cotswolds countryside and thousands of tourists came to view the many attractions, including the railway museum – housing some of the finest steam engines. All were magnificently preserved.

In restoring these locomotives, future generations would have access to the transport systems of an earlier age. During school holidays the engines were dressed up as cartoon characters and wheeled out of retirement, stoked up, and great billows of white smoke would force their way out of the newly painted funnels.

The dilapidated carriages, filled with excited school kids, would then be shunted half a mile down a rusty track.

Ricky wondered why they spent all that time and effort on the engines but none on the carriages and track.

A new leisure centre housed all the latest equipment and the football club had an agreement enabling the players to have full access to all the facilities.

Browsing through a shop window Billy saw the latest mobiles. 'Let's get in and take a look.'

The girl assistant came over. 'Can I be of help?'

'We're thinking about changing our 'phones,' said Billy, peering down her cleavage.

'Are you on contract?'

'Probably need to change. Just pay-as-you-go at the moment but it's getting plenty of stick,' he said, eventually making eye contact.

'Right. There's many contracts to tell you about but have we to look at a few models first?'

'We saw a couple in the window,' said Billy.

'Hold on.'

As she moved to the other side of the store Billy said, 'Eh up. You're in there mate. Just like a burglar. She blimped you, no danger. Ask her for a date.'

'What right here? Leave it out. Bit tasty though, in't she?' said Ricky.

'And what do you two do?' said the assistant as she put several 'phones on the glass surface.

'We're footballers,' said Billy, immodestly.

'Yeah right,' said the dubious assistant.

'No it's true,' insisted Billy. 'We play for the City,' he added, fumbling with the photo system.

'What's your names?' asked the girl.

'I'm Billy Pointer and this is Ricky Grant.'

While putting away some of the models she said, rather dismissively, 'Never heard of you.'

'We're youth team players,' said Ricky.

'Played in the reserves as well,' jumped in Billy.

'So I've got two superstars in the shop,' said the sceptical assistant. 'I'll have to go and have a lie down.'

'You're not taking the piss are you?' said Billy, becoming a little riled.

'Would I do a thing like that?' she said, taking the heat out of the situation. 'Now do you fancy any of these or do you want to look at something else?'

'Maybe we'll have a think about it and come back later,' Billy said.

They left the premises and Billy clipped his mate on the head. 'Get in there, you muppet. Must have a chance.'

'With you there? I'd get slaughtered.'

'So you might sneak back?' suggested Billy.

'Who's to say?'

'If you do, see if she's got a mate.'

'You're on.'

'What'd you fancy doing now?'

'How about some eats?' said Ricky. 'Fancy a Basil?'

'Basil?'

'Basil Fawlty. Balti.'

'Curry?'

'Right on.'

At the café they ordered cheeseburgers, chips and milk shakes. They found a table overlooking the river where most of the tourist boats were moored up for the winter – all except one, which slipped past with a handful of passengers.

On a cold gloomy winter's day, a boat ride on the choppy waters wasn't for everybody.

'Not a bad place, is it?' said Billy.

'Better than where I live. That's the pits,' said Ricky, taking a drink. 'I tell you what Bill, if I do make it, first thing I'm going to do is get my mum a decent house.'

'I'd get one of those penthouse flats,' said Billy, squeezing tomato ketchup over everything. 'You know, looking out over the city with all the latest mod cons. Press buttons for everything. That'll do me.'

'And all blinged up?' asked Ricky.

'Too right. The diamond in the ear 'ole. Diamonds everywhere.'

'And a tattoo?'

'Now you're talking mate,' said Billy, animated. 'I fancy a snake going all the way down the back.'

'Top of the arm for me. Something artistic,' said Ricky, fantasising. 'Italian. Got to get the biceps first.'

'Rattlesnake. I'd get a reputation as a big ugly defender who splatters strikers. Might get one on me pecker.'

'No way,' laughed Ricky. 'No room is there? Might just get its head on.'

'Oh yeah. What about you? Not exactly mister elephant trunk are you?' said Billy as he emptied the rubbish. 'Fancy another shake?'

'What about a chewy toffee?' suggested Ricky.

'You what?'

'Coffee.'

'No. Come on we'll get moving.'

'Or your chalfonts'll start playing up?'

'Chalfonts?'

'Chalfonts St Giles – piles.'

'Hey you might be right.'

'Tell you what. Why don't we go down the snooker club?'

'Sounds good. Then we can see what's on at the pics.'

'They might be doing your life story,' said Ricky zipping up his tracksuit top. 'Casablanca.'

'The original?'

'No cockney version.'

'Bastard.'

36

After the Saturday victory against Bristol City in the fourth round of the FA Cup, Jake went into training on Monday morning high as a kite. Things were ticking over nicely and the guys were playing out of their skins. As the gaffer told them, 'Go with the flow, you never know what's round the corner. Enjoy it.'

The belief was there – could they maintain the momentum, a little while longer?

He showered, collected his mail and made his way up to the players' lounge to watch the draw live. Spurs came out of the hat. A tough one, no doubt about that, but at least they had home advantage. After signing autographs he headed for the car. He checked his mobile – his agent had a couple of things he wanted to discuss.

Jake had asked the PFA to represent him – the Professional Footballers Association Player Management Agency, to give the organisation its full title. He'd heard the stories circulating around the dressing room of dodgy dealings by some agencies and he was confident – with the PFA's knowledge of contracts, regulations and negotiations – that he'd be guided correctly.

There was also a message from Tess. Could he get round that afternoon? 'Business and pleasure.' The emphasis was very much on the pleasure side. Things couldn't be better.

Taffy had mentioned 'the zone'. Well he'd hit it, early doors. Only nineteen and he couldn't want for anything else. Captain of a Premier League club, money coming out of his ears and seeing a magic bird who had no hidden agenda. They were both getting what they wanted – no frills, no heavy commitment, no complications. A blissful physical relationship, with no strings attached.

Was he available? Too damn right he was.

In the parking area of the training ground, he opened his car door and threw his letters onto the passenger seat. He texted Tess to say he'd be round later – spruced up and showered.

After his afternoon 'session', he went home to check the emails on his computer. He half expected one from Marie. He knew she'd moved on from Australia and her next port of call was somewhere in the Far East. Was it Laos or Cambodia? But there was nothing. He switched off, poured himself a glass of orange juice and started sorting his letters. A bundle.

He was receiving more and more and he'd be at it for the next hour at least. Some of them asked stupid questions like 'What do you have for breakfast Jake?' or 'What's your favourite girl group?' 'Will you wave towards me when you next score – I'm in the Family Enclosure?' Yeah right, course I will.

He was halfway through when he came across an airmail envelope. It was hidden between two large brown ones. He slit it open. He recognised the handwriting immediately.

Jake, I just had to write to you. I just couldn't email this stuff. It's all too personal. We are now in Thailand, which was hit by the Tsunami disaster.
How they suffered! Just unbelievable!
We met some people who lost their entire families. One woman told us she had to go away for the day and visit someone a few miles away. She felt kind of strange that day. There had been a full moon. When she returned she found out her complete family had been wiped out – husband and three kids. Can you imagine what she must have been thinking? She wanted to be with them. Why did she go on that day? She said she couldn't cope with the reality of it. She wanted to be with her sons.
Helen and I listened for hours. She kept going over and over. Why me? Why that day? And she was such a lovely lady. Somehow we weren't able to comfort her the way she wanted. We just sat there. Silent. We wept buckets. The courage of this woman was amazing. Talking about it has helped – she reckons it's good therapy – but for her it's still a living nightmare.
Others who witnessed the disaster said it was like someone had pulled a plug on the ocean. A really strange feeling – like the sea receding down a big hole. But then, within seconds, there

came this massive wall of water. Everything in its path was flung into the air like feathers in the wind – boats, buildings, trees, people.

One guy told us, 'We were up there on the top floor of the hotel. We couldn't go anywhere but we knew we were going to be hit. In that split second we thought we were going to die. Then it hit. This giant moving mass. The noise was deafening. Windows were smashed. We found out later that others weren't so lucky. They were killed by flying debris.'

One said he'd been to a celebration. It was his parents' wedding anniversary – they had been married for 40 years. He never saw them again. Their bodies were never found. This guy is on heavy medication – his life has been destroyed. He told us he used to be happy, smiling. Now he's just a wreck.

Like that lady, he wished he'd been taken as well.

Lots of others who survived felt the same. One woman was with her two friends and the building she was in collapsed, trapping her underwater. She was swept towards a palm tree but her clothes caught hold and she held on. She doesn't know how she clung on. Water lashed around her but from somewhere she got the strength. The water receded. She survived with only a few cuts. A boat rescued her. The other two, who were with her in the building, died.

Devastation was all around. It just sounded so frightening and begs the question – how could anyone survive?

There were so many brave people that day. A man risked his own life to carry a woman, who was trapped in a basement, up three flights of stairs, before the place was completely flooded.

A honeymoon couple did survive. We saw them yesterday and they had to return to the scene. They were two of the lucky ones. They'd been walking on the shoreline at around 7.30 in the morning, after breakfast. It was warm, with a clear blue sky; an almost perfect start to the day but they both felt a strange feeling. Couldn't put their fingers on it but both noticed it. Then everybody starting shouting, 'RUN! RUN! They got back to the hotel then they heard this awful noise and a huge bang.

They thought it was a terrorist bomb exploding. They told us they clung on to each other – thought they were going to die. 'We'd just got married, wanted to spend the rest of our lives together and we thought it was going to end – just like that. That day. We kissed each other, we prayed, we cried. We said our goodbyes.'

At the airport they saw all these pictures of missing people. Could anybody help? Has anybody any information?

They told us the Thai community was fantastic – organising food, clean water and medical attention. The rescue services went in with no thought to their own safety. Unbelievably brave.

Some were not so lucky. A baby boy was found the following day. Alone on the beach. Nothing within 100 yards of him. He was at peace. After the carnage, the destruction and the death – came the silence.

Jake – 8,000 died in Thailand alone. 400 villages were severely affected. It destroyed the livelihoods of over 100,000 people. In financial terms the Tsunami cost Thailand $2.1 billion in damages and losses.

I'm telling you all this because it could have been us out there – couldn't it? It makes you realise just how short life is. We can't mess about thinking we've got plenty of time. It could all end tomorrow – couldn't it? And where would that leave us? You and me?

I said before I left, that being away from each other would be a test – a test of what we felt for each other. A test of our feelings and what we wanted from life. Do we want to be together? That sort of thing. Well, I've got to tell you, when I sent all those emails I tried to put a funny side to it all. But the fact is, I'm missing you like crazy. I think about you everyday. I miss you so badly, it hurts. Almost too much.

I wanted to turn round as soon as we got to the States. But I put on a brave face. Didn't tell Helen 'cos she would have taken it badly. I was determined to see it through and not bottle out. But it's been tough. Every time you contact me and tell me how *things are, I wish I was there with you, taking everything in – being with you, supporting you, loving you. And now you're captain. I'm stuck over here.*

But I can't blame anyone else, can I? It was my call. I chose to go – not you. I know you didn't want me to go – but did I listen? No. I thought I knew it all and that we were too young to be thinking about a deep, long-lasting relationship. Hey! what do I know? Sweet bugger all! Why didn't I listen?

Jake, you know when we had that meal in Spain and we talked about love and things and whether we really knew what we felt for each other? Well – the longer I've been away my feelings for you have just got stronger and stronger. I realise what a special person you are. And what a wonderful, wonderful, handsome, truly special boyfriend I've got.

When I get back I'd like to sit down and talk it through. Just you and me. How do we feel about each other? Do we want the same things in life? I've put my side – do you feel the same? Has anything changed for you? One thing I'd like to do is think about getting a place of our own – to see how things pan out. A step at a time. Is it what you want? To see if we might have a future together?

Being here has really knocked me sideways. Whether it's been a good experience or not I don't know – but at least it's made me think long and hard about the important things in life. And the people who are nearest and dearest to me.

And at the top of the pile is you!

I know I've prattled on a bit. But I feel so emotional.

Lots and lots of hugs and kisses. I might feel better tomorrow when we leave for Vietnam. By the time you get this letter we'll probably already be in Cambodia.

For fully five minutes he stared at the paper. He then reread the letter. All of it. There was nobody in the house – it was 3.35 in the afternoon – and there was a deadly silence. He just sat there in a state of shock.

Everything was going through his head. The one thing he kept repeating to himself was, 'Am I a complete plonker or what? What am I doing? Have I ruined everything?'

It all sunk in. The realisation. What he was doing, his lifestyle, had far reaching implications. If Marie found out about the affair she'd go absolutely ballistic. Out of sight, out of mind – that's what he thought. 'What she doesn't know won't hurt her, will it?'

He'd been wrapped up, full of his own importance, protected by the bubble he was living in. All it took was one slip up. That's all. Just the one. And everything could come crashing down.

It's what the academy staff were on about every day. 'They're out there. Just waiting. Any bit of gossip – it's readies for them. Just a 'phone call away and – wham – major news! It's gone in two weeks but not with the player. It sticks. And it'll affect you. No doubt about that.

Don't ever think it won't because it'll be on your mind every second and will affect your play. It'll take away that little bit of magic. Doubts will creep in. What was instinctive, instead, you'll start thinking – choosing the wrong option. It will take that five per cent off your performance and that's all it takes.

And if you can't get it back then you'll be like everyone else – a journeyman player – picking up a contract here and there, moving on every twelve months. Scratching around for a living. Is that what you want? No? Well keep your nose clean guys. Don't get involved in any scandal. Keep smart.'

He felt sick.

He went to the bathroom and splashed cold water on his face and looked in the mirror. 'You little prat, Jake. You little prat. Someone out there could have already made that call. "Bonko Watko – Affair with married woman." You just couldn't see it through could you? You just couldn't give it a go. And you could have lost the most precious thing ever, to have come into your life.'

Within twenty minutes he had made a 'phone call and sent a text message. On one he said it was over. On the other, he said 'I love you'.

37

For the next game against Coventry City under-18s, Lewis decided on an unconventional line-up. 'Right lads. I'm giving you something to think about today. Seven of you lot are playing out of position.'

The players didn't react apart from Billy who shouted, 'I don't fancy going between the sticks, Lewy.'

'Don't worry on that score. Ossie is one of the few who'll play in his normal position. But for the rest of you, listen up.'

The lads had gone through their pre-match routines and were sitting in the dressing room – some nervously fiddling with their boots, others exchanging encouragements. 'Dave, you'll come in from right back to play alongside Jonno at centre back. Willie will play in midfield.

'The two centre mid players will play wide. Billy, I want you to go and play up front alongside Ricky. Right then. Concentrate. I still want you to pass the ball about but you can use Billy as a target and play off him to mix it up. This'll give you something else to think about Billy. What strikers don't like. But generally play the same way. Last week you pinged it about for fun.'

Lewis glanced at his clipboard, before reassuring the players. 'Don't worry about your positional play, guys. You are all good players. You know what they said about the Dutch side in the '70s? Obviously not – you weren't born then, were you? But they were all footballers, not inside forwards or defenders. They could play in any position.

'That's what I'm looking for from you lot today. You've shown me already this season that you're a talented bunch. Now let's see if you understand other people's problems. If you're going to have decent careers then you're going to have to be versatile. Look on it as a challenge.'

After starting hesitantly, when they found themselves behind, Mexter settled and began to knock the ball about confidently. Neutrals on the touchline wouldn't have known of any positional changes as they'd overturned the deficit by halftime to go into the break leading 2-1.

Billy scored with a towering header for the equaliser and a direct corner avoided everybody to put them in front. In the second half Ricky showed all his trickery. He loved the freedom in the more advanced role, dropping deep to pick up possession to attack the Coventry back four.

The Sky Blues were on the back foot for the rest of the game. One cracking drive hit the bar before another was palmed to the feet of Billy who tapped in. Ricky completed the scoring. A knock down from his digs-mate found him twelve yards out and his crisply taken strike flew in. Four-one it finished. The dressing room was alive.

'I tell you what,' said Lewis, after the match. 'Some of you guys crapped it before kick-off but it just shows what you can do if you apply yourselves.'

'Magic coach,' said Jonno. 'The only player who didn't get a kick in the second half was Ossie.'

They laughed.

'Hey, I'm not complaining. Watching you lot was the business,' said the 'keeper putting his gloves in his bag.

'That's not going to happen every week but it gives you a chance to see it from another angle,' said Lewis, helping Ricky to remove his sweat-stained shirt. 'You defenders now know how hard it is as a striker. Getting kicked all afternoon. Isn't that right Billy?'

'Give over coach,' said Billy, grinning. 'Piece of piss playing striker. They get all the glory for knocking it into the net? Do me a favour.'

'But what about the service?' asked Lewis.

'What service?' he said, grabbing a water bottle.

A smelly sock came flying over and landed on Billy's head. The contents of the ice bucket quickly followed. 'Cool, man, cool,' chuckled the big man.

That afternoon the first team were playing Southampton. Billy, Ricky and the rest of the lads watched from the stands.

'Bill, was it right you got in the first team back end of last season?' said Ricky flicking through the programme.

'Couple of charity games,' said Billy, singing along with the crowd.

'Testimonials. I got on for the last bit.'

'What did the gaffer say?' asked Ricky trying to get him to sit down.

'Said I did well. Told me to keep improving and I'd get another chance.'

'Simon Haworth reckons the club has always pushed the young players. The club's reputation is all about developing its own.'

'Always been like that. The number they've produced is staggering, but a lot had to be sold to balance the books,' explained Billy.

'When they were relegated a few years ago?'

There was a massive roar as the teams came out.

'Almost a complete team,' shouted Billy, trying to be heard above the noise. 'They had to get the money in. Even those on Bosman's had to go. They wanted to play top flight football.'

'That's not bad for the likes of us?' said Ricky checking his watch.

'If they think you're good enough then you'll get in. Or at least be given a chance.'

They met up with Fred and Mary after the match. 'Good match boys? We did okay?' said Fred fiddling with the car keys.

'One-one? Not a great result, was it?' said Billy.

'Missed loads of chances though and the ref was a buffoon. How many did he book?' added Ricky.

'Must be five from each side,' said Fred, finally manoeuvring out of the car park. 'Reckon you lads could hack at it at this level?'

'No danger,' said Billy, confidently. 'When me and my mate get that chance they won't know what's hit 'em. In't that right Ricky?'

38

Tim Ward faced some difficult decisions when he arrived at the training ground on Monday morning. He shared his worries with his sounding board, Aidy Newton.

'We're going to have to throw a few kids in on Saturday. It's getting desperate. The injury situation and suspensions have really thrown us.'

'And it's been looking so good,' said Newton slipping on his tracksuit bottoms and picking up his whistle from the desk drawer.

'We can't even bring anybody in on loan with it being a cup tie. I'll have to wait till next week.'

'I'll back the eleven who'll start to give anybody a game,' said Newton, checking the list of players available for the morning session. 'These kids won't let us down. They're looking the business.'

'It's a tough ask though, isn't it? said Ward, looking out of his window onto the pitches below.

'Yeah. But it's a great incentive for them, Tim,' said Newton. 'If we get through this one, it's the quarters. That'll give everybody a boost.'

'Right then,' said Ward turning to face his number two. 'Bring these four into the squad. Ossie John will have to be on the bench 'cos Pete is still a fortnight off being fit. Billy Pointer, he's a strong lad. Physically can handle himself and from what I've seen deserves his chance.'

'I'd agree with that. His attitude has been superb.'

'The other two will be Alan Merrick. He's got pace and a trick. Gets away from people. And Ricky Grant.'

'The only thing I worry about with this lad,' said a concerned Newton, 'he's having to take such a lot of stick.'

'But he's quickening up all the time. In the reserves last week he skipped away from two crunching tackles. Read it so well.'

'I know. Don't get me wrong. He's a great talent,' added Newton.

'But we've still got to protect the lad. I know he's got to be given his head sooner or later. I just wonder if the timing is right.'

'Is it ever?' queried the manager.

' We've all had to go through it. I'm sure he's itching to get a start,' said Newton, opening the door.

'I'll think it over. See how he reacts this week.'

The fifth round FA Cup draw had them paired with Stoke City at the impressive Britannia Stadium. In the previous two rounds, non-league opposition had provided a comfortable passage. The carrot was a place in the quarter-finals and the possibility of facing a glamour club.

When their names were read out that Monday morning they could-n't speak. Billy and Ricky looked at each other with mouths open.

Then Billy shouted at his digs mate.

'******* hell'

'Hey, Points, give me twenty press-ups,' called out Newton. 'Bad language.'

Ossie joined regular 'keeper Gavin Halford for a specialist session with goalkeeping coach Sam Parton while Billy, Ricky and Alan Merrick made their way over to the rest of the first team squad.

A generous round of applause greeted the youngsters on a cold February morning. Their shorts were unceremoniously yanked down. Welcome to the big league. Piss-takers all.

Little was said to any of them. They went straight in, expected to pick up the drills quickly. All three were on their toes. They concentrated hard, no one wanted to mess-up, but with the blood flowing through their veins at one hundred miles an hour, it wasn't easy to take everything in their stride.

One thing they had decided on beforehand – they'd encourage each other.

Nick Proctor, the leading scorer, pulled up Billy after one challenge, which left the star performer on his backside.

'******* hell Points mate. Leave it out,' said Proctor rubbing his ankle furiously.

Ricky had little difficulty adapting to this company. Better the player, better his touch. He wanted to test himself against the best and in a twenty-minute keep possession game, he didn't lose it once. Drew in opponents and released it – his touch was immaculate and timing perfect.

One piece of skill left the squad gasping, full of admiration for the young kid, when he dummied to clip the ball over to the far side of the square and then, with some outrageous footwork, dragged the ball backwards with the sole of his boot giving him time and space to knock it off effortlessly.

'Well done Ricky, great play son!' shouted skipper Mike Sadler. In that split second, the senior players recognised what a talent he was. Their attitude towards him changed. They knew he would be a huge asset to the football club and one who could help them achieve things. He could do things with the ball, they could only dream about. This lad was special. The opposing players started backing off. They didn't want to look foolish.

Back in their digs Billy and Ricky tucked into risotto.

'So you trained with the first team did you? What, both of you?' said Fred applying a blood-pressure amount of salt to his plate.

'And it was brilliant.' said Billy.

'You're in the squad for Saturday?' asked Fred, passing the bread rolls to the boys.

'Nothing's been said yet but we must be in with a chance,' said Billy.

'The only one who'll definitely be in there is Ossie,' said Ricky, taking a swig of orange juice. 'He's the only fit 'keeper after Gav so he's bound to be on the bench.'

'Unless the boss goes with five outfielders.'

'Wouldn't do that, would he? Not in such an important game,' said Fred.

'You never know what he's thinking,' said Ricky.

'I tell you what, Fred, Ricky was dynamite today,' said Billy. 'You should have seen him go past Speaky. Nut-megged him as well.'

'He wouldn't like that would he? Not Speaky.'

'Took it well. Just said "well played". But the next time Ricky got it he steamed in. Put him on his arse,' said Billy laughing.

'Had to get rid early doors after that,' said Ricky. 'You going to the match Fred?'

'Wouldn't miss it for the world, lad. Already got the tickets. Me and Mary are going to make a day of it. Our daughter lives nearby so we're going to stay overnight. You boys will be all right, won't you?'

'Billy can make some boiled eggs on Sunday morning.'

'Leave it out.'

As the week went on the importance of the game began to sink in. How would they cope in such an atmosphere? But they'd face it together and they knew each other's game.

The manager had hoped that a few of the injured players would be available for selection – but the game had come too early. He'd have to rely on those who'd been together all week.

On Friday morning he announced the side before the training session. Billy would make his debut at centre back to partner Phil Speak. Ricky, Ossie and Merrick would be on the bench. They were well pleased for their mate. All four had make significant steps forward in their careers.

Ricky and Billy, dressed in club blazers and distinctive red ties, mounted the team bus taking them to the hotel for the overnight stay. After the meal they hung around the lounge area watching the senior pros playing cards before they went to their rooms. The young stars tried to get some sleep but everything was whizzing around their heads.

'You asleep, Ricky?'

'Wide awake.'

'Must have got some kip?'

'What time is it?'

'Just after three. I've been dreaming. Kept seeing me slicing a corner into my own net,' said Billy.

'I get off the bench and trip over the linesman,' said Ricky turning over. 'He doesn't see an offside and they score the winner. What's all that about?'

They laughed.

'Fancy a brew?' said Billy.

'Just water.'

'The gaffer seems pretty calm, doesn't he?' said Billy opening the bottle and spraying some on his room mate.

'You pillock,' said Ricky, wiping his face. 'Must be a lot of pressure on him.'

'They expected the play-offs this year. But it'll have to be a hell of a run to do that.'

'Can't see it myself. No way.'

'Tomorrow's all that matters now,' said Billy, spooning in the sugar and returning to his bed. 'Get through that. Worry about the rest later.'

'Better try and get some more kip.'

'Here goes. One sheep, two sheep, three ******* sheep.'

39

Burding's eagerly awaited fifth round tie at home to Tottenham Hotspur turned out to be a huge anti-climax. Neither side could take the initiative or looked like scoring. A snap shot by Marco Cornelio, comfortably held by 'keeper Paul Robinson low down to his near post and an inswinging corner which clipped the top of the bar in the second half were the closest Town came to opening their account.

Spurs, for all their flair and outrageous talent, threatened even less. A 30-yard effort from Jermaine Jenas skimmed across the surface but wide of the post and Ledley King, from only ten yards out, fired over the bar when well placed. Only occasionally were the near capacity crowd lifted from their seats.

The cautions dished out by referee Dave Frost also cancelled each other out. Michael Dawson picked up a yellow when he ploughed through the back of Juan Torres and Jake Watkins was cautioned for clipping the heels of Robbie Keane, marring an otherwise impressive performance.

So the players had to settle for a disappointing stalemate. Spurs would obviously be favourites to win the replay and go through to the quarter-final stage. For Burding? Perhaps their best chance had gone. They would certainly need more inspiration in the return if they were to stay in the competition.

40

'Good luck Billy,' said Ricky giving him the high fives in the away dressing room. 'Any probs, get it out of there.'

'Right out the ground mate,' said Billy, rubbing Vaseline onto his knees.' No way am I trying any fancy stuff. It will be wellied and in some style.'

Sadler led the troops onto the pitch in their blue away strip. The stadium was ablaze in red and white on all corners of the ground with only a few hundred Mexter City supporters wearing their replica away shirts.

It was a disastrous start for the Mexter boys after Stoke took the lead inside the first ten minutes. They failed to clear a long punt down the middle and Halford was beaten at his near post. It was a soft goal to concede but they recovered and stood firm to halftime. Ricky handed the drinks round as Ward spoke to his players.

'I'm not seeing enough belief in you lads. Okay, you're knocking the ball around and you don't look in any trouble at the back but we've got to do more if we're to stay in the competition. And that means somebody's got to step forward and be counted. You've all got your talents but you're not stretching yourselves. We need more and that means from all of you.'

They raised their game in the second half and put Stoke under a lot of pressure. Mexter were clearly the better side but the goal wouldn't come. Chances went begging and it looked like being a sad exit.

'Ricky, get warmed up son,' shouted Ward, from his position in the technical area.

Ricky took off his track suit bottoms before jogging up and down behind the referee's assistant. He did some stretching by the corner flag and a few sprints. The manager signalled him over.

'You're going on. Play just behind Nick,' said Ward grabbing hold of Ricky's arm. 'You've got a free role. Last third of the field, I want you to do some damage. Have a real go at them.'

The fourth official held up the board. 'Number 29, Ricky Grant, will replace number 8, Reg Davies.'

Ricky ran onto the pitch tucking his blue shirt into his shorts. He looked a player.

The pitch was in surprisingly good condition for that time in February. After a mild few weeks there was a good covering of grass which made the bounce true and with his first touch Ricky played a neat one-two off Proctor and clipped it to the far corner for the overlapping full back, Danny Barnes.

The cross came to nothing but it was a promising start. Ricky then went deep to pick up from Billy on the halfway line, wriggled his way past an opponent to carve out a chance for Jody Young. The shot was struck with plenty of power but missed the target.

Mexter had a let off five minutes later when Stoke were gifted the chance to put the tie to bed – the crossbar intervened. Within minutes Mexter were level. A long throw deep into the area was headed out to Ricky fifteen yards from goal. With his second touch he rifled it left footed into the bottom corner. His teammates engulfed him. Billy joined in the celebrations.

'Hey, roommate, what was that? A rocket launcher or what?'

But more was to come. Quick thinking by Sadler, with an instinctive threaded pass, found Proctor, who ran on to slip the ball past the 'keeper. Two-one, and Mexter were through to the next round of the FA Cup.

Billy and Ricky were made up. The atmosphere in the dressing room was unbelievable and after the coach journey home they were on a high like they'd never felt before.

'Hey what about a party at our place? Mary and Fred are away, aren't they?

'How's about it?'

Ricky smiled. 'All I'm ready for is bed.'

'Leave it out. After what we've done today we've got to celebrate.'

'I'll tell you about it later, Points. I've got to keep my nose clean,' said Ricky, stepping off the coach.

The two youngsters started walking from the ground to the taxi rank in the centre of town.

'Anything I can help with?' said Billy.

'I've got a bit of baggage.'

'Haven't we all?' said Billy. Phil Speak drew up alongside, wound the window down to ask, 'Do you want a lift? I'll drop you off.'

Billy, sensing that Ricky wanted to talk, said,' We're fine, mate. Thanks anyway '

'See you Monday. Eh, and well played you two. Bloody magic.' Speak drove off and Billy turned to Ricky. 'Speaky helped me so much today. Talked me through the whole 90 minutes. Anyway, is it your folks causing the aggro?'

'Sort of,' said Ricky.

'They're all the same, Granty. On different bleeding wave lengths, aren't they? Cloud cuckoo land mate. Look, we've all had shit. Growing up's shit, isn't it? Who'd live at home anyway? All kids would move out when they're twelve if they could. It's all hassle. Look at me. I didn't have great time you know.

'Nothing was handed to me on a plate, no way. There were five of us and the old fella was in and out of jobs. It was hand to mouth and we all had to go out and get something in. Anything. If you didn't, you didn't eat. That was it.'

'Did he drink?' asked Ricky.

'He had a drink but he wasn't pissed all the time if that what you mean. He was just a plonker.'

'And your mum?'

'Kept out the way. Didn't want to know. Anything for an easy life. You know what I got one Christmas? A cardboard box. A bleeding cardboard box.'

'You're taking the piss.'

'Seriously. I'm not joking. I opened it up and there's nothing in it. We'd had a row the day before. It was a car with a trailer. He'd taken the toy out and wrapped it back up again. Do you know what that felt like? He said it would teach me a lesson. What a tosser. I wanted to hurt him so badly. I just wanted to put his head in a vice and tighten it until all his brains spewed out. I hated him.'

'Every time Ronnie came near, my skin would crawl.'

A couple of supporters, walking in the opposite direction, spotted the lads and asked for autographs. 'Brilliant guys. That goal was a cracker, Ricky. I'm going to get bladdered tonight. Thanks again boys, you've made my day.'

'No problem. See ya,' said Ricky.

'Ronnie? He's your dad?' said Billy.

'No way.'

'The guy your mum's with?'

'You know what,' said Ricky, attempting to flag down a taxi, ' I went home one day and he was laid out on the settee rat-arsed. I told him he was a disgrace. He gets up and says, "We'll see about that," and starts taking off his belt. Swings it at me, but falls over.

'I just looked at him – an excuse for a human being. I could have taken him out right there. Put him away permanently. The world would have been a better place. But what did I do? Lifted him back on the settee, switched on Thomas the Tank Engine and went through the door.'

'Sounds a right bastard. What's he like now? Now you're doing good,' said Billy, zipping up his jacket.

'Haven't heard from him for ages. He's in a clinic, drying out.'

'Sounds like my old fella and him were out of the same box. He'd smash anything I'd made at school. Woodwork, metalwork. I'd bring them home and he'd say, "What's this rubbish?" He'd take them out back and stamp on 'em or burn 'em. Told me I'd never do anything in my life. Told me I was a waster.'

'Bird-brain,' said Ricky.

'I knew I'd prove him wrong. Being big and physical, I was able to get rid of that anger. Did a bit of boxing. I could knock people about. Gave me confidence.'

It started to rain and the boys quickened their walk.

'Is he around now?' asked Ricky.

'They're divorced. I don't see him,' said Billy. 'But you know what?'

'Go on.'

'When I joined City he got in touch. Wanted to meet up and sort things out.'

'And did you?'

'No way. Told him I never want to see him again. So where's your dad?'

'Never met him,' said Ricky. 'He's Italian, that's all I know. My mum's told me stuff about him. Said he's a great guy.'

'You don't know where he is?'

'I know where they met, that's all.'

'Bit of a shock for him if you do find him?'

'Tell me about it. Eh, I think I will have that drink, Bill.' It was raining heavily and they dived into the Dog and Duck.

'Good on you Rick, mate. When you crashed home that first one I could have given you one,' he said laughing.

'Ha Ha. Too risky. If I score in the quarters I'll keep well away from you Points Baby. Don't want to catch anything nasty,' said Ricky, as they sidled up to the bar.

'Don't worry. I'll leave well alone,' said Billy, shaking off the rain. 'I'll be counting the bonus.'

41

With the exception of Dan Jones, Les Whitehead had a full squad to choose from for the replay. He settled for a 4-4-2 formation with Juan Torres partnering Marco Cornelio up front, Ivor and Smidgy on either side of Sean and Jake in midfield and top Scot Craig Hennessey leading the troops from the back.

In the dressing rooms, deep in the recesses of White Hart Lane, Whitehead briefed his side a quarter of an hour before kick-off. The team were stripped and ready. They had returned from their warm-up, changed into their match kit and had gone through their final individual preparations. Liniment, sweat and smelling salts filled the air. Simmo, hampered by goalie gloves, turned off the stereo.

'According to the experts this game is a foregone conclusion,' said Whitehead, sleeves rolled up and clutching the team sheet. 'They've even suggested we may as well have stayed at home. Well – let me tell you one thing. They know sweet bugger all. I've been in the game too long to know this is going to be no cakewalk for them.

'And I'll tell you why. Because of you guys. I wouldn't swap any of you lot. And that's a fact. If you apply yourselves, individually and collectively, then you've a great chance. You have the qualities to give them plenty of problems. I have every confidence in you to do the business. The only thing I want you to have is belief in yourselves.'

The players stood up. The sound of studs reverberated around the tiled floor. 'COME ON LET'S DO IT'. Jake went round to every player. They embraced, high-fived and shook hands. He then spoke to Sean. 'It's up to us Con to get a grip on the game. We must keep together, no matter what. Keep each other going.'

'No problem mate.' Jake was handed the captain's arm band and stood by the dressing room door. He turned. He looked into their eyes.

The buzzer went and the teams ran out to a crescendo of noise. After the presentations the referee blew the whistle and Spurs took early control. They appealed for a penalty when Darren Bent was

226

brushed aside by a strong challenge but the referee waved play on, indicating it was a legitimate shoulder charge.

First blood went to Burding. A right wing corner was delivered to the far post and when Craig Hennessey rose majestically to nod back across the six-yard box, Juan tapped the ball in from a few yards. The mass of Spurs supporters at that end of the ground went silent and the Spanish galactico wheeled away in jubilation. Burding retained their lead and returned to the changing room at halftime in good spirits. Whitehead was well pleased.

'What you've shown me out there, has been nothing short of magnificent. But there's another forty-five minutes to go. We're going to have to dig deep and stand up to a lot of pressure. Concentration is the key. That's what'll win you the game. I'm going to make a couple of positional changes. We're going to switch to a 4-1-4-1 formation.

'Jake, I want you sit in front of the back four, Juan you'll drop into the right mid position. I want you to use your pace down that flank. Give us an outlet. Ivor, you'll move inside to play alongside Sean and Marco will be on his own through the middle. Any questions? No. Good.'

The boss took Jake to one side. 'Jake they're dangerous at dropping deep from those striking positions so I want you fill that hole,' said Whitehead moving counters on the tactics board. 'Don't allow them to receive easily and have a go at our back four.'

'Okay boss. I've done that job before.'

'Good luck. If they score early on I may want to change it again. So watch for the signals.'

For the first twenty minutes of the second half Burding couldn't get out of their own half, so intense was the pressure exerted by the home side. Some of the football played by the Londoners was exquisite.

Simmo produced two outstanding saves and the Town goal led a charmed life and relied on resilient, defensive play to keep the score intact. Jake was right in the thick of it, leading by example. He covered every inch of the pitch, anticipating passes, breaking up attacks with crunching tackles and regaining possession.

But they couldn't hold out indefinitely and with only fifteen minutes left Spurs got their due desserts and equalised. Dimitar Berbatov sprinted clear to expertly steer the ball inside the far post. White Hart Lane erupted. One-one and all to play for.

Although Spurs held the upper hand they couldn't find a winner. One hundred and eighty minutes of football and the teams still couldn't be divided. Extra time and substitutions failed to end the deadlock and as the clock moved deep into the St Valentine's night the dreaded penalty shoot-out beckoned.

Jake won the toss and elected to take the first spot-kick. He strode up towards the end occupied by the mass of Spurs supporters. The long walk from the halfway line to the 18-yard box was never-ending. He cleared his head and made his decision. Were his legs really feeling tired or was it just nerves?

He was soon to find out. As he placed the ball on the penalty spot the goal seemed to have shrunk with Spurs 'keeper Paul Robinson filling every square inch. As Jake turned for his run up, he stood and looked up to the leaden skies.

The ball was driven firm and true and nestled into a devouring net. The noise from the home fans abated. Jake jogged back to the halfway line. Heart racing. Job done.

Spurs scored with their first but then Burding missed, Robinson producing a magnificent save from Ivor's placed shot. Spurs scored their next and so did Sean. Simmo then took centre stage. His antics on the goal-line outwitted the next two kickers. First he anticipated correctly to fingertip around the post, and then he punched the air when the next effort struck the woodwork and flew over.

As Jonah had netted with his spot-kick Smidgy had the responsibility of completing the job. Was he up to the task? He went for the direct hit.

Straight down the middle. Robinson made a brave attempt and got a strong hand on the power drive, but the ball, to the anguish of the home supporters, inched over the line.

The lads went berserk. The tiredness in the legs had disappeared as they leapt on their veteran 'keeper in a heap of steaming bodies. This was Jake's proudest moment so far in his young career. They were through to the quarter-finals of the FA Cup. How far could they go?

42

It had been a topsy-turvy few weeks for Jake. The Spurs result was magnificent – extra time, penalties, the full Monty. Nerve-wracking or what? They'd got the breaks and he'd been lucky not to fluff his spot-kick.

If he'd missed, it would have been the pits. Now for Fulham at home in the quarters – all 26,000 tickets were sold within twenty-four hours.

The town was buzzing and the anticipation around the club was at fever pitch. Jake saw smiling faces wherever he went and, for a short period, the fans forgot about their dull, monotonous routines.

Businesses in the area were booming and massive sales figures reported; the feelgood factor had clicked in. The locals were convinced that an appearance at Wembley was a foregone conclusion. And why not?

Jake could see the roller-coaster spinning out of control – but then even he started to wonder. Could they get there? What would it be like leading the troops out in front of a full house at the home of English football in the most famous club knock-out competition in the world?

It was on the personal front that things had taken a bit of a battering. He'd read the letter from Marie every day – digested every word.

It could have been us out there – couldn't it? ...You and me.

Us together, reflected Jake. We're as one. No question about it, she believes we're an item.

...thought they were going to die ...thought it was going to end – just like that. Devastation was all around. ...We kissed each other, we prayed, we cried. We said our goodbyes.
Some were not so lucky. A baby boy was found the following

day. Alone on the beach. Nothing within 100 yards of him. He
was at peace. After the carnage, the destruction and the death
– came the silence.
We can't mess about thinking we've got plenty of time. It could
all end tomorrow – couldn't it? And where would that leave
us? You and me?

'Has anything changed?' Jake asked himself. Just about everything.
What to do? Tell her? Be up front? Be totally honest?

Jake sat at home, clutching the crumpled pages, wondering which
way to go. ' If I tell her what's been going on, how's she going to react?
Could I risk it? Would she understand?'

'It's okay Jake, you've had a fling, don't worry. I forgive you. It was
bound to happen. Let's put it down to sowing wild oats. Don't think
anymore about it.'

Yeah, right! But this was the real world. How many girls would
react like that? But if he decided to bluff it out – say nothing about
Tess – and Marie got wind of it, he was bound to be dead meat. Trust
would be out the window – the relationship would be well and truly
over.'

At least he'd talked to Tess. He'd taken the line he didn't want
to be the one to break up a marriage and felt their 'fling' was going
nowhere. And he reasoned that as they had to see each other on the
committee, it would lead to an impossible situation.

Tess understood. She was upset, pretty miffed to be honest, but
agreed. No bones about it, she'd had a fantastic time – just like Jake.
But she was intelligent as well as being very attractive and she knew
what the consequences would be if they continued the relationship.
'Not even a quickie, now and then?' she laughed after it was finally
sorted.

The attraction between them faded just as quickly as it had
begun.

After mulling it over, Jake finally came to a decision. He would
play it cool. What was the point of telling Marie what had gone on?
She's on the other side of the world. It's not as if they could discuss it
in any depth, could they?

It would make her miserable and who knows what would happen?

So he emailed to smooth things over. Told her he was thinking about getting his own place but would now put that on the back burner until she returned – and they could choose together. He felt sad that he hadn't been there with her to share the grief.

He understood that listening to all the personal accounts must have been horrendous. She had chosen to go but he backed her all the way. He had total respect for her courage. And in a few weeks time, she'd be coming home – and they could pick up where they left off.

He finished by telling her all about the Spurs game and what a special night that was. 'Awesome.' Yeah, he actually used the word. 'And send some more photos.'

Prior to the cup-tie, Town were away at Everton where they lost 2-0. Jake had to be subbed midway through the second half with a calf strain.

The following morning Jake was in pain. He hobbled into the treatment room to find Jimmy more upbeat.

'Right, get the strides off and hop on the bed. Let's have a look at the damage,' said Jimmy switching on the various machines. 'Any problems sleeping last night?'

'No I was okay but when I got up this morning it was stiff,' said Jake.

'Morning glory, that mate,' said Smidgy, laughing. He'd popped in to have a dressing changed on a head wound. 'Girl friend's been away for a bit now, hasn't she?'

'Good one Smidge.'

'Let's take a look,' said the physio. 'Bend your knee.' Jimmy felt around the muscle, pressing and massaging. 'Does that hurt?' he asked.

'No.'

'And that?'

'Yeah, that's the spot,' said Jake in obvious distress.

'It could be there's a small tear or just a slight strain,' said Jimmy moving the ultrasound machine to the side of Jake's bed. 'Can't be too careful so we'll get it checked out. Just precautionary to see exactly what we're dealing with.'

Smidgy, flicking through the papers, shouted, 'Bastards.'

'What's up?' said Jake, moving to a more comfortable position.

'I only got five in this paper. Five out of bleeeding ten,' said Smidgy, frowning. 'You get five for turning up. Didn't they see all those blind runs I was doing?'

'That's the problem. Nobody saw 'em,' added Jake.

'They reckon the four who'll go through to the semis are Charlton, Villa, Fulham and Pompey,' said Smidge, removing a blood-stained dressing above his right eye. ' We don't get a shout.'

'What do they know?' said Jimmy, applying the gel to Jake's muscle. 'It might be the year of the underdog.'

'The draws have favoured the lesser teams this year, haven't they?' said Smidgy, returning to his bed after placing the plaster in the bin.

'Who'd have thought all the massive clubs would be bombed out at this stage?'

'About time a lower division club got a look-in,' said Jimmy, setting the timer. 'Mexter are still in with a chance, aren't they?

That young kid Ricky Grant is supposed to be a whiz kid. See him yesterday? Magic bit of skill. And he's only seventeen.'

'Looks a bit special,' said Jake.

Smidgy agreed. 'The way he went past the last two defenders was different class.'

'Can't rule them out with him in the side,' piped up Jake.

'A team from outside the top division getting through to the final? It's been done before,' said Jimmy, gently finding the right spot. 'Who was the last?'

'Millwall,' said Jake.

'Correct. And for a bonus point who was the last team from outside the top division to actually win the trophy?'

'Bloody hell Jimbo. Ring Taffy, he'll know,' said Jake.

'Give up lads? Sunderland. They beat Leeds against all the odds back in 1973. Jim Montgomery made a fabulous double save,' said Jimmy, obviously pleased with himself.

'Excuse me, Mr Know-it-all but you've made a right ricket there,' chipped in Smidgy.

'Come on then, mastermind, who was it?' said Jimmy, a little annoyed.

'Southampton did it in '76 but West Ham were the last in 1980.'

'Where the hell have you got that from?'

'It's here, in the paper,' said Smidgy, happy to put one over on the intelligentsia. 'Second Division winners FA Cup. You can't argue with that.'

'I was in short trousers, wasn't I?' said Jake. 'I remember my dad telling me about the Sunderland game.'

'I'll ask you one more about the cup,' said Smidgy. The question was directed towards Jake. 'Four clubs have all lost the FA Cup final at Wembley and been relegated in the same season. Who are they?'

'How the hell am I supposed to know that?' said Jake.

'Have a guess.'

'I've got one,' said Jimmy. 'Middlesbrough in the late '90's.'

'Correct well done. One-nil to Jimbo.'

'All right I'll guess at... ' Jake was really struggling. 'Southampton.'

'Wrong. But one is a team on the south coast,' said Smidgy giving them both a massive clue.

'Brighton.' Both Jake and Jimmy shouted in unison.

'Back in 1983. Only two to get. And one's not far from us.'

'United.'

'No. Manchester City in 1926. The last one is a midlands club.'

'Coventry, Derby, er Birmingham?' said Jake.

'Carry on,' encouraged Smidge.

'Villa, Leicester,' guessed Jimmy.

'Yeah, Leicester City in '69. Got there in the end.'

'How's that feeling Jake?' said Jimmy, wiping the excess gel off his leg.

'Feels easier. It's settled down. Not aching as much.'

'It's going to be a close call for Saturday,' said Jimmy, moving a heat lamp towards the affected area. 'We'll have to see what you're like on Thursday and test it out.'

43

After his spectacular appearance Ricky was suddenly in big demand. He rang Simon.

'Simon? You okay?'

'Not as good as you lad from all accounts. Well done, absolutely bloody brilliant.' Haworth was on his hands-free 'phone in his car, driving down the motorway for a business appointment in London.

'It went well.'

'I should say it did from what I saw on TV,' said Haworth switching to the inside lane after flashing lights warned of delays ahead.

'It's been kinda hectic these last few days.'

'From zero to hero?' said Haworth.

'Something like that. Simes, I'm looking for a bit of advice.'

'At your service,' he said, changing to a lower gear. 'Fire away.'

'There's been a lot of agents on, wanting to represent me.'

'No surprise there. They'll be falling over themselves to get you signed up.'

'Well that's the problem,' said Ricky. 'What to do?'

'The agent who looked after me was a guy called Walter Snape. I had him for five years and he never let me down. There's some wasters about but he's not one of them.'

'Is he still in the business?' asked Ricky.

The slight holdup disappeared and Haworth once again accelerated. 'Yes. If you like, I'll tell him to get in touch.'

Ricky got a 'phone call within the hour.

'Ricky, it's Walter Snape. Congratulations on last week's game. I suppose your world has turned upside down?'

'You could say that.'

'Do you want to have a chat? I could call round tomorrow night. I take it you've no game?'

'No. But the thing is,' said Ricky, collecting his post after the training session, 'I'd like my mum in on the talks.'

'No problem.'

'I'm going home this weekend. Can you get round on Sunday?'

'Give me your address. What's a good time?'

A distinguished, middle-aged grey-haired man wearing a dark blue suit and carrying a black briefcase was standing at the front door of the flat. He introduced himself. 'Hi. I'm Walter.'

'Good to see you Walter,' said Ruth, shaking his hand. 'I'm Ricky's mum, Ruth. We've heard a lot about you. Come in.'

'So this is the wonder boy, is it?' How you doing, Ricky?' said Snape, glancing around the humble surroundings.

Client or no client, the sooner they were out of that place, the better.

'Pity the game was postponed yesterday,' added Snape. 'You'd have wanted to follow up that great performance.'

'It's frustrating. But, to be honest, I think I'd have been back on the bench,' said Ricky switching off the TV.

'I suppose your lives have changed just a little bit,' said Snape.

'You could say that,' said Ruth. 'The 'phone has never stopped ringing. Come and sit down. Can I get you something to eat?'

'No thanks. But could I have a glass of water?' said Snape, placing his case on the floor.

'Of course,' she said, making her way through to the kitchen.

'What an impact, Ricky,' said Snape. 'What did the manager say to you before you went on?'

'Just to enjoy myself and be confident. Things couldn't have gone much better.'

'You're telling me. Nice to see yourself in the press?' said Snape, making himself comfortable.

'It's kinda strange. Unreal. The players have taken the mickey a lot. Presented me with a cake on Monday morning – with one candle on it. I had to make a speech. Just about got through it without looking a complete berk.'

'What did you say?'

'That I couldn't have done it without them. That sort of thing. I know it sounded well crap. But I had to say something, didn't I?

Then Billy Pointer came over and lifted me over his shoulder. The rest of the lads whacked me on the arse.'

'Ha! Ha!' laughed Snape. 'Sounds like the squad's really taken you on board. Fancy yourself in the next round? Charlton's a good side.'

'I suppose they'll be the favourites but at least we're at home.'

'I'm hoping to take the game in. League debut first?'

'That'll be something special,' said an excited Ricky. 'If it's at home? Can you imagine?'

'Billy looked good,' said Snape, taking the glass from Ruth. 'You wouldn't have thought it was his first game.'

'He's a good mate. Sound guy.'

'Great stuff. Anyway, let's get on. How can I be of help?'

'To be honest, we're a little in the dark about agents,' said Ruth. 'How does it work?'

'Well, we're there to help both with the football side and also the financial side,' said Snape. 'The important part is the football. If a player is successful then all the other things tend to fall into place.'

'I've heard stories about agents upsetting the apple cart and making life difficult with the club,' said Ricky.

'That can happen. Of course it can. I'd be lying if I told you it didn't. There are some bad agents just as there are some bad teachers or bad solicitors. But I've got to say the vast majority are very professional.'

'So what's the next step?' asked Ruth.

'To be honest, Ricky probably doesn't need an agent right now. But the thing is as his career progresses then he will need one at some stage. There's no question about that.'

'That's what Simon said,' chipped in Ricky.

'My relationship with Simon was excellent,' said Snape, opening his case and taking out some leaflets. 'He was a good pro. Did well on the field and was very popular off it. So he was an ideal player to manage. You see, it's got to be right from both sides. We have to trust each other. I take it you signed your first contract this season?'

'Yeah. It's for two years.'

'Right then, there's no hurry to change anything. Just keep doing what you're doing. What I suggest is I'll keep in the background and advise you from afar to start off with.

'I'll definitely come and see you play and you can always get in touch whenever you feel I can help. We'll take it slowly and not rush into anything too soon. You'll know yourself when you need that guidance, then it's just a case of sitting down together and talking it through.

'By then, I'm positive we'll be on the same wavelength. I'll leave a bit of info about our agency. All the contact numbers are there.'

After only seven games the club wanted to renegotiate Ricky's contract. During that time Mexter had been undefeated and a 2-0 victory over Charlton saw them reach their first ever semi-final. Ricky had been included in every game, making his League debut against Plymouth Argyle in a goalless draw.

'Walter, can we meet up?'

44

Even with intense daily treatment the injury didn't improve as quickly as Jake had hoped. At home he sprawled on the settee watching TV, depressed.

Chloe was in her final year at school and was preparing for her GCSE exams.

'Are you going to be fit for Saturday?' she asked, laying out her books on the dining room table.

'Don't know yet,' said Jake grumpily. 'Physio reckons I've got a chance.'

'I'm not going if you're not playing.'

'Whatever.'

Jake wasn't fit. Whitehead was desperate for him to be in the starting line-up but it would be suicidal to even consider him. He got his skipper in on the Thursday afternoon.

'Doesn't look good Jake. Can't risk it. If I do it'll put you back weeks.'

'I know, gaffer. I couldn't give my best. It's still tight and I feel it when I jog. It's a lot better since Saturday but it's not right.'

'I still want you in the dressing room before the game,' said the manager, already thinking about who would replace his star performer.

Whitehead juggled his team around to accommodate the loss of his talented captain and decided on a 4-5-1 formation, packing the midfield in an effort to get a stranglehold on the game.

Before kick-off Jake had a word with all the players 'Good luck mate. Keep 'em going Ivor. Get the tackles in, Sean.' He wondered over to Craig Hennessey who had been given the captain's armband. 'All the best Scotty.'

Jake was left in the dressing room with the manager, coach, physio and kit man after the players made their way onto the pitch.

'Want to sit with us Jake or go in the stands?' asked Whitehead, putting on his quilted Town jacket.

Jake picked up a programme. 'On the bench boss, at least I'll be able to shout.'

'Come on then,' said Whitehead. 'Let's see what the next ninety minutes have in store.'

For Jake it was agony. Every time Fulham went within thirty yards of the Burding goal he was convinced they'd score. Every time a cross was whipped in towards Simmo he was convinced the big man would spill it. Every time one of their players dribbled into the 18-yard box he was convinced a flying boot would send him crashing and a penalty be awarded.

On the field he could get involved and do something about it. Stuck there in the dug-out, he couldn't do a thing.

The occasion seemed to have got the better of the players and it became obvious that the longer the game went on the first goal would be crucial. And so it proved. Town broke quickly down the left flank and Holty's cross was met twelve yards out by Ivor who had come inside from his right mid position. His first touch was excellent and with the second he slotted the ball into the far corner.

Jake was as nervous as a kitten. All he could do was pray for the final whistle. Finally it came. Burding's organisation saw them through – to put them out of their agony and into the semi-final.

The draw was made by two footballing legends of the '70s and '80s, Bob Latchford and Ian Rush. Both were prolific scorers who wore the No 9 shirts with distinction for the Merseyside rivals Everton and Liverpool.

'Did you ever get to a final Bob?' asked host Gary Lineker, himself an ex-Evertonian and FA Cup final goalscorer.

'Closest I came was three semi-finals,' said Bob, looking distinctly trim. 'Boys against men when I played for Birmingham City against Leeds in 1972, then controversially got turned over by Rushie's lot in '77 and lost again to West Ham in 1980.'

'And what about your recollections, Ian?'

'I was very lucky to win it three times. The games against Everton in '86 and '89 stand out and, of course, scoring at Wembley. What a feeling that was.'

'Gentlemen, great to have you with us today,' said Lineker. 'It's a simple draw. Only four teams left so if I could ask you Bob to draw the first number please.'

A shuffle of the balls and Latchford called out 'Number Three.'

The FA communications director followed up with 'Burding Town'.

'Hey, first one out the hat. Hope that's a lucky omen,' said Jake, watching the draw from the club canteen with the rest of the squad.

'All we need now is Mexter,' said Ivor.

Ian Rush pulled out ball number two.

'Will play Portsmouth.'

'All to do then,' was the response from Frank Hart.

'Number One'

'Aston Villa will play...'

'Number four.'

'Mexter City.'

'These games will be played on Sunday April 10th with kick-offs and venues to be decided. Gentlemen, once again thank you for your help this afternoon. That is the conclusion of the semi-final draw.'

45

'Right, let's get to the nitty gritty,' said Snape, taking a seat at the kitchen table. He took out a writing pad from his case and a pen from his inside jacket pocket. Ricky sat opposite with Ruth to his left. 'At present your basic is £300, you're on £250 appearance in the first team and bonuses. Is that correct?'

'Yeah, that's right,' said Ricky.

'Well first of all they'll be offering you improved terms. I know it's difficult for a young lad to talk money. You feel honour bound to sign for whatever they offer – but this is where I come in. You deserve the going rate after what you've done. They won't think any the worse of you during the negotiations. I've dealt with the club many times before.'

'The thing is,' Ricky pointed out, 'they've been great to me.'

'I know – and I have no intention of aggravating anyone. But if we can come to some agreement pretty quickly then everyone can get on with winning football matches. What would you be happy with? Any ideas?' said Snape, scribbling down some numbers.

'I haven't thought about it,' Ricky said, moving the pepper-pot to one side.

'You must have something in mind?'

'Well, I thought they might increase my basic to say around £400. But you tell me. Am I asking too much?' It suddenly became dark and Ruth switched on the light.

'It's not just the basic pay to consider. What length of contract would you want? Maybe a signing-on fee could be included. We can't do anything about bonuses. They're already sorted. But what about representative honours? You know, if you get picked for the international squads say at under-19 or under-20 level?'

'Would they include that?' said Ricky, surprised.

'Of course. It means the player is worth more on the transfer market. But let's not start thinking too far ahead. Playing regularly is what it's all about.'

Ricky agreed. 'So where do we start?'

'I would try for a new two-year deal because if you do well the club will want to re-negotiate after twelve months. That's if you keep improving. I think we should be asking for a basic of around £700 with an increase to £800 the following year. With appearance money we're talking around £1,000 a week. How does that sound?'

Ricky was clearly shocked. 'Mind-blowing. What do think mum?'

'A thousand pounds a week? For playing football?' For a moment Ruth was flustered. 'I don't believe it. Does he still get paid if he's injured?' she asked.

'Every week, fifty-two weeks of the year,' confirmed Snape.

'That's unbelievable,' said Ruth, obviously finding it difficult to take everything in.

'Well that's what we'll be going for and I'm sure with all the negotiations I've done, we won't be far away with those figures. Leave me to sort out those England clauses. I'll have another think about it.'

'You do know I've got dual nationality? My dad was Italian.'

'More options. Interesting,' said Snape writing it down.

'Is there anything else that Ricky needs to think about?'

'It'll all come later on, Ruth. I have contacts in other areas, like financial advisors who can sort out pensions and mortgages. Once Ricky passes his test for instance, and is looking for a car, we might be able to get someone to sponsor him. But one step at a time.'

'There's one thing I've got to ask, 'cos Ricky won't,' said Ruth slightly embarrassed. 'How much is all this going to cost? Your fees I'm talking about?'

'The ballpark figure is around five per cent but as it's Ricky's first contract I'm prepared to take less. In the future, if things go well, then we can both be rewarded. Is that okay?'

'Seems fair to me,' said Ruth.

'Fine,' said Ricky, circling the table to shake hands.

'Deal done?'

'Deal done,' said Ricky. 'I'd better start scoring a few goals.'

'It would help.'

After negotiating with the club secretary and one of the directors, Walter arrived to tell them the good news.

'The meeting went well. The club's really buzzing with the Villa game coming up and they obviously think very highly of you. The manager even popped in during the negotiations and you could see he was keen to get it all sorted.

'Anyway they've come up with a package, which I think you'll be happy with. They've offered a three-year deal starting at £800 basic for the first year, £925 for the second and £1,050 for the third. £250 appearance money for each first team game plus bonuses.

'If you break through into an international squad you will receive £5000 and into the full international squad £10,000. After fifty first team games the club said they were willing to renegotiate an improved contract. What do you feel about it?'

'Brilliant,' said Ricky, beaming from ear to ear.

'Thanks very much, Walter,' said a very happy Ruth. 'It's really put our minds at rest.'

'But just to put the icing on the cake,' said Snape producing a bottle of champagne from his briefcase. 'I've saved the best till last.'

'There's more?'

'The club has said it would pay my fees so you won't have to shell out anything.'

'Couldn't be better,' said Ruth, looking for suitable glasses. It came as no surprise that the fluted variety were missing.

'Now the only thing you have to concentrate on, is out there on the pitch.'

'Too true. I'll give it my best shot.'

'That's what I like to here. Things are in place, son. It's now up to you.' Snape took a sip and said, 'Good luck, Ricky.'

'I hope I'm not rubbish in my next game,' said Ricky with a short laugh.

'In that case, we'd better sign this deal fast, or they might welsh on it.'

'Where's the pen?'

Ruth and Ricky showed Snape to the door and hugged each

other. 'I'm proud of you Ricky,' said Ruth flushed but relaxed. The bubbles had found the spot.

'I can't believe it mum. I've been so lucky,' said Ricky.

'They say you make your own luck.'

'Not this type. I was coming from a long way back.'

'It was my fault in many ways,' said Ruth, clutching him tightly. 'I got involved with a wrong 'un and it brought a lot of unhappiness.'

'Don't say that, mum. You weren't to know what he was like.'

'Ricky, I've got to tell you something. I got a 'phone call this morning. Ronnie died last night.'

Showing little emotion, Ricky said, 'It's not like it was unexpected, was it? I've got to say I won't shed too many tears.'

'He got in touch with me last week,' said Ruth moving through to the kitchen. 'Sent me a letter.' She took an envelope out of the top drawer and slipped it into Ricky's hand.

Hi Ruth

The docs have given me a 50-50 chance. My liver is knackered. My guts are well bad. But I'm hanging in. The stab cut has healed. But I can't stop the hands shaking. Nurse Kelly is writing this for me. She's been great.

It's not easy for me say – but I'm sorry for all the pain and the aggro I've caused. The booze got in the way.

I've been thinking a lot lately. Since I've sobered up. About how I've wasted my life and the pain I've caused – especially to you and Ricky.

I've got a chance to start again and I'm going to give it my all. I want to do the simple things in life – watch Ricky play football and do things with you Ruth. Time together. As a family.

I treated the lad badly and I know what he thinks about me. And he's right. But tomorrow is another day.

Now I'm out of the prison of my addiction, I want to enjoy the freedom. The freedom with you and Ricky.

Whatever happens from now on in I'm going to do it sober. I've said goodbye to the bottle. Never again. I've wasted so much of my life.

I thought I could beat it myself. Not accepting my illness. I've gone over it so many times. Why didn't I listen? To you? I know how you tried to help. But I thought I knew what I was doing. You know what Ruth? – it's good to be free from the lies, the violence and the cheating.

I'm a changed man. Honest. I am. I've learnt so much in here. The counsellors have been fantastic. They'll all been through what I'm going through. They know what it's like. And they've given me everything. Even when I told them where to get off. They came back for more.

No more guilt. No more remorse. I hope I can make you see that I'm serious about what's going to happen. No more drunken Ronnie – the violent piss artist. It's all in the past.

What do you think Ruth? Can we try? One day at a time. We felt something for each other at one time didn't we? I know we did. I've never stopped loving you.

It's not too late – is it? To give it another go?

Dignity is a word that's been mentioned a lot in here. It took some time to sink in. With me. But I've begun to realise how important it is.

At least I know one thing. Whenever it finally happens – if my liver packs up or my heart crashes – tomorrow, next week, maybe even in 5 years time – I'm determined to die sober.

And when I do I hope you're not a million miles away.

Love from Ronnie

Placing the letter on the table Ricky said, 'Would it have made any difference?'

'No, no. I'd already decided. I couldn't trust him again. He was a dangerous man.'

'Now he's gone. It's a new start.'

'I know, love. I know,' she said, tears flowing down her face.

46

Hi Jake. Thanks for all the nice things you said. It'll be great when I get back and we can plan ahead and see what we want to do. Coming away has made me think long and hard. It's given me a new perspective on everything. It's not long to go now.

Sorry to hear that you missed the game. What's going on? You weren't fit? That's awful. How did you cope? Must have felt rotten. Are you going to be fit for the semis? It would be a disaster if you weren't. Tell that physio to get you right otherwise he'll have me to answer to.

We are now in Cambodia. I've got to tell you this. We went to a Sports Bar – thought there might be something on about the Cup games. There's one called 'Sprinters' so we went down, ordered a drink, but something wasn't quite right. There were lots of very young girls drinking with some very dodgy old men. Found out it was the town's brothel and 'sports bar' meant something very different to what we thought. Got out of there in double quick time although Helen did say, if we hung around for a bit, we could have ditched the rucksacks and gone 4 star for the rest of the trip! I told her you wouldn't be too happy about that!

Vietnam was very beautiful but very stressy. Everywhere you go in Hanoi, somebody is trying to sell you something. – postcards, books, even glue for your shoes! And crossing the road was an experience in itself. There's no traffic lights and no places to cross. Just hundreds of motorbikes and scooters. What you have to do is step on the road, walk very slowly and hope the scooters swerve past you!

Went on a 2-day boat trip to a place called Halong Bay, a couple of hours away from Hanoi. Hundreds of tiny islands that you sail around. Really lovely but we had a guide on our boat who wound everybody up. An irate Canadian threatened

246

to smash his face in and called him a cheat and a liar. Oh dear.
Some people are just not suited to going on holiday and others
shouldn't be tour guides!

And in the paper:

BURDING GO TO TOWN
On a bright sunny day with a cool wind, Villa Park staged
a marvellous game, which kept the 42,000 fans engrossed
throughout the 90 minutes.
And what a refreshing change it was to witness two sets of fans
exchanging friendly rivalry instead of the vile obscene insults,
which usually occur during these sporting occasions. 'Seems like
a nice boy' was one example of the instant wit shown by the
Pompey supporters when well-rounded 'keeper, Alan Simpson,
replaced his ripped shorts midway through the second half.
Both teams had chances in the opening 15 minutes. A clever
dummy from Matty Taylor presented a shooting opportunity for
Pompey midfielder Pedro Mendes. But Tommy Holt managed
to get a block in and the shot was deflected for a corner.
Burding soon retaliated. They broke down the left flank after
a long clearance from Clive Jackson and when the cross was
delivered to the far post Jonah Sonsissko was only inches wide
with a powerful header. In fact, all Burding's best work was
coming down that side of the field and Pompey were quick to
spot the danger, moving Mendes into a slightly more defensive
role.
The game was played at a cracking pace and in the right
competitive spirit and from Burding's next attack Marco
Cornelio's 20-yard strike clipped the far post. At the other end
a poor back pass almost embarrassed the Burding 'keeper.
The opening goal came after 25 minutes and it went to Burding.
A right wing corner was delivered to the far post and Craig
Hennessey dispatched it into the roof of the net.
Pompey didn't have long to wait for the equaliser. A long throw
into the six-yard box from ex-Arsenal defender Lauren put the

Burding defence under intense pressure and when they failed to clear, Benjani crashed home from close range.

A move involving Burding skipper Jake Watkins and his midfield partner Sean O'Connor ended with a shot from Sonsissko, which was cleared off the line. There was some doubt as to whether the ball had actually crossed the line but the assistant referee was in the perfect position.

Welsh international Ivor Smeeten became the unlikely goal-scoring hero after he started and finished the move that would take his club to Wembley. Smeeten, whose goal defeated Fulham in the quarters, fed Watkins on the left wing and when the cross fell nicely in his path, side-footed the ball into the net from ten yards. Pompey came back strongly but for all their pressure the Burding back line held firm.

The atmosphere at the final whistle was fantastic – or at least for one half of the ground. The Burding players went into a collective huddle before acknowledging their ecstatic fans. Music played over the tannoy – 'Hi Ho Silver Lining!' – and Jake and the boys danced away in front of the fans. Scarves and hats were thrown down from the stands.

One banner said 'Les's Blue and White Magicians' – another, 'Town's Terrors.' Back in the dressing room, the chairman dished out the champagne. He had a huge smile on his face and informed the players, 'we're all going cruising round the Caribbean' – if they returned with the cup in May.

The gaffer was doused in water – the first time he'd not been bothered about his hairstyle! Cameras, photographers, radio, TV – the lot. It was bedlam. When Jake got in the showers it finally hit home what they'd achieved. 'Captain of a cup final team! At nineteen.' He shouted to Sean. 'Can you imagine what it'll be like if we win the bloody thing?'

Hello Capitano. Yabadabado! Fantabidosey!!!!!! I couldn't believe it. Watching you and the lads leaping about in front of the fans. With that big smile on your face. Unbelievable. Me and Helen just screamed right through the whole game. We went mental.

We watched it with two Pompey fans – husband and wife – decked out in their colours! Which are the same as ours. When we told them who we were they went crazy. Wouldn't let us buy a drink. Of course they were gutted but pleased for us. They were great fun. Watching the game together thousands of miles away was unreal. Little England in Cambodia.

It was a good game, wasn't it? We were very nervous. We had to keep going to the bathroom. But when we found out its condition we crossed our legs instead!

We thought you deserved to win (well we would say that wouldn't we?). We celebrated by staying in a 5 star hotel for a couple of nights, which cost 10 quid. It was incredible. Sampled a few bottles of the finest Cambodian plonko! We got talking about you and they said we could stay another two days without paying! So in every restaurant from now on, you'll be mentioned.

We are now in Siem Reap, which has the largest religious temples in the world. Very famous place to visit in Cambodia. Angelina Jolie filmed Tomb Raider here. There are lots of $2,000 dollar a night hotels, which we can't even afford to walk past. Perhaps that Sprinters isn't a bad idea? Only joking!

Congratulations skipper. You must feel on top of the world and you deserve it. You've worked so hard. Keep up the good work. Off to India next week. If you win it'll be free curries for life. Lots of love from your No 1 fan – M.

47

The atmosphere inside Old Trafford for the second semi-final between Aston Villa and Mexter City was electric with both sets of supporters hell bent on shouting their heroes all the way to the final on May 20th.

In front of a capacity crowd of over 75,000, Mexter made two changes from the team that defeated Charlton in the quarter-finals with Jody Young returning from injury and Jim Moore coming in at right back.

Aston Villa, in their all white away strip, kept to the line-up that had been undefeated in the last four games.

Heavy showers preceded the kick-off but as the players emerged from the dressing rooms the stadium was bathed in glorious sunshine.

A cold blustery wind, however, circulated around the 'Theatre of Dreams' making the conditions far from ideal for such an important game.

The pitch had been recently re-laid and was in immaculate condition.

Mexter started the game positively and in their first attack should have taken the lead. Intricate two touch football in midfield opened up the Villa defence and full back Danny Barnes made an excellent run on the blind side; but his touch was poor and Villa 'keeper Thomas Sorensen was quickly out to thwart the danger.

After their lethargic start Villa had one or two bright moments but it was Mexter who had the next sight on goal. They gained a free kick just outside the 18-yard box and when Ricky Grant ran over the ball Mike Sadler whipped in a dangerous cross, which Nicky Proctor just failed to convert.

Villa then forced a corner, which avoided everybody and went for a throw-in on the far side. A lucky escape for Mexter – manager Tim Ward was visibly unhappy in the technical area with the way his team had defended the set play.

But Mexter were still enjoying some excellent passages of play and when a long throw was launched into the six-yard box Phil Speak got the slightest of touches but, agonisingly for the veteran defender, the ball flashed the wrong side of the post.

The crowd was certainly playing their part and was determined not to let the occasion pass quietly.

And it was the Mexter fans who had more reason to celebrate when their side opened the scoring. A free kick taken on the halfway line was hoisted into the 18-yard box and what should have been a formality for the Villa defence, turned into a defensive mix up.

The ball landed to Sadler at the edge of the box and he instinctively lobbed it into an unguarded net. A soft goal to concede but no more than Mexter had deserved. One-nil, fifteen minutes gone. Game on.

Villa responded immediately and their extra urgency resulted in a caution for Billy Pointer for a late challenge on Gareth Barry. The young defender could have no complaints about the decision – lucky in fact not to have been shown a straight red card.

The windy conditions didn't help Villa's free flowing football and they were making too many misplaced passes and elementary mistakes. They needed to regroup and quickly.

Some success was to follow. A long through ball wasn't dealt with by Mexter's centre back pairing and Ashley Young raced clear. A fiercely hit strike from the former Watford player looked like arrowing into the bottom corner but Mexter 'keeper Gavin Halford flung himself horizontally and with a strong left hand tipped it away for a corner. It was the best Villa had shown and gave hope to their loyal fans.

They had another chance soon afterwards when lovely skills from Gabriel Agbonlahor saw him bearing down on goal. Mexter midfielder Dario Maricco seemed to have clipped his ankle but Agbonlahor tried to stay on his feet in an attempt to steer the ball home. Sadly, he stumbled and the chance was gone.

From the stands it looked like a legitimate shout for a penalty. In his technical area animated Villa manager Martin O'Neill took issue with the fourth official. If the score stayed the same, no doubt the Villa contingent would have other choice words to say at the final whistle.

Mexter went into the break leading 1-0.

Big decisions and crucial calls had to be made. Would Mexter try to hold onto their lead or go all out for the second goal, which would surely seal the win? And what of Villa? Would substitutions be made or even a change in formation?

No changes were made by either side at the break but within five minutes of the restart Villa made a double substitution. Striker Luke Moore and midfielder Craig Gardner came on and the formation changed into an attacking 4-3-3. Villa had clearly set out their stall and within minutes their positive approach almost brought dividends. Moore got around the back in a tight area and whipped in a great cross, which somehow the Mexter back line shovelled away for a corner.

Mexter were now under pressure and when Sadler needed attention for a shoulder injury, the players grabbed the opportunity to take in fluids and instructions from the manager.

Villa had at last grasped the initiative and worryingly for Mexter their early dominance was now a distant memory.

Mexter had reverted to hitting long balls and the fluency of the early part of the match had disappeared. Manager Ward had seen enough. Midway through the second half he sent on another defender, Ian Mills, and reverted to a 5-3-2 formation. Villa knew this was their best chance to keep Mexter penned into their own area and force an equaliser. Mexter were under siege.

Somebody had to grasp the nettle and it was the skipper Sadler who led by example. With help from the promising young Grant and Italian Maricco, he managed to stem the tide. But the Mexter strikers were continually losing possession.

Ward made another tactical change. He moved Grant into an advanced position with Proctor playing deeper. The third formation in the game.

After applying so much pressure Villa were still unable to find a way through the Mexter rearguard and left themselves open to a quick counter attack.

Grant received the ball wide on the right flank, attracting two Villa defenders and showing great composure he extricated himself from the tight position to slip the ball through to Proctor who ran on to score. Two-nil.

A skirmish ensued as Proctor removed his shirt in celebration. The referee reacted quickly, cautioning the Mexter goal scorer and shepherding the players back to the halfway line.

The papers summed it up.

So Mexter will line up to play Burding Town in the Final on May 20th.

Make no mistake about it. Mexter enjoyed huge slices of luck in this match after being put under the cosh by a very good second half Villa performance. Villa will be devastated to lose after dominating for long periods.

But that's now in the past and it's the underdogs who look forward to the biggest day in the club's history.

Can they win it? If they enjoy the same amount of good fortune as they did on this blustery day in Manchester, then anything's possible. But, on this evidence, it will be Burding Town who'll start favourites to lift football's most famous knock out trophy.

48

'Could you tell me which ward Ellen Whitlow works on, please?' said Jake holding a bunch of flowers.

He was slightly embarrassed when hospital staff came up to him asking for autographs and wishing him good luck. He posed for photographs.

'She's on men's medical,' said the receptionist. 'Go left and follow the red line.'

He made his way along the hospital corridors, painted in a mushroom colour. If anything were to make the patients feel worse, that would be it. He spoke to one of the nurses.

'She's just taken a patient to the loo,' she said, checking the work schedule. ' Won't be long. Mind you it is Alfred and he tends to write his memoirs in there.'

Jake spotted her at the end of the corridor, chatting away, wheeling her patient back to his bed.

'Well blow me down with a feather,' said Ellen, surprised. 'If it isn't Captain Fantastic.'

'How are you Ellen?' asked Jake.

'Fine as nine pence and yourself?'

'Good, thanks.'

'I should think so. Alfred, do you know who this is?' said Ellen, leaning over to grab his attention.

Startled, he said. 'Is he the porter?'

'Not quite,' said Ellen, laughing. 'Have another guess.'

'Your lad?'

'Ha ha. I wouldn't be working in here if he was. I'd be home with my feet up. No it's Jake. Jake Watkins, he plays for Burding Town. They've got through to the cup final.'

'Is this him?'

'Yes. So you've had a treat today, haven't you? A special visitor.'

'He hasn't brought me paper up, has he?' said Alfred, getting to the important issues of the day.

'It's already arrived,' said Ellen moving to the other side of the bed. 'Look, here.' She released the foot rest. 'Come on let's get into bed.'

'Are you going to join me?' said Alfred, chuckling.

'See Jake? Alfie is very cheeky. Aren't you love?' said Ellen, patting his face. 'Still got that twinkle in his eye.'

'Can I help?' volunteered Jake.

'I think we're all right Alfie, aren't we?' she said, helping him to sit on the bed. 'We've had a lot of practice.'

Once Alfred was settled, Ellen asked, 'who are the flowers for? I'll put them in a vase if you'd like.'

Handing them over, Jake said, 'They're for you.'

'Me?' Ellen was genuinely shocked. 'Nobody buys me flowers.'

'They're for looking after me so well,' explained Jake.

'But it's my job. I don't want anything.'

'I know you don't,' said Jake. 'But if you don't want them I'll give them to one of the nurses.'

'Give 'em to me,' said Alfie. 'Missus will fall in love with me, all over again.'

'No, no. They're beautiful, thanks ever so much, Jake,' said Ellen, now a little flustered. 'Come on, I'll find something to put them in.'

Jake sat down while Ellen took the flowers out of the paper, opened the cupboard and found a glass vase. Turning on the tap she said, 'I've been watching out for you, Jake. You've come a long way.'

'It's gone well. I've had no problems with the injury at all, touch wood. It's spot on.'

'And of course you're the captain now, aren't you?' said Ellen trimming the longer stalks.

'It was a surprise when the manager told me; I've got to say. But it's working out well,' said Jake glancing at a chart showing all the vital organs. 'How are you doing anyway?'

'Plodding on. I've been on this ward for three weeks and the patients are some of the best I've come across. How's that girlfriend of yours, Jake? What's her name?'

'Marie.'

'That's it. Lovely girl. Are you still together?'

'Sort of.'

She stared at him. 'What kind of answer is that? It's either yes or no, isn't it?'

'She's gone off around the world,' said Jake, fingering a delicate gold chain that hung around his neck.

'Where is she now?'

'India, doesn't get back until the end of June.'

'You're not telling me she'll miss the game, are you?' said Ellen, shocked.

'Looks like it, yeah. It's all tied in. Can't change the flights. Said she'll watch it in some hotel in Delhi, drinking herbal tea.'

The nurse came back in. 'Sister I'm going to need some help with Henry. He's being a little awkward.'

'I'll be right there.'

Jake rose from his seat and fumbled with his wallet. 'I've kept you too long,' he said. He placed something in her hand.

'What's this?'

'Take a look.'

'Tickets for the FA Cup final,' said Ellen, startled. 'You are joking, aren't you?'

'Not a bit of it. You deserve them. Kept me going when I was down. I must have been a right pain the backside. Thanks for what you did.'

'Right then. Thanks ever so much,' said Ellen, picking up her handbag and putting the tickets in the purse. 'Good excuse for getting that stingy old fella I live with to get his moth-balled money out of his back pocket and book a nice weekend away.'

She smiled. 'Just make sure you bring that cup back.'

'I'll do my best.'

'I'm sure you will. Come here and give me a kiss,' she said, hugging him. 'I'm not too old, you know.'

49

Hi Jake. Hope plans are going well for the final. I suppose everybody's asking you for tickets. It must be hectic. At least there's only a week to go now. You finished the season well, so everybody must be confident. Has your Mum got a new outfit for the game? If she can't get glammed up for that, she never will.

Anyway an update. India is very different from back home. It's very beautiful but very, very hot and the sewerage system isn't quite what it should be. So if the wind is blowing in the wrong direction it's dire. Mumbai was heaving, so we arrived very late one night and left the next morning. We then went to a little island called Diu, which is a Portuguese colony. And lovely. Very different from the big cities we have seen so far. Since then we visited the Taj Mahal, which was fantastic.

Everything is very bureaucratic. They have at least 5 people for every job. Getting a train ticket was a task in itself. Turn up at the station and get a ticket? Easy? No way. There were 40 windows. We got to window 13 (lucky or not?) and were asked lots of questions. Where you want to go, how old are you (?) how many people, and when you've answered them they tell us we are at the wrong window and must go to window 20. So we go to window 20 and get asked all the same questions and guess what? It was the wrong window. We must go to window 43, which is up the stairs, turn left, second door on the right. Anyway, we get there at window 43, which is the foreign tourist window.

Couldn't understand why they didn't tell us that in the first place. We then had to fill in a form, which has about million questions on it. After all that you pay your money and you get a ticket! Hallelujah! The whole process takes about an hour and half. But what a feeling when you get that ticket in your hands. It's like winning the lottery.

I'm reading about Gandhi's life and, as everybody knows, he was a supporter of non-violent demonstrations. Obviously he had never bought a train ticket in his beloved country!

Fascinating man. Got married at 13! Yes. The girl's name was Kasturbai and guess what? She was the same age. But in those times it was no big deal. Seems like you and me are ancients.

In one respect though, I'm similar to the great man. He had his problems at school. In one report in 1886, it said his general knowledge was 'faulty' and his English 'painfully inaccurate'. And he only got 59/175 for maths. So you never know. I might stay here and be the next Prime Minister!

The only animals we seem to see are cows. They are respected holy figures and wander around the towns and streets as if they own the place (which they do!). So you could be driving through a busy city and suddenly a cow pops its head around a corner and all the traffic diverts away to give it room to walk by. Apparently it's very bad for your karma if you kill one and if you mention, 'I could murder a burger' your next life won't be a good one!

We are now in a town called Manali, which is beautiful with lots of mountains and very clean.

We've been to a couple of yoga classes, which have been great. Couldn't quite understand what the instructor was saying this morning. It sounded like 'straighten botty, straighten botty'. Well try as we might we weren't sure how you could straighten your bottom but thought we'd give it a damn good try. But he kept on about it and I thought, you can only straighten your bottom so much... turns out he was saying 'straighten both knee, straighten both knee'. He must have thought we were right idiots with our knees bent and our bottoms doing God knows what!

Lots of love – M.

50

Prior to the final, the views expressed in many of the press conferences were fairly predictable. Burding manager Les Whitehead, however, was quick to dismiss the result was a foregone conclusion.

'We're under no illusions we can steamroller Mexter because they've done brilliantly. We know we will be billed as the favourites, there's nothing we can do about that, but we also know we've got to go there and do a job. If we play to our capabilities, I'm confident we can get the right result. If we don't, we'll get turned over.'

In Mexter's press conference, a question from one of the red top journalists was directed towards manager Tim Ward, flanked by captain Mike Sadler and full back Danny Barnes.

'The fact that a lower division team has forced its way through to the final suggests that other higher profile clubs haven't looked on the competition as one of their top priorities,' said a reporter, fiddling with his laptop. 'Would you agree or is it a case of your team taking all before them?'

Ward was matter of fact. 'Quite frankly, I'm not too concerned about other teams but judging by their reactions when they were knocked out, they were all very disappointed. All I can say is we're delighted to be in the final and thoroughly deserve to be there.'

A question from one of the broadsheet reporters highlighted Mexter's current form in the second tier of domestic competition.

'Your results have certainly taken a turn for the better towards the end of the season. Only one defeat in six since the semi-final win. How much is that due to the introduction of Ricky Grant who many people are eulogising over, saying he's the most naturally gifted young player to have come along in years. Probably since Wayne Rooney's introduction.'

'Eulogising?' said Ward smiling. 'Not a word I come across every day but if it means what I think it does, I'll have to agree. His performances over the past few weeks have been nothing short of sensational and he's turned a mediocre season into something quite extraordinary.

'He's an absolute gem – what every manager dreams about. Someone who comes into training every day and lights the place up. You see this lad doing things, which are world class. So it puts a smile on everybody's faces. We all want to come into work.

'I believe in all my players and they have never let me down. But only my skipper here knows what it's like to win in a top final. The rest haven't tasted that success but they do have the hunger and desire to try and achieve it. The team spirit is second to none. Winning that first trophy would give us all a massive lift.'

'You must have read the predictions?' said another journalist. 'That Mexter had no chance of winning. "Sacrificial Lambs to the Slaughter" was one headline. What's your take on that?'

'It is a chance to silence our detractors. None of them thought we could get this far. At every stage of the competition we've been the underdogs. We've had to take the knocks and let those who want to have a go, get on with it.

'But one thing is for sure. We'll give it our best shot. We may not be the best team in the country but no one can criticise us for our lack of commitment. It got us this far. Who's to say it can't take us one step further?'

Defender Barnes recalled the first players' meeting at the start of the season.

'The manager got us together and boosted our confidence straight away. He told us he rated us very highly and that was good for our self-belief.

'He trusted us to do the business. He got the younger players together and talked to them separately. Told us he liked young players with fire in their bellies who were prepared to go the extra mile. It's a new journey for a lot of us.

'We're going into unknown territory but we're not afraid. In fact, we're looking forward to it. Personally I've a lot to be thankful for from the manager. He's taught me so much. It's all a learning process but I feel we are developing a strong winning mentality and desire to see it through, no matter what.'

Mexter's only concern surrounded the appointment of referee Andy Culshaw. Boss Ward was happy to play the psychological card ahead of the game.

'This guy is a Premier League referee and as such is in regular contact with top players week in week out,' Ward was keen to point out. 'He's only been in charge of one of our games this season and that was a League Cup game when we went down to Arsenal.

'We felt in that game we lost out in all the big calls. We were denied a penalty when he gave a free kick outside the box. TV pictures clearly indicated the offence was well inside. So we were done twice as the offending player should have been red-carded.

'It was a crucial moment in the game. And then the referee's assistant flagged for a corner, which was in fact a goal kick. Straight afterwards they scored their second. I'm not suggesting for one minute that Mr Culshaw isn't totally honest but sometimes I wonder if there is that bit of pressure from the top clubs.'

'Would you say that Mexter will go into this game totally relaxed because there's far less pressure to deliver?' The question came from a BBC radio reporter.

'Burding are favourites,' said Ward, looking smart in a club blazer and sipping from a bottle of water, 'and as such carry a heavy burden of responsibility for their expectant fans.

'We are going into the game in fine form, with no injuries to worry about. A settled, confident squad of players who are looking forward to the game. I have complete faith in each and every one of them.'

The next question was directed towards skipper, Mike Sadler.

'You've got a winner's medal in the trophy cabinet at home, Mike. Will your experience of playing in that kind of atmosphere be important on the day?'

'I can't wait to get started. I played in the final two seasons ago for my old club as you know but only came on for the last twenty minutes. I'd been out for three months with a leg injury so they didn't want to change the side.

'I got on but things went bad for me, even though we scraped home 1-0. It was a real dogfight. Towards the end we were battered but somehow hung on. From a personal point of view it was very unsatisfactory. I felt I hadn't contributed at all.

'Afterwards it was a little weird. We'd won but I felt empty. I had it in my mind that I would score the winning goal and be cheered by the fans and saluted as the match winner. But now I have another chance to make an impact and I'm determined not to let the occasion pass me by.

'Now I want to get one over on my mate Simmo who is in the Burding goal. I roomed with him once for an international game and he's bet me I won't score.'

One article analysed some important issues.

'There will be many crucial individual battles around the pitch. A little bit of magic or a slip-up could be the key to success or failure. Both keepers, for instance, have made individual mistakes this season but are also recognised as two of the best in their respective divisions. Could it go all the way down to a penalty shoot-out with one coming out the hero? The centre-back pairings have been models of consistency and have got better as the season has gone on, hardly putting a foot wrong, dealing with all the pressure and showing excellent leadership qualities. Craig Hennessey has been a terrific buy for Burding. His performances have meant that influential defender Dan Jones, who's been absent through injury, has hardly been missed. Hennessey's partnership with Clive Jackson has been the backbone of the side.

But most supporters are relishing the prospect of seeing the clash between those magnificent youngsters, Jake Watkins and Ricky Grant, who have burst on the scene this season in such superb style.

Ex-Town player, Jeff Partridge, assessed Watkins' contribution. 'No one should ever underestimate this lad's importance to the football club. His attitude is superb and he's always wanted to learn from the very first moment he joined as a schoolboy. There is an honesty about the lad I admire. Anybody who saw the game a few weeks ago wouldn't have given them a prayer of getting back into the game after conceding two soft goals just after the break. But single-handedly Jake picked up his teammates by their bootlaces and got them back into the game, firstly by rifling in a magnificent twenty-five yarder into the top corner and then creating a last gasp equaliser for Jonah in the dying minutes.

'I looked at him at the end of the game and pride was etched all over his face. He clasped his fists, kissed the club badge and no one could ever doubt his love for this football club. It means everything to him.'

For Watkins to dominate this final he will have to be on top form because in direct opposition will be one of the most gifted players of this or indeed any other generation. Ricky Grant has taken the football world by storm since his introduction to the professional game and it seems like he is destined for a wonderful career. Nothing is impossible for this 17-year-old wonder kid. The sky's the limit.

Plucked from obscurity after a chance meeting with an ex-international and the rest is history. He has the cockiness and self-belief to inspire Mexter to even greater heights through his outrageous ability, vitality and pace. This lad has the qualities to be the match winner.

The managers have important roles to play, making the right calls, tweaking the tactics and the personnel. An odd word here, a change of face there. Tim Ward is a quiet man, a thinking manager who doesn't show too much emotion during the game. To some observers, this shows a lack of passion; to others a thoughtful, intelligent approach. One thing is for sure: he is an outstanding professional and his knowledge of the game is without question.

In the other dug-out Les Whitehead is a sub-editor's dream, never far away from controversy through his actions and forthright opinions. His one-liners are legendary, often interpreted by the football authorities as 'bringing the game into disrepute'. Seen by many as arrogant, he has gained total respect from his players and is the first to protect them from controversial situations. With his slick hair and tailored suits, there is no doubting he is 'The Boss'.

But, there can only be one winner. A bit of jiggery-pokery or a subtle word could bring the ultimate reward. It's finely balanced and only a whisker separates the two teams. Let battle commence.

51

CUP FINAL HERO IN DRUGS SENSATION
World Exclusive
Mexter City's teenage star Ricky Grant and I smoked crack

Ricky Grant, dubbed the next Wayne Rooney, is today exposed as a drug-taking drop-out.

His teenage pal Joey Rowlands tells the Sunday Graphic about how he and the teenage sensation smoked marijuana and crack cocaine in a notorious crack house.

Grant, who has taken the football world by storm since his introduction as a substitute in the cup game against Stoke City only three months ago, has been outed as a lay-about who indulged in class A drugs.

'Ricky used to hang out with us guys. No way was he pressurised. He was full of it. Wanted to be one of us, like. One of the crowd,' says Rowlands

'There were a gang of us. We used to hang out wherever we could. In an old warehouse or boarded up places. Sorta used to squat.

'Ricky was up for it no danger. Smoked grass and a bit of brown. Whatever there was. He was there, like man. Blew his mind. He was out of it.'

Rowlands added, 'There were girls as well. I don't know which ones Ricky got shacked up with. But he was there, like, with the rest. We were all out of our brains, man.

'Then one day, he sorta disappeared. None of us knew where he'd gone. Then we'd see his face all over the papers and on TV. We knew straight away. It's Ricky. It's the same guy who hung around with us.'

These revelations will be a major concern to manager Tim Ward on the eve of biggest game in Mexter's history. Grant's performances have revitalised the club leaving them just outside

a play-off position and into a glamour FA Cup final against
Premier opposition Burding Town.
With this expose, Grant may have blown his chances of being
one of the youngest players ever to feature in the world's greatest
knockout final.
The FA has a strict monitoring system and the authorities will
want to drug test Grant before the final.
Ward was unavailable for comment last night.

Ward contacted his star player. Clearly it was a distraction for the club, one they could have done without.

'Listen Ricky, it changes nothing,' said Ward who had arranged the meeting in his office. 'You were totally honest when you signed and from what I've seen this season, I've no doubts that you've kept your side of the bargain.'

'Spot on, boss,' said Ricky, eager to sort out the problem.

'That's what I thought. You couldn't have put in those performances if you'd been on the razz. Then again, maybe for one game!' he said laughing.

'This sort of muck raking is only to be expected. We know journalists have a job to do. They're all looking for bits of gossip before a big game, to stir things up. But we're going to have to deal with it.'

'I know.' Ricky agreed.

'I think it's best we have a press conference and issue a statement. That okay with you?' asked the manager.

'Fine with me.'

'They wouldn't expect anything less,' explained Ward. 'And I think it'd be better coming from you. That's if you're up to it?'

'Okay with me,' said Ricky.

'Good. Right, I'll set it up for tomorrow. Watch out for the rest of the day.'

'Why's that, gaffer?'

'Because you and me will be on opposite sides in the five-a-side,' said Ward, smiling. 'I'm going to be all over you like shit to a blanket. You won't get a kick!'

'No way,' said Ricky making a swift exit. 'You'll never get anywhere near me.'

Ricky sat next to his manager on the top table in a packed press room surrounded by microphones and TV cameras. The powerful arc lights shone directly into his eyes and for a split second he was blinded. The manager opened a bottle of still water. He handed a glass to Ricky. 'Just take your time son. Don't rush it.'

The manager addressed the room.

'Thank you gentleman, and ladies, for attending this meeting. After the articles published last weekend, Ricky felt he'd like to set the record straight. He has prepared a statement, which he will read to you in a few moments. There will be no questions after the statement and neither Ricky, or myself will be making any further comments.'

Ricky, his mouth dry, hid his hands below the table to stop the press from seeing them shake. He had a drink of water and started hesitantly, to read.

'I must admit when I was younger, it wasn't the happiest time of my life. I experimented, got in with the wrong crowd and made a lot of mistakes.

'Perhaps I'm lucky to have made those mistakes when I was young. It was a hard lesson in life but it's definitely made me stronger, more determined not to go down that same path again. I realise what my responsibilities are now. I know it's important not to let my teammates down, the fans or the manager of this wonderful club.

'I know people will always bring things up about the past, the messing about, the aggro. All the negative stuff and I can't stop them. But football is my passport out of my other life. I'd be a fool to throw it all away now.'

52

The night before the final Ricky couldn't sleep. His roommate Billy was well away, out like a light – snoring like a pig.

Ricky picked up his mobile and wandered into the bathroom. He phoned Simon.

'Can't sleep mate?' said Simon. It was 1.35 in the morning.

'The game's going over and over in my head,' said Ricky.

'And you're the match winner every time?' said a yawning Simon.

'Just the opposite. Couldn't get a kick and was subbed after twenty minutes.'

'You'll be fine.'

'All that TV and stuff. Millions watching.'

'Bit scary?'

'Too right.'

'Rather be playing in front of ten old geezers and few stray sheep?' said Simon, now wide awake and getting angry gestures from his wife.

'Magic that. Playing for the cup with no speccies.'

'Not the real world, I'm afraid,' said Simon checking the noise hadn't wakened the kids. 'Though you could try blanking your mind.'

'What with ninety thousand screaming at you, expecting to be entertained?'

'You're not there to entertain, Ricky,' pointed out Simon. 'They've got opera singers and a pop group for that. And a gymnastic display team. They're the entertainers. You're there to do a job.'

'What if I have a 'mare?'

Simon made his way to the kitchen and switched on the kettle. 'Do the simple things early on, ten-yard passes to feet, don't complicate it. Make sure you get into the game.'

'It doesn't stop me worrying.'

'Course it doesn't,' said Simon placing a teabag in his favourite mug. 'You wouldn't be human otherwise. You're bound to be nervous. But everybody's in the same boat. Maybe they don't show it but it's all churning up inside.'

'Eh, Simes, I'm talking to you sitting on the bog.'

'Ha! Ha! Nothing like a cup final to act like a laxative.'

'I hope Billy doesn't wake up and want to use the bathroom. He'll die.'

'You've just discovered that adrenalin is brown?' said Simon, adding the milk.

'You'd better believe it.'

'Listen son, whatever happens tomorrow it'll be the best day of your life,' he said, positively. 'You've come a long way in such a short time. So try to enjoy it. What's the worst thing that can happen? You're not going to die, are you?'

'Hope not.'

'Course not. If you lose so what?' said Simon taking a sip. 'As long as you've given it your best shot. But wouldn't it great to win? What a feeling that would be?

'You're fit, you're in the team on merit and the manager and players rate you highly. So go for it.'

'I know you're right.'

'Do you want a bit of advice?' said Simon, wanting to end the conversation and get back to bed.

'Go on."

'Forget the game.'

'Sorry?'

'It'll take care of itself. You've got more ability in your little toenail than ninety per cent of the players so focus on something else.'

'Like what?'

'A random act of kindness,' said Simon turning off the light and climbing the stairs.

'You've lost me, said Ricky, confused.

'A random act of kindness and a senseless act of great beauty.'

Ricky was certain he'd lost his marbles. 'You been puffing away on the wacky baccy or what?'

'People will forget what you did,' said Simon, 'they'll forget what you said but they will never forget how you made them feel. Think of others. It'll take the pressure off yourself.'

'Like who?' asked Ricky.

'Come on,' said a stunned Simon. 'You're not telling me you don't know anybody who deserves a surprise?'

'Course I do.'

'Well then, do something about it,' demanded Simon. 'And another thing.'

'What's that?'

'I'm in row JJ so if you have to clear your lines, try and find me.'

'The only thing I want to find right now is some bog paper.'

'A good clear out,' laughed Simon. 'Just what you needed. Nice one.'

Ricky switched off his 'phone and crept back into bed.

Simon snuggled up to his wife. 'Who was that?' she asked bleary eyed.

'Ringing up at this time of night?'

'Someone who will one day be one of the greatest players this country has ever seen.'

53

On a gloriously sunny day the teams emerged from the dressing rooms of the new Wembley Stadium to a tumultuous welcome. Skipper Jake Watkins followed his boss onto the pristine playing surface, casually bouncing a ball in an effort to relieve the tension.

What had the old-stager Bill Anderson said? 'Take it in lad, best you can. But don't forget, it's what happens after the whistle blows, that's important. Everything else will take care of itself.'

Ricky Grant was next-to-last in Mexter's line-up. Points just in front of him. The strapping centre back turned and shouted, 'Pinch me, mate, pinch me. I think I'm dreaming.'

They were desperate for the action to start but were kept waiting until the national anthem was played and the dignitaries introduced.

Mexter, playing in their home colours of red shirts, white shorts and red socks, started with a 4-5-1 set up with Nick Proctor their lone striker and Ricky playing in the left centre mid position. Burding plumped for a 4-4-1-1 formation with Jake tucked in behind leading scorer Marco Cornelio. They lined up in their familiar colours of blue and white striped shirts, blue shorts and white socks.

The lower division side enjoyed more possession in the opening quarter of the game and used their extra man in midfield to good effect, showing excellent composure, touch and movement. Burding, however, were far more adventurous whenever they had the ball. They attacked with purpose and pace down both flanks but didn't create any goal scoring opportunities. The keepers were largely redundant.

But that was about to change. A quick break out of defence found Juan Torres down the right flank. It was questionable whether he had strayed offside but the assistant gave him the benefit of the doubt and the referee waved play on. An early cross found Cornelio near the penalty spot and with a deft spin and low shot he found the bottom corner. The far end of the ground erupted. One-nil to Burding, twenty-two minutes gone.

On the balance of play Mexter were unfortunate to have conceded but the Premier League club had taken full advantage to ease in front with a clinical finish. Jake was in his element and looked completely relaxed in the surroundings. As one commentator exclaimed, 'Watkins looks class.'

During a break in play when Ivor Smeeten needed treatment, the Mexter players jogged over to the touchline. Tim Ward had a word. 'Keep playing. Sooner or later we're going to get a break. They can't keep nicking it in those tight areas.'

It was well documented that the Mexter manager had expressed concern about the appointment of referee Andy Culshaw but he couldn't complain about the official's handling of the early part of the match. Culshaw let the game flow, pulled up the bad tackles and was on top of every controversial incident. He also kept the yellow cards firmly in his pocket.

Ten minutes before the break, Town struck again. Jake strode forward majestically from the halfway line, played a neat one-two with Marco and struck a brilliant 20-yarder which flashed by 'keeper Gavin Halford's right hand. An absolute pinger.

The fans rose as one to acclaim their hero. Jake was mobbed by his teammates over by the corner flag and as the referee shepherded the players back to the halfway line, the giant TV screen replayed the classic strike.

The Mexter fans were mortified; 2-0 down, only thirty-five minutes played. Their greatest day was turning into a nightmare. Tears were seen on the painted faces of their youngest supporters.

Jake skipped back to the halfway line feeling like a million dollars.

'Bloody hell, what a goal!' he thought to himself. 'You little beauty.' Big Scotty grabbed hold of him. 'Magic, Jakey, give us a kiss. It'll make all tomorrow's papers.' Jake had never felt as high. The adrenalin was flowing so fast, it was frightening.

The Mexter manager replaced full back Jim Moore with Luke Porter, a decision forced on him after Moore picked up a knee injury. The second goal was a major blow and the early dominance enjoyed by City had all but disappeared.

One thing was for sure. They had to get to grips with Jake Watkins, otherwise they had little chance of getting back into the game. His foraging runs from deep positions were causing all sorts of problems. He was on top form and action had to be taken.

A signal went out for rugged Italian, Dario Maricco, to man mark him. 'Stick to him like glue son,' ordered the manager. ' If he goes for a crap, you go with him.' For the final few minutes of the half, the tactic worked.

Jake was coming in for some rough treatment. After one particularly nasty foul he complained to the referee. ' What's all that about?' Physio Jimmy, shaking the ice-cold spray, said ' Jake, there's only five minutes to go. Just get through to halftime.'

'This guy's doing a hatchet job on me.'

During the latter stages of the half, Ricky Grant, who had been fairly quiet, was becoming more influential.

The whistle blew for the break and the Burding players jogged off to a rapturous ovation. They had expended a lot of energy but were only forty-five minutes away from glory. Was there any way back for the unfancied Mexter side?

Tim Ward sat next to Ricky in the dressing room. 'You're doing well, son, but we've got to get you more involved. Take a few chances. When you're around the box have a go,' said Ward patting him on the leg. 'Take people on. We've got to get after them.'

'Okay, boss.'

That's what Ricky wanted to hear. Licence to express himself.

The manager then turned to Reg Davies. 'I'm looking to get Ricky on the ball in more advanced areas. With Dario on Watkins, I want you to give that bit of protection.'

In the second half, it was vital Mexter got an early break. And they didn't have long to wait. Ricky gained possession 40 yards out, skipped past a couple of weak challenges and nicked it through to Jody Young who had come inside from his left wing berth.

Ricky went on the overlap, received the return pass but was then confronted by Clive Jackson who had moved across to cover. A lovely step over by Ricky took him clear into the box before a lunge from an outstretched Craig Hennessey brought him crashing down. All eyes were drawn to the referee. Immediately, he pointed to the spot. Penalty.

Burding players, convinced there had been minimal contact, were outraged and menacingly stood over the youngster. From their reactions they certainly felt he'd gone to ground too easily but TV replays told a different story. It proved to be a correct call.

Mexter had a problem. Regular penalty ace Jim Moore had been substituted and not too many of his teammates were eager to step forward and take the responsibility. Ricky was badly shaken from the challenge and was receiving treatment when captain Mike Sadler came over. 'Fancy it Ricky? If you do, it's all yours. If not, I'll take it.'

Ricky got to his feet, picked up the ball and placed it on the spot.

Manager Ward desperately tried to relay instructions to his skipper but in the pandemonium his message went unheard.

Ricky took a few strides back. 'This is it. I'm never going to get a better chance to score in a cup final. Relax, keep your head down. Make sure you hit the target.' Deep down, he knew he was going to score.

Ricky looked directly at Alan Simpson, who had an impressive record for saving spot-kicks. He looked huge in the Burding goal. The referee made sure the rest of the players were outside the area before blowing his whistle.

Ricky jogged forward confidently to whip the ball, left footed, a yard inside the right hand post. Simpson was transfixed. He didn't move. The Mexter crowd rose as the ball nestled in the back of the net. Two-one, and City were back in the game.

What would the next forty minutes bring?

Both managers were getting more and more agitated in their technical areas. In the next serious attack Mexter gained a free kick five yards outside the box. It was vital that Burding didn't concede a second in double quick time. Ricky again took up the mantle. It was in a nice position for a left-footed player.

Simpson lined up the wall to protect the near post and then took up a position by the far post. Ricky wondered if the best option was to curl the ball over to the unprotected side. In the end, he decided to go for the 'keeper's side and hoped that Simpson would be unsighted.

Ricky struck it beautifully to the far corner but the ball clipped the post before going behind for a goal kick.

A long clearance down the middle brought their next chance. It fell to Proctor who volleyed it first time – unfortunately, straight at the 'keeper. Burding were coming under severe pressure and were penned into their own half, frantically holding on to their 2-1 advantage.

The Burding fans were becoming very edgy and it was time for action. Manager Whitehead sent on Jonah Sonsissko to replace Juan Torres and switched from his 4-4-1-1 formation to a 4-5-1 moving Jake deeper to bolster an overstretched midfield. Mexter continued to press and probe and threw caution to the wind looking for the equaliser.

The pressure had to tell and it did. Another flowing passing move, started on the halfway line, ended with Ricky's snap shot on the edge of the box. Simpson fumbled it straight into the path of the alert Proctor who prodded it over the line. Two-two. What a come back!

The underdogs had regained the initiative and had put themselves in a winning position. Approaching the final few minutes, Burding were hanging on, hoping to force extra time.

They defended stubbornly and cleared their lines but had no answer to the skills of the wonder kid Ricky Grant. His touches were breathtaking and he was threatening to win the game on his own.

Then a moment of magic won the game. Jake won possession on the edge of his own 18-yard box, skipped past his marker and sprinted clear. Socks rolled down, he fed Jonah on the right flank who made ground and jinked his way past Danny Barnes. There wasn't another blue shirt in sight.

But Jake had gambled and had eaten up the yardage. His exceptional fitness took him clear.

'This could be our last chance. I've got to get in there. Put it in, Kiddo. Just put it in the box.'

Jake accelerated and timed his run to perfection. His 6 foot 1 inch frame leapt high, eyes focused, aggression etched on his face.

The towering header flashed into the top corner.

The stadium erupted; the noise was deafening. But Jake wasn't to witness his greatest moment. As the header was unleashed, Halford's punch caught Jake on the side of the head. He fell – poleaxed. The Burding fans who watched the ball soar into the net were on their feet cheering and celebrating.

Gradually their attention was drawn to their goal hero lying motionless. The players rushed over to congratulate, but then fear and panic took over as they frantically signalled to the bench. Jimmy sprinted onto the pitch and knelt beside Jake.

The paramedics were sent on. They immediately put on a cervical collar and moved Jake gently onto a backboard stretcher to support his spine. The club doctor left his seat in the directors' box to make his way onto the pitch.

'Oh my God!' shouted Linda, on her feet and looking down from the main stand. 'What's happened?' Steve wrapped his arm around her. 'Please God don't let him die,' she said. 'Not after that.'

'I'm sure he'll be okay, love,' said a comforting husband.

'I feel so helpless,' said Linda, watching the giant screens. 'I want to be with him.'

'He's getting the best attention,' said Steve, anxious himself to get a closer look. 'Let's just see. Then we'll go down.'

Unconscious, Jake was carried to the waiting ambulance.

'Jake can you hear me?' The paramedics attached the oxygen mask and checked the blood pressure. 'If you can, squeeze my hand.' Two police motorcyclists escorted the ambulance to the neurology department at the city hospital.

The last five minutes of the match ended in a blur. Dan Jones came on for Jake as the Mexter players piled forward looking for an equaliser. Successive corners found the eager head of the former skipper who rose majestically to clear the danger. It was agony for both sets of fans. Little constructive football was played. Burding were happy to whack the ball to the four corners of the ground.

The referee blew for full time to end an enthralling match. The Burding fans went wild. For one player it proved to be a perfect swansong. Dan Jones, who had served the club with such distinction through his long career, fittingly collected the trophy to the cheers of the Blues' supporters.

54

St James's Hospital received the call and the emergency team, headed by neurosurgeon Francis Duberry, prepared for Jake's admittance.

'Fill me in,' said Duberry, a short stocky man, with wispy hair and frameless glasses.

'Severe blow to the temple playing in the cup final today,' said staff sister Louise Boyle. 'Unconscious in the ambulance, pulse is stable, blood pressure and respiratory rate normal.'

'A kick?' said Duberry, glancing round the operating room.

'No,' said Boyle. 'A punch from the goalkeeper.'

'What was the score by the way?' said Duberry, reaching into his pocket for a pen.

'Burding won 3-2,' said Boyle. 'Jake Watkins received the injury heading the winner.'

'So he's the hero,' said Duberry, opening the door and walking through into the corridor. 'And we'll have the media crawling all over us very shortly.'

'I should imagine so.'

'What time did he receive the injury?'

'Ten to five,' answered Boyle, checking her watch. 'Nine minutes ago.'

'Any history of head injuries?'

'No, we checked with the club doctor.'

'What is the eta?'

'Five minutes,' confirmed Boyle.

'Right. Get the team in place,' said Duberry, striding purposefully towards the reception area.

The ambulance arrived at the main entrance and the paramedic, club physio and doctor jumped out. Jake was wheeled into the emergency room, an oxygen mask covering his mouth.

He was very carefully lifted onto the bed. The neck brace was gently removed.

'Right, check his bp, pulse and respiratory again; and then take his temperature, blood glucose and oxygen saturation readings,' said Duberry, leaning over to get a closer look at Jake's head. 'Early diagnosis, it doesn't look like a skull fracture. And please take off his boots.'

Linda, Steve and Chloe were waiting in the family room with the club's medical team. After what seemed like an eternity, Duberry came in and introduced himself. 'I take it that you were all at the game?' he said.

'Yes,' said Steve.

'I'm told Jake was the match winner? Excellent.'

'How is he, Mr Duberry?' asked Linda, worried.

'He's had a nasty blow to his head. We don't think he's fractured his skull but at the moment he's still unconscious. He is resting. But the CAT scan has come back clear.'

'CAT scan?' asked an anxious mother.

'Sorry let me explain,' said Duberry, lowering his voice. 'It's something we do to diagnose the pressure of blood clots or fluid in the brain to see if there's any brain damage. Any trauma to the skull will produce a movement of the brain rather like a jelly on a plate and so the damage is often sustained to the opposite side from where the initial blow occurred.

'It's good news. It looks like everything is clear. We hope that he regains consciousness very soon. That's all there is at the moment.'

'He is he going to be all right, though, isn't he?' asked Steve.

'There's a very good chance but until he comes round, we won't know for certain. When we've more news, we'll let you know.' Duberry was alerted when his beeper sounded.

'Sorry, I must go.'

55

The Mexter dressing room was subdued. City had come a long way and to miss out at the final hurdle was a real letdown. Many of the champagne bottles remained unopened and even the manager's consoling words and lighthearted gestures failed to raise morale.

First is first, second is nowhere. The players sat shaking their heads – physically drained and hugely disappointed.

Ricky took off his red shirt bearing the inscription 'FA Cup Final 2008 Mexter City v Burding Town'. He wrapped his socks and shorts inside the shirt and placed them in his bag. He made his way over to the showers, squirted the shampoo onto his flowing locks and started to massage thoroughly.

Billy turned on the next shower. 'All right mate? What about that goal? What a killer.'

'Couldn't do anything about it,' said Ricky, applying conditioner. 'Came from nowhere.'

'Too right.'

'I feel a bit sick Bill,' said Ricky looking drained. 'Must be all the emotion.'

'Go and see the physio,' advised Billy. 'He'll get you something.'

As Ricky towelled himself down, the players were slowly coming to terms with the result and the realisation they'd been involved in one of the greatest ever finals.

Ricky was sweating and his white shirt clinged to his body. He applied hair gel, knotted his tie and put on his black club jacket. He got some paracetamol from the physio.

The manager told him he'd been voted Mexter's man of the match and the media requested an appearance in the interview room.

Ricky rang Walter Snape who was in the players lounge. 'I'm going to see the press. What should I say?'

'Speak from the heart, son,' said Snape finding it difficult to hear. 'You've shown everybody what you're about on the park. Brilliant. Just be honest – but don't slag anybody off.'

A PR man – earpiece attached to his left lobe and resembling an FBI agent – escorted him to the interview room where Ricky faced the massed ranks of the world's media.

The first question came from a broadsheet reporter. 'Well played Ricky. You seemed to handle it without any problems. Very mature performance. How did you find it?'

'I just tried to do my best. I'm gutted that we didn't win. There are a lot of disappointed players in our dressing room. After getting back level we all thought we might nick it. But after saying that I think it was a great team performance.'

'I think we'll all agree with that,' said the Sky Sports reporter. 'Did you have any nerves when you took the penalty?'

'The skipper, Sads, took the pressure off to be fair. He said if I didn't fancy it then he'd take it. But it was my best chance of scoring. I'm glad it went in.'

'There was a lot of stuff written about you before the game. Did that put extra pressure on you?'

'Not really. I always knew it would come out sooner or later,' said Ricky with a hint of a smile. 'I spoke to the gaffer and he supported me, which was great.'

'Where do you go from here, Ricky?' was the next question.

'I want to be involved in other big games. It will take time I know but promotion is what we'll be looking for next season. Then we'll see. But I believe our time will come. We lost the game today. Today it was all about Jake Watkins – for me, a brilliant player. He was the difference. I just hope he recovers fully and we meet up again very soon.'

Ricky got up from his seat to be surrounded by a group of photographers.

His head was in a spin. It had been a surreal day. In the players' lounge, well-wishers, all wanting a piece of the action, congratulated him – the new kid on the block. Mike Sadler and his wife came over and other players and their families added their best wishes.

He saw Billy standing at the bar with his brothers. 'Get me a drink mate,' said Ricky. 'I'm parched.'

'No probs.'

He moved through the throng and made his way over to the

seating area. His mum grabbed hold of him, tears in her eyes. 'Come here you.' She squeezed him tightly, oblivious to all in the crowded room.

'I'm so excited. You were wonderful Ricky,' kissing him on both cheeks. 'Just wonderful.'

'Thanks, mum. I enjoyed it apart from the result,' said Ricky taking a drink. 'I tell you what, you look fabulous. Absolutely beautiful.'

'Well I had to make an effort didn't I?' she said, grabbing his arm. 'Come over here.'

She led him over to where other family members were seated. Walter Snape was first to get up and shake him by the hand. 'Well done son. Brilliant.'

Ricky handed his mother an envelope. 'What's this,' she asked.

'We're going on holiday, to Italy. Back to where I was conceived.' Simon was right, a random act of kindness did feel good, although Ricky was aware how much he owed his mother.

56

'Mr and Mrs Watkins, it's good news,' said Duberry, smiling. 'You'll be pleased to know that everything with Jake is fine. You can go in and see him now.'

Linda, Steve and Chloe hugged each other. They rushed in to find Jake sitting up in bed. 'Get me out of here!' he shouted.

'What are you like?' said Chloe, racing over to throw her arms around her now famous brother.

'You score the winning goal and you don't even hang around to collect the trophy? What's that all about?'

'When I woke up,' said Jake, 'I thought what am I doing here in my match kit?'

'Well done son,' said Steve. 'Absolutely bloody marvellous. Everybody around us was going berserk.'

'I take it the header went in, said' said Jake laughing. 'Still haven't seen it on TV yet. What a cross from Jonah.'

'Like a bullet,' said Steve. 'The 'keeper had no chance. Then it was straight off. Paramedics, physios the lot. You were well out of it.'

'How are you feeling now, love?' said Linda, leaning over to touch the side of his face.

'Good, mum. A bit of a headache – that's all. They said I've got to stay in overnight but all being well, I'll be out of here first thing.'

'In time for the celebrations?' said Chloe.

'I don't know what they've got planned. There's a dinner at the hotel tonight then they're going back to Burding tomorrow. I suppose they'll organise something. Who collected the cup anyway?'

'Jonesy,' said Steve. 'He came on for you for the last few minutes. Nice touch that.'

The nurse came in and told Jake he had another visitor. 'It may be someone from the club, mum. Would you see who it is?'

'Course love,' said Linda moving off the bed and heading towards the door. 'If it's a reporter I'll send him packing.'

'Steady. They're my bestest buddies now,' said Jake.

As Linda stepped outside Steve said, 'Mr Duberry told us everything is clear. No brain damage. All the tests have got the green light.'

Linda popped her head around the corner. 'Steve, Chloe have you got a minute?'

'What's up?'

'Nothing important,' she added. 'I won't keep you long.'

Jake shuffled around to try and get a little more comfortable and then poured himself another glass of water. While he was fidgeting with his pillows, the door opened.

'Now then Mr Watkins, what's going on?'

'MARIE! What are you doing here?'

She hugged him tight, smothering him in kisses. 'You didn't think I was going to miss out on your greatest day, did you?'

'Great to see you,' said Jake. 'How did you sort it?'

'I was in touch with your mum and dad straight after the semis,' said Marie, stroking her hands through his hair.

'Enjoy it?'

'What do you think?' said Marie, her teeth looking strikingly white against her tanned complexion.

'You were brilliant. Two goals – I just went crazy. But when you went off I was frightened to death.'

'Bit scary?'

'Scary? You better believe it. But what an atmosphere. What was it like playing?'

'Different class. Everything about it. From the buildup this week to leading the team out.'

Jake's eyes were intense. 'Meeting royalty before the game. And to score the winner. But I thought we were going to bottle it.'

'That young lad's a good player.'

'Ricky Grant? Yeah he'd be good for us,' agreed Jake. 'Don't suppose we could afford him.'

'You and him in the same side? You'd win everything.'

'So you're back for good? No more gallivanting.'

'I'm glad I went. I've learnt a lot about myself. But I must admit I've had enough of backpacking.'

283

'It's good to have you back,' said Jake, holding her hand. 'What's the first thing you did when you got home?'

'Had a bath. It was heaven,' said Marie rolling her eyes. 'And I'll never slag off my bed ever again.'

'Is your bath big enough for two?'

'It could be.'

'Well we've a lot of talking to do – you and me,' said Jake folding his arms around her. ' What could be better? Sorting out our futures while you give me one of your special massages.'

'As long as it's reciprocated.'

'Don't get carried away...'

57

They came in their tens of thousands to salute the cup winners after one of the greatest finals in the history of the famous competition.

Fans shinned up lampposts and trees; they hung precariously from every vantage point, to get a glimpse of their heroes. The open top bus crawled along the five mile route on its way to the Town Hall surrounded by a sea of blue and white and a cacophony of noise from blaring horns and piercing whistles.

Some were already wearing victory T-shirts. Local tradesmen were having a field day with every piece of memorabilia snapped up by the jubilant crowd.

'Town's Cup.'

'Burds Are Flying.'

'Blue Heroes.'

'Captain Courageous.'

Inflatable Cup replicas were seen flying about after escaping from the tender grasps of the younger supporters.

But through it all, match winner Jake Watkins was in everybody's thoughts.

When the team bus, decked out in blue and white, finally arrived, the players made their way up to the town hall balcony to acknowledge the cheers of the fans below.

The mayor, Tom Clarkson, spoke first. 'It has been a privilege and an honour to be mayor during this great time of celebration. The manager and players have put Burding on the map and their success will have a significant impact on this town for many years to come. Congratulations on this wonderful achievement.'

A tumultuous roar came up when manager Whitehead stepped forward holding the magnificent trophy.

'Thank you everybody. Thank you for your support yesterday. The players mentioned it in the dressing room and it spurred them on when things were getting tight. So in many ways you proved to be an excellent twelfth man. Let's hope it's the start of many more exciting times at this club. We will be trying very hard to repeat this success.' He let the applause die down before saying, 'I know that you will all be wondering how Jake is. Well I've got some very good news.'

From the Mayor's reception room, out stepped the Burding skipper, waving to the thousands below. A massive cheer echoed around the town square.

'There's only one Jakey Watkins, one Jakey W-a-t-kins, there's only...'

The manager passed the gleaming trophy to his skipper and Jake held it aloft. After minutes of thunderous applause, the noise eventually subsided allowing Jake to say a few words.

'Thank you very much. And thanks your support. As the gaffer said, we couldn't have done it without your help. It's a great feeling holding this cup. I seem to have missed out on it yesterday. But I feel fine now and the doctors have given me the all clear.'

Another huge cheer greeted the news. 'Supa, supa Jake! Supa, supa Jake! Supa, supa Jake! Supa Jakey Watkins... Supa... !'

'It's a big honour to be captain of this great club,' he continued, 'and we all hope that we'll enjoy more success in the future. You're the best supporters in the country. Enjoy the summer and we'll see you all next season.'

With the club song blasting out into the night air the official party left the scene. The fans reluctantly started to wind their way home after a weekend they'd never forget.

For two young men it was only the start. Their adventure had only just begun.

About the author

Martin Dobson was a 19-year-old striker when Bolton Wanderers decided he wouldn't make it as a professional footballer. But Burnley thought otherwise, converted him into a midfield player and he went on to play more than 600 games in a career which lasted nearly 20 years.

His first spell at Burnley saw him play 224 games and score 43 goals. In 1974 Everton then paid a British transfer record fee of £300,000 to take him to Goodison Park. He played 230 games, scoring 40 goals, before returning to Burnley in 1979.

After another 186 games in his second spell (20 goals) he ended his career at Bury (61 games and 4 goals).

He played five times for England, first being picked by Sir Alf Ramsey.

He led Bury to promotion as player-manager and then became manager of Bristol Rovers. He was also Academy Director at Bolton Wanderers.